D0389651

Presented to:

Edwina Mom Cirelli
WITH THE LOVE OF THE
LORD JESUS CHRIST,
Peter, Abigail,
Elizabeth, Jonathan,
FROM
and Daniel
JUST BECAUSE WE LOVE
YOU AND FOR MOTHER'S
OCCASION DAY!

Sunday, May 14,
DATE 2000

FOCUS ON THE FAMILY®
presents

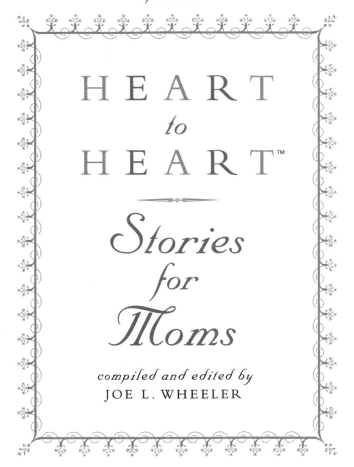

HEART
to
HEART™

Stories
for
Moms

compiled and edited by
JOE L. WHEELER

TYNDALE HOUSE PUBLISHERS, INC.
WHEATON, ILLINOIS

Visit Tyndale's exciting Web site at www.tyndale.com

Author photo by Joel D. Springer.

Heart to Heart is a trademark of Tyndale House Publishers, Inc.

Focus on the Family is a registered trademark of Focus on the Family, Colorado Springs, Colorado.

Woodcut illustrations are from the library of Joe L. Wheeler.

Designed by Jenny Destree

Published in association with the literary agency of Alive Communications, Inc. 1465 Kelly Johnson Blvd., Suite 320 Colorado Springs, CO 80920.

Library of Congress Cataloging-in-Publication Data

Heart to heart stories for moms / compiled and edited by Joe L. Wheeler.
    p.   cm.
  ISBN 0-8423-3603-6 (sc)
  1.Mothers—Fiction. 2. Mother figures—Fiction. 3. Short stories, American. I. Wheeler, Joe L.
PS648.M59 H43 2000   99-052555
813′.01083520431—dc21

Printed in the United States of America

05   04   03   02   01   00
7   6   5   4   3   2

Dedicated to

BARBARA LEININGER WHEELER

My story-loving mother not only
addicted me to sentimental Judeo-Christian
stories but is herself the prototype of the
best stories in this collection.

CONTENTS

ACKNOWLEDGMENTS

"Introduction: Motherhood—Yesterday, Today, Tomorrow," by Joseph Leininger Wheeler. © 1996. Printed by permission of the author.

"Beauty for Ashes," by Anna Brownell Dunaway. Published in *The Youth's Instructor,* May 26, 1925. Text used by permission.

"All Joy Gone," by Reva I. Smith. If anyone can provide knowledge of the earliest publication and date of this old story, please relay the information to Joe L. Wheeler, in care of Tyndale House Publishers.

"His First Step." Author and original source unknown. If anyone can provide knowledge of the origins of this old story, please relay the information to Joe L. Wheeler, in care of Tyndale House Publishers.

"The Golden Chain," by Josephine DeFord Terrill. Published in *The Youth's Instructor,* 1931, and in *Red Letter Day and Other Stories,* © 1942 by Review & Herald Publishing, Takoma Park, Md. Text used by permission.

"'Ketched,'" by Ida Alexander. Published in *The Youth's Instructor,* Feb. 21, 1928. Text used by permission.

"A Sandpiper to Bring You Joy," by Mary Sherman Hilbert. Published in *Our Family,* Oct. 1979, and in *Reader's Digest,* June 1980. Reprinted by permission of the author and the Reader's Digest Association, Inc.

"Houses and Homes," by Martha F. Simmonds. Published in *The Youth's Instructor,* March 12, 1929. Text used by permission.

"Billy Brad and the Big Lie." Author and original source unknown. If anyone can provide knowledge of the origins of this old story, please relay the information to Joe L. Wheeler, in care of Tyndale House Publishers.

"Applesauce Needs Sugar." Author and original source unknown. If anyone can provide knowledge of the origins of this old story, please relay the information to Joe L. Wheeler, in care of Tyndale House Publishers.

"Their Father's Wife," by Priscilla Hovey. Published in *The Youth's Instructor,* May 29, 1928. Text used by permission.

MOTHERHOOD—YESTERDAY, TODAY, TOMORROW

Joseph Leininger Wheeler

The mother's face is the child's first heaven.
—Mrs. C. T. Cole

*M*other—on earth, the ultimate source, the bedrock of our existence. She is the soil one germinates in, the inner sun and rain one flowers to.

Her voice is the first ever heard. She is the moon that summons and dismisses the tides of life, the pitch pipe that sets the melodic base, the rhythm that sets the beat.

By her health or lack of it, one either builds a life upon an unshakable rock—or is doomed to a lifetime of spinning helplessly in loose shale.

Her temperament becomes ours.

Her heartrending screams of anguish are the prelude to one's symphony of life. It is in the crucible of this agony that mother love is born; in that seething cauldron of pain are extinguished all vestiges of self-centeredness, perhaps explaining why mothers find it harder to deny children their heart's desire than do fathers.

Lydia H. Sigourney put it this way:

> Observe how soon, and to what degree, a mother's influence begins to operate. Her first ministration for her infant is to enter, as it were, the valley of the shadow of death and win its life at the peril of her own! How different must an affection thus founded be from all others!

Even after birth, life continues at her breasts—life itself still dependent upon the mother. The resulting bond is more intense and lasting than anything a father could possibly offer. Tactile memories—the earliest we know.

Never has the world needed mothers more than today. Their love is, after all, the deepest, purest, and most altruistic we know—second only to God's love itself. In that respect, what an

object lesson Christ gave us; in His dying agony on the cross—
scourged, beaten, bleeding, burdened with the weight of our
collective sins though He was—His last worry, His intense and
heartfelt concern . . . was for His mother!

> Near the cross of Jesus stood his mother, his mother's sister,
> Mary the wife of Clopas, and Mary Magdalene. When Jesus
> saw his mother there, and the disciple whom he loved stand-
> ing nearby, he said to his mother, "Dear woman, here is your
> son," and to the disciple, "Here is your mother." From that
> time on, this disciple took her into his home. (John 19:25-27)

MOTHERHOOD IN THE NINETEENTH CENTURY

In order to fully comprehend the complex choices women face
today, it is necessary to first step back into the past and study what
motherhood was then. In truth, it was both worse than it is
today—and better.

Worse, in that, through the centuries, the male-dominated
British legal system (the base from which American jurisprudence
sprang) so boxed women in that there was little they could call
their own. Young women experienced relentless parental and
societal pressure to *marry! marry! marry!* Not to marry was to be
stigmatized as a spinster, someone who was supposedly so unattrac-
tive that no man would marry her. When a woman *did* marry,
all legal control to anything she had previously owned passed
to her husband. Should he cast her off, she had virtually nowhere
to turn. Should he predecease her, his property went to the closest
male heir—and she could be evicted from her own home!

Her role in life was predetermined. As a child she was

conditioned to believe that marriage and family represented her only option in life. On the frontier and in rural America, chances were she would be married by fourteen, fifteen, or sixteen, after having completed perhaps three to six years of formal education—if she were lucky, she might get eight. Should she come from a more affluent family, she would be sent to a finishing school or seminary, there to be immersed in the classics, the arts, and religion. But afterward, the result was the same: marriage and family.

Once married, a woman was kept "barefoot and pregnant," with children coming at predictable two-year intervals. Her life expectancy was short (the average man would go through three wives during a lifetime), mainly because of death from childbirth complications. Just walk through any old graveyard and see how many women died in their prime.

This mind-set has been with us far more recently than one might think. Browse through family magazines of the '30s, '40s, and '50s—magazines such as *Saturday Evening Post, Collier's, Woman's Home Companion, Ladies' Home Journal, McCall's, Good Housekeeping,* and *Country Gentleman,* and read the fiction.

Again and again, you will find women portrayed as lovely to behold, charming, endearing, creative, lovable, rather intelligent in certain areas—but utterly helpless and incompetent in the male-dominated career world.

The jokes in all the magazines of those days were full of put-downs about women, usually lovable incompetent wives or shrewish mothers-in-law.

There were some compensations, however. Next to *God* and *country,* the most sacred word in the English language was *mother.* As the "weaker vessels," women were protected, respected, eulogized, pampered, and adored.

A woman knew clearly what her domestic portfolio included and what it did not. First and foremost, she was weighed in the balances and judged on how well she performed the duties and obligations of being a mother. That meant preparing meals on time (time set by the head of the household), making or purchasing suitable clothing, directing the children's education, apprenticing the daughters in the art of motherhood and housewifery, and providing spiritual leadership and direction for the family. Second, she was a wife, meeting her husband's needs and demands. She was her husband's support system, the oasis he returned to for regeneration after doing battle in his male-dominated, career-world jungle.

If she had time, she would lead a number of worthy causes: community betterment, educational strengthening and enrichment, church support, intellectual growth through organizations such as lyceum and Chautauqua, music, art, drama, etc.

The male of the species made the living. The female did the rest. Since that was so, the nineteenth century's deification of women is quite understandable. After all, she was the support system for both husband and children, and she almost single-handedly set the children's domestic, intellectual, artistic, and spiritual agendas. It was a world that both preserved the home and provided the basis for a society that was predominantly peaceful and productive. It was safe to walk the streets. It was safe for children to play in the front yard. Almost anywhere, night or day, a woman was as safe as she would be in church.

THE NEW WOMAN

In recent decades, all the rules have been rewritten. When I teach Great Books and get to *Don Quixote,* I point out to my students a very strange development in the book: the "quixotification" of

Sancho Panza and the "sanchification" of Don Quixote. Just so, during the last hundred years, we have begun to see the feminization of man and the masculinization of woman—and the resultant blurring of the sexes we label "unisex," sort of a biological Esperanto.

During both World War I and World War II, women were asked to step in and fill the job vacuum left by men in military service. Such responsibilities brought with them a very special sense of making a real difference in those troubling times. Many women wished to continue in career tracks when the wars were over; many did not and gladly returned to their home-based priorities. Certainly advances in birth control gave women options not available before. And medical research breakthroughs enabled women to live not only as long as men—for the first time in millenniums—but longer.

All these developments contributed to the changing status of women, bringing both good and bad consequences. Has the pendulum swung too far? Many women feel it has. They worry that their victories in the career marketplace may have cost them their femininity and destroyed both the family and society in the process.

We have seen during this unprecedented period of career growth for women the proportionate deterioration of marriages (one out of every two ending in divorce), a frighteningly large percentage of households being headed by only one parent, and the even more appalling fact that one out of every three children is born out of wedlock!

The term *new woman* has been with us a long time. In the September 24, 1896, issue of a venerable old magazine, *The Youth's Instructor,* was this observation by Max O'Rell, the celebrated French lecturer:

The Anglo-Saxon "new woman" is the most ridiculous production of modern times and destined to be the most ghastly failure of the century. She is par excellence the woman with a grievance and self-labelled the greatest nuisance of modern society. The new woman wants to retain all the privileges of her sex and secure, besides, all those of a man. She wants to be a man and remain a woman. She will fail to become a man, and she may succeed in ceasing to be a woman.

My use of the term *new woman* (in the Christian sense) applies to a radically different composite than O'Rell's. I am speaking here of the Christian woman who stakes out a centrist position. She is sophisticated, streetwise, earthy, funny, verbal (both in speaking and in writing), well read, computer literate, inner-directed, and self-assured; she has real integrity, is service oriented, knows where she is going, wants to be fulfilled as a wife and mother or in a professional career—or both, wants to be respected for her mind, skills, and talents but still admired as a woman, wants to have a good marriage that will last a lifetime and be supportive of a husband who will also be supportive of *her,* wants to raise a family and be at home with her children during those crucial formative years—and she loves the Lord.

What she seeks in marriage is neither the old nor the new but rather a synthesis. She most certainly does not want a return to second-class citizenship, and she is determined never to be walked on as her predecessors often were. But on the other hand, neither is she seeking to dominate. In that respect, she welcomes men's movements such as Promise Keepers, for she yearns for a man who is strong yet tender; one who believes in his own gifts and skills but does not look down on hers; one who will be an equal partner in parenting responsibilities—not a throwback to the past who will dump them all on her, one who loves the Lord and views marriage as a lifetime commitment, one who will continue to cherish her for her inner qualities even after her external beauty fades away.

She looks at the disintegration of the family and society . . . and is frightened. She distrusts the immoral messages of the omnipresent media so much that she is likely to be among the first generation of Christian mothers who will either pull the plug on the TV during their children's formative years or have the guts and stick-to-itiveness to rigidly monitor every program they watch. And she is looking for a mate who is strong enough to help her pull it off.

She is also willing—nay, eager!—to spend quality time with her children: reading stories to them; studying the Bible with them; helping them develop their talents and creativity to the fullest; encouraging them to broaden themselves through hobbies, wide reading, nature study, walks, trips, visits to museums and galleries, attendance at concerts, oratorios, and lectures. And most important of all, together with her husband, she desires to make the Lord and church attendance central as the children are growing up.

MOTHER SURROGATES

moth-er. 1. A female parent. 2. Mother-in-law, step-mother, or adoptive parent. 3. An old or elderly woman. 4. A woman looked upon as a mother, or exercising control or authority like that of a mother: *to be a mother to someone.* 5. The qualities or characteristics of a mother, as maternal affection. 6. Something that gives rise to or exercises protecting care over someone else. 7. Of, pertaining to, or characteristic of a mother: *mother love.* (*Random House Dictionary of the English Language,* 1974)

As supremely important as biological mothers are, in each of our lives are other women who also have a major impact on us. When we are young, grandmothers, aunts, older sisters, etc., become an integral part of our extended family support system. Mother surrogates such as stepmothers, stepsisters, stepaunts, and stepgrandmothers may exercise key developmental roles in our maturation. The same is true for unrelated women who "mother" us in any way.

Second only to the impact of the biological parent is that of the mentor. There comes a time—usually beginning in the teens and ending in the twenties—when we begin to build bridges away from our parents to other adults whom we admire. It is said that we learn more from our mentors than from any other source. Because we idealize them, we will imitate them; because we imitate them, we will someday become *like* them. Actually, mentoring never ceases: We are always either emulating a mentor or being one.

The stories in this collection feature all of these precious relationships: mothers, stepmothers, surrogate mothers, and mentors.

MY DREAM

It is my earnest hope that this collection of stories, along with the other books in this series, will enable you and your family to begin building a large collection of wonderful old stories. Stories that convey strong Judeo-Christian values; stories that are virtually impossible to put down once you start reading them. Stories that, when their values are internalized, will result in the kind of character we want our children to grow up with. And to those of us who are a little older, these stories will remind us of what life, the Christian walk, and our daily ministry to those around us are all about.

CODA

Each reader of this collection is invited to help us compile additional volumes by searching out other stories of equal power, stories that move the reader deeply, stories that illustrate the values this nation was founded upon. Many of these stories will be old, but others may be new. Please send me copies of the ones that have meant the most to you and your family, including the author, publisher, and date of first publication, if at all possible. With your help, we will be able to put together additional collections centered on other topics. You may reach me by writing to:

Joe L. Wheeler, Ph.D.
c/o Tyndale House Publishers, Inc.
P.O. Box 80
Wheaton, IL 60189-0080

May the Lord bless and guide the ministry of these stories in your home.

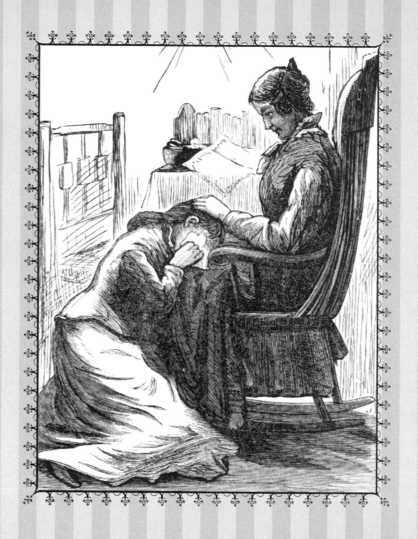

BEAUTY
FOR ASHES

Anna Brownell Dunaway

To red-haired, freckle-faced, green-eyed Bea Rainey, plainness—nay, worse than plainness!—was a curse almost impossible to endure. The last straw, however, was having to suffer through the senior class beauty contest, knowing full well she was the homeliest of all. So it was that she fled to her mother, imploring answers.

*I*f only Great-Aunt Lydia Fain had not wished her looks on me!" sighed Bea, thrusting hairpins into her red topknot. "Red hair, freckles, green eyes—I'll never be killed for my beauty." She snapped her barrette and continued plaintively:

"If I might only cover up a few defects with rouge and all that. But Daddy and Mother are so old-fashioned—there, stay down, you ugly things, you!" She gave a vicious stroke to her eyebrows. "I'd like to pluck 'em, like the girls do, every one out by the roots—"

"Bea—" It was her father's voice at the door, following a quick knock. "Can you hurry down this morning? Your mother has one of her blinding headaches."

"I'll be right down, Dad," called Bea cheerfully. She shook a small fist in the direction of the mirror. "For shame, whining about your looks with Mother sick. Just because tonight's the senior reception and you know you'll be a wallflower—there are the twins, at it again!"

She burst into the kitchen to find the twins engaged in a rough-and-ready tumble over the warmest place. Her father was halfheartedly putting on the teakettle. Ben was scowling over an obstinate necktie. The kitchen, bereft of Mother's customary presence, emanated gloom.

"Cheer up!" cried Bea. "If the sun has set, it will, as someone once observed, rise again. Now, I'm going to open some peach jam and make muffins. And there's gingerbread—"

"Hooray!" exulted Ben. *"Gingo, gingere, gingi, gimmesum."* His scowl had vanished before a sunny smile.

The twins, who stood nearby, giggled admiringly.

"He asked for gingerbread in Latin," marveled Belva.

Ben threw out his chin haughtily. "Latin is my middle name," he explained with condescension. "It is my mother tongue."

Everybody laughed. The teakettle sang. The table, laid out in its blue cloth, was inviting. From the oven came a tantalizing odor. Bea flew about with scarlet cheeks. Everyone drew up to the table merrily.

"You're your mother's own daughter, Bea," said Mr. Rainey, splitting a muffin. A look of relief had replaced his worried frown. "Do you suppose, Bea, you could run over to Aunt Sheby Buffalo's before school and get her to come and stay with Mother?"

"Of course," laughed Bea. "Aunt Sheby's heart's in the right place even if she does murder the King's English. The other day she called Mother's salvia 'saliva.' She—"

"Say, Bea," broke in Ben explosively, "I got to cram for an English exam. Can you give me a good example of enumerative inductive syllogism?"

"Let me think," murmured Bea distractedly. She was here, there, and everywhere, tying the twins' ribbons, hunting for mislaid books, wiping up milk that had been accidentally spilled. "Let me see, enumerative inductive—"

"Oh, Bea, the old cap's come off my shoestring," wailed Elvy.

"Wait, honey, I'll dip it in glue and dry it."

"My arithmetic!" cried Belva with tragic afterthought. "She gave us ten long problems; I forgot 'em. Bea, won't you work this one for me? I don't understand it."

"Tempus does *fugit,"* announced Ben. "Leave it, Belva; you're out of luck. Better hurry, Bea." He grabbed his cap and was off with a rush, as usual.

"I'll have to take the car," murmured Bea. She was hastily stacking the dishes, brushing up crumbs, getting things in order. At the last possible minute she gathered her books and ran across to Aunt Sheby's.

"You hadn't ought to run that way, Child," expostulated Aunt

Sheby when Bea had stated her errand. "You look as done out as a wilted spittoonia. I 'lowed to go over to the Aid dinner at the Disposition Building. They got contention tables extributed all over it. But then, lawsy, it's no matter. It don't make me no difference. I'll run right over and look after your ma—"

"Oh, thank you, Aunt Sheby," called Bea. She was already at the gate, signaling her streetcar. It was passing, and she caught it just as the doors closed. Two girls in the seat ahead of her were talking animatedly. They were very much rouged, and their ears were hidden under elaborate earmuffs. Bea recognized them as two sophomores.

"The seniors are going to hold their class election after school. I hear Beulah Gordon is to be put up for class beauty."

"For class beauty!" Bea repeated the words to herself with a little stab of pain. She remembered that today was the senior election as well as the class reception. And Beulah Gordon was to be accorded that great honor! She pictured Beulah, pretty, graceful, flaxen haired. To be acclaimed the prettiest girl—Bea sighed.

"These elections are all cut-and-dried affairs," the voice went on. "I hear Velma Doran is slated for the wittiest girl and Anne McConnell for the most charming and Mayme Bedford for the most artistic."

"Mere sops to disappointed beauty candidates," laughed the other, "consolation prizes, as it were. Here's where we get off."

Bea followed in their wake, nodding as she passed them in the hall. In the locker room, from the other side of the tier of lockers, she heard their frank comments.

"Isn't it too bad Bea Rainey is so plain—"

"And so old-fashioned. My dear, did you ever see such long skirts? They are positively to her ankles."

The first voice replied condescendingly. "If she'd dab a little rouge on those freckles and use a lipstick—"

They moved away, giggling. Bea, like an ostrich protruding its head, emerged from her locker with tears of humiliation in her eyes. Every vestige of color had left her face, and in the semi-darkness the freckles stood out like little golden flecks of light.

"If I could only be beautiful," she sighed with a half sob. "Oh, Aunt Lydia Fain—"

"Why, there's Bea!" A merry group of girls bore down, literally surrounding her. "Say, Bea, class election's at three o'clock sharp."

Bea nodded, winking back the tears.

"And, Bea, Bob Anderson's going to bring his city cousin to the senior reception," cried Velma Doran. "Just think, an Easterner from New York!" Velma adjusted an imaginary monocle. "Think how this Midwestern burg must look to him. There goes the warning bell. Hurry, Bea, help me with this translation."

"'How doth the little busy bee,'" broke in Anne McConnell. "Hold, minion—" she waved a haughty hand in Velma's direction—"I have a message to deliver. Bea, Mrs. Pitts wants you in the auditorium after English VIII. She needs you to take Jane's part in the chorus; seems Jane's got the mumps. And Miss Oliver wants you to referee the sophomore basketball game."

"My translation," urged Velma.

"If Latin were my long suit," declared Bea, laughing.

"Everything's your long suit," declared Velma. "It's Bea Rainey this, and it's Bea Rainey that."

"'First in war,'" chanted the girls in jubilant chorus, "'first in peace, and first in the hearts—'"

The clanging of the last bell scattered them. Bea's spirits rose subtly under their loving banter. But they fell again as she recalled the locker-room episode.

I will not go to the class election, she said to herself with a firm little set to her chin. *I'll run along home. Mother's illness is a good excuse.*

So at closing time, she donned her wraps hurriedly. Catching up her handbag, she fairly flew through the hall to avoid meeting the girls.

When she arrived home, her mother was resting easy on the lounge, Aunt Sheby in charge.

"You are home early, Little Dame Burden." Mrs. Rainey smiled.

Bea sat down soberly beside her. "Mother, why did I have to look like Aunt Lydia Fain?"

"Why, Bea—what is it?" For the tears were trickling in little rivulets down each side of Bea's nose.

"Mother, Mother—" It was out now, the burden that had suddenly grown too heavy to carry. "Mother, why did I have to look like her? Homely and freckled and gooseberry-eyed—and—with eyebrows that meet and a mouth like a catfish—"

"Aunt Lydia Fain," Mrs. Rainey broke in musingly, "once took the prize at a beauty contest. Everyone thought her beautiful. It was the beauty that shone from within. She had the oldest of beauty formulas found between the covers of an old Book—'to give unto them beauty for ashes.' And you are like her, Bea. We wouldn't trade those freckles for a king's ransom. And your eyes—they are limpid like a green sea."

"But, Mother, if you had overheard—" Bea's voice caught in her throat.

Mrs. Rainey was of the understanding kind. She guessed intuitively the hurt of careless speech. "No woman is beautiful," she said gently, "unless born so. Even then, without the soul, it is like frozen music. Anything can destroy beauty of features—illness, accident—"

Aunt Sheby Buffalo put in her head. "The cat," she imparted solemnly, "has took a fit and run up the viscera vine and fell in the system."

"She means in the cistern," gasped Bea and went into gales of laughter.

"It was a good honest cat," reproached Aunt Sheby, "as ever."

"There now, I'm over my doldrums," declared Bea. She wiped her eyes. "I'll rescue the cat and set the table. After that I don't mind donning the garments of mourning and being a wallflower at the senior reception. And when I'd decided not to go, too. But you positively can't pity yourself when you've laughed till your sides ache."

"No more you can't," agreed Aunt Sheby. "When I'm downheartedlike, whether I want to or not, I go 'round grinning like a Jessy cat."

"It's better than lipstick," averred Mrs. Rainey.

Later in her room, Bea slipped into her filmy green party gown.

"All it lacks is a train," she said whimsically. As she reached for a pin among her scattered belongings, her eyes suddenly encountered something strangely unfamiliar.

"Beulah's vanity case!" she gasped. "I must have picked it up by mistake! The very idea!" She opened it curiously, and an array of articles fell out. There was a bottle of liquid powder and a tiny box of rouge. Half guiltily, she moistened her finger with the liquid powder.

Recklessly she dashed the liquid powder on her face, and with an artistic eye rubbed some of the rouge into her cheeks, her lips, the lobes of her ears. She looked older, insincere. Bea could not imagine that artificial person laughing at the antics of a cat.

"Bea—" it was her father's voice from the hall below—"some girls are here for you. Are you ready?"

"Ye-es, Father," she called and took a long, searching look in the mirror. Above it, Aunt Lydia's pictured face seemed to gaze down in gentle reproof. Bea rushed into the bathroom and began scrubbing and splashing. With a laugh of relief, she caught up her coat and ran downstairs.

"Bea Rainey! The idea of your staying away from class election! But it didn't do you any good. You were elected the best all-around senior in Central High. Unanimously. And a reporter from the *News* is coming out to take a picture of you."

"Of *me!*" stammered Bea.

"Can you feature that?" exploded Ben.

Bea, glancing back as they danced out, saw him bumping the twins' heads together in an excess of delight. She had a composite picture of her father's proud smile, her mother's eyes, and Aunt Sheby's important air.

The reception was in full swing when they entered. Bea found herself presently ladling out fruit punch to thirsty friends. Between whiles, behind a huge palm, she tried to look with cheerful animation at the fairylike scene.

"Did you see Bea Rainey in that green gown?" The words drifted to her. Bea ducked her head quickly. "I saw her serving punch," the voice went on. "Do you know, I never knew anyone who could carry off red hair and freckles as Bea does. She is positively pretty."

They moved away. Bea's eyes followed them. "Can you— 'feature' that!" she mused.

"Are you too busy to serve some more punch?" inquired a voice at her elbow.

Bea started. The immaculate youth before her was none other than the fabled New York cousin. She cheerfully extended him a cooling drink.

"Oh, no," she offered calmly. "I am only walking a slack rope across Niagara Falls."

The youth laughed, and Bea laughed, too.

"I'm Jimmy Boyd," he said. "Do you mind my saying that I didn't know there was a girl like you left? I see plenty like them—" he flipped a thumb in the direction of the games—"but you—and Mother. She's—well, you know, sort of old-fashioned. Mother says I've been looking for your sort in the wrong places. That they'd be bending over cots in hospitals, paring potatoes, and—and—"

"Blooming as wallflowers," supplied Bea.

Jimmy Boyd laughed.

"A fellow gets sort of fed up on the other kind," he said and drained his fifth cup.

Several hours later, Bea blew a kiss in the direction of Aunt Lydia Fain's portrait. "So much," she whispered jubilantly, "for our fatal gift of beauty. You win, Aunt Lydia, even if your formula is as old as Holy Writ."

One of the most frustrating aspects of story anthologizing is that you fall in love with a writer, often on the basis of only a story or two, then discover that virtually everything else that person ever wrote has apparently disappeared from the face of the earth. In my case, this has been true with Anna Brownell Dunaway; other than three short stories and one book, I have met with a solid wall. Other than learning that she also wrote greeting-card messages prolifically, I have met with just as solid a wall there too. But I shall not give up! This has long been one of my all-time favorite stories. Aunt Sheby's malapropisms alone make the story a classic!

ALL JOY GONE

Reva I. Smith

Although this old story is very short, the message it packs is not. The careless words that cut like knives . . . never stop cutting, no matter how many years go by.

*J*enny awoke to the song of a robin—or was it to the yellow green shaft of sunlight that came filtering into her eyes through the crack between the window shade and the window frame? She listened for people sounds. No, Bobby wasn't up—no chatter, no clatter of toys. Daddy must be gone—he was never home when she awoke, for he had to be at work at six o'clock in the morning. And Mommy . . . she listened again. There was a familiar hum coming from the basement. Mommy must be doing the washing.

Jenny slipped out of bed and pulled back the window shade. How lovely was the world! Long blue-green shadows covered the lawn, with little patches of golden sunlight here and there, and soft whispering air that begged her to come out. She stood entranced, smiling to herself.

A happy thought struck her. *I'll surprise Mommy! I'll get dressed all by myself and go out and help her hang up the clothes.* Then another thought sobered her for a moment, but her smile soon returned. *Maybe she'll let me do it this time 'cause I'm bigger than I was that other day.*

She found the little dress she had worn the other day. After many struggles she turned it right side out and pulled it over her head. Fortunately it buttoned in the front. Now her panties and her sandals (the buckles finally surrendered to her four-year-old fingers), and she was finally ready to greet Mommy and the robins and the new day.

Softly she stepped out the front door into a fairyland of damp green, shining with silvery drops of dew. *Uh-oh!* she thought, *Mommy wouldn't want me to get my sandals wet.* Down on the bottom step she sat and laboriously unfastened the sandals. And the first step into that cool, soft wetness was worth every moment of buckle struggle! She slowly marched around the yard, watching the design her feet made in the grass. Then she stood perfectly still, smelling, listening, looking, feeling—the robin song again, the tickly grass, the flickering light between the leaves of the big catalpa tree, the sweet perfume of its blossoms. Her heart fairly burst with joy.

Then she started to the backyard to surprise Mommy, to help her with the clothes. Mommy would be proud of her. Mommy would be happy; she would laugh.

Mommy's back was toward her. Jenny slipped up behind her and encircled her skirt, as much of it as her short arms would encompass. "Mommy! Look! I got dressed all by myself." The beaming little face was turned up expectantly to Mother. But alas! No smile of approval was forthcoming, no praise for dressing all by herself, no approbation for remembering to remove her shoes before walking in the wet grass, not even a chance to say she had gotten up early to help Mother. Only a frown and the words, "Oh, Jenny! What did you put that dress on for? I was just going to wash it!"

Mother never knew the pain that stabbed that little heart, never saw the tears that welled up in the blue eyes. Jenny silently turned away and hurried back through the fairyland—but no, it was not pretty anymore. She could not see it through tear-dimmed eyes; she could not smell the catalpa blooms; no longer did the robin sing to her. Only the echo of a scolding voice filled her ears, her mind, her heart as she slowly ascended the stairs to take off the offending dress. She did not understand—she only felt.

Through fifty years the stab of pain is still poignant as Jenny, now a teacher, remembers that day. The sudden tears of a second grader brought it to her forcefully one day. Valerie was punching holes on sheets of construction paper where Teacher had marked them. She was rewarded with a smile as she handed Teacher the punched pages for the scrapbook the class was making. Then Valerie took another twenty sheets and made what she thought were properly spaced holes in them. But this time, instead of a smile of approval, her efforts were met with a stern, "Oh, Valerie, why did you do that? Those holes aren't in the right places—now all that paper is wasted!"

Valerie was crushed, and the tears quickly overflowed. Then suddenly the teacher's heart was again stabbed with the old pain of her childhood. Quickly she lifted Valerie to her lap and held her close, begging the child's forgiveness. And how willingly it was granted! Smiling through her tears, Valerie returned Teacher's hug with a fervent, "I love you, Mrs. Smith."

HIS FIRST STEP

Authorn Unknown

This story goes back a long way, and like a number of the best ones . . . somewhere, somehow, through the years, it lost its roots. I've searched for years but have been unable to find out who wrote it, and when and where it was first published—if indeed it has ever been published before.

Suffice it to say that it is one of the most moving stories of them all, one that my mother never got through without tears—and neither have I.

*T*he ward was cool in the half-light of early morning. The other children were asleep, but Tucker lay wide-awake. This was a special day—the day that Jim was coming again after four long months!

At the thought of seeing Jim, Tucker swallowed hard. He felt like crying, he was so glad; but a big guy, seven years old, who'd been through what he'd been through, couldn't cry just because his dad was coming, could he? Well, maybe he could—if his dad was all he had, and especially when Jim was the best dad in the world.

The ward was lighter now. He looked across the aisle. That girl was still asleep. Tucker eased himself up on his elbow and looked at her. Boy, she was pretty! Fat yellow curls, and he could see her eyelashes clear from here. He looked at her for a long time, for he was always interested in that bed. The bed across the way was the only one he could get chummy with. Suddenly the girl opened her eyes and looked straight at Tucker. He grinned at her. "Hi!"

She regarded him curiously, then said cautiously, "Hello."

"What's the matter with you?" Tucker asked. He had to know that. If it was just tonsils, she'd not be worth bothering with. Tonsils only stayed a day, but if she was an operation for a St. Vitus or something, she'd be here for a while. She was too quiet for a St. Vitus, though.

The girl looked him over carefully before she answered. "I've had pneumonia. Up on the fourth floor. I'm better now and was lonesome, so the doctor said I should be moved down here with the others to keep me from getting—uh—out of hand."

"Oh." Tucker didn't know just what "out of hand" was, but the girl seemed to know.

"What's your name, and how old are you?" he asked.

"Brenda Forsythe, and I'm seven."

"So'm I!" Tucker beamed. "And I've been here two years. A horse fell on me and hurt my legs. I've had bunches of operations," he added, seeing the gratifying amazement in her eyes. "Say—my dad is coming today! I haven't seen him for four months."

Brenda pushed her curls back loftily. "Well, my daddy would never leave me for four months, and my mother never left the hospital when I was so sick. I had three special nurses."

There was respect in Tucker's voice. "Well, Jim had to take care of the farm, or he wouldn't have left me either. And—" his chin lifted bravely—"I—I never had a mother."

There! She knew now. He'd told her. He lay back so he wouldn't see that look on her face. The lump was in his throat again, too. His cowlick waved defiantly as he burrowed into the indentation that his black head had made in the pillow. What if she did feel sorry for him? What if she did have a mother and—and—well, what did he care? Jim was coming. He was enough for anybody!

Doctor Holden had said that Tucker would be able to walk again soon and go home to the farm. At the thought of the farm, Tucker felt a warm, quivery feeling, but he refused to think about it. They were all so sure that he was going to walk, but he knew differently. He knew he never would because—well, he hadn't prayed like they had told him to.

Maybe God couldn't hear little boys that lived too far from church to go on Sabbaths, or maybe He was just too busy, because if He could hear, why didn't He answer? Tucker had prayed ever since he could remember, and it was always the same prayer. A prayer for a mother. He'd been so sure of that prayer! For a long time he'd climbed eagerly out of bed every morning and run downstairs to see if she'd come yet. But she had never come. And he'd never told Jim about it, because Jim trusted God so much.

So when Miss Lacey said every night, "Don't forget to ask God to help you, honey," Tucker just smiled, remembering that other prayer. And he had never asked Him to help him walk. He was afraid to.

The door opened and Miss Dawson came in carrying a pitcher of hot water. "Well! Wide-awake, Early Bird? And you, too, Brenda?" Miss Dawson looked tired. Tucker wondered how she managed to stay awake all night.

"Miss Dawson, my dad's coming today!"

"So I hear, Tucker. Come on now and get washed before breakfast." She popped a thermometer into his mouth as she sponged his hands and face. Tucker liked her, even if she wasn't as nice as Miss Lacey. But then—no one could be as nice as Miss Lacey. Miss Dawson was prettier, but Miss Lacey's gray eyes were kind and soft, and her brown hair fluffed under her white cap. He knew that taking care of little boys was fun to Miss Lacey.

When the nurse had gone, he cautiously moved his legs under the covers. Now that the heavy casts were gone, they felt like legs again and not big logs tied to him. He was supposed to wiggle his toes for exercise, but he'd never had the courage to try for fear that they really might not wiggle. But he would try sometime. Sometime . . .

He heard a quick, light step and looked up into Miss Lacey's twinkling eyes. "Two minutes past seven and three minutes until breakfast, Tucker Todd!"

"Oh, boy! It's Tuesday—and stewed apricots! Miss Lacey, what time do you s'pose Jim will come?"

"Jim?"

"My dad. You didn't forget he was coming today?" His voice was horrified until he saw the teasing laughter in her face.

She leaned over and smoothed his unruly dark curls, and her

voice was gentle. "No, I didn't forget, Tuck. I'll bathe you right after breakfast so you'll be all ready. Now let's prop up your pillow. Upsy-daisy!"

He liked the feel of her arms about him, and he liked the clean smell of her uniform.

The day swept on. Miss Hemstreet, the supervisor, was going over the charts at the desk; the voices of the other children hummed beneath the wailing of the baby down at the far end. Tucker, clean and shining, lay happily between smooth sheets. He closed his eyes. It was almost ten o'clock—

"Tuck!"

Tucker's eyes flew open, and for a breathless instant he looked up into the face so much like his own. Then he was clasped in strong, hungry arms and heard himself sobbing, "Jim! Oh—Jim!"

"Tuck, you little scamp! I believe you're getting fat!" Jim's voice trembled a little.

Tucker's eyes shone. Even if Jim's brown face did look a little thinner and more tired under his black hair, there wasn't a dad in the world as good-looking!

Jim's hand squeezed around the little white ones he held so tightly. "How're you doing, anyway, Skipper?"

Just then Miss Lacey came out from behind Brenda's screen. She saw Jim and smiled as Tucker said proudly, "This is my dad, Miss Lacey. This is Jim."

The smile deepened as she looked from one face to the other. "Yes," she said, "I can see that."

She came close, and Jim said, "You weren't here the last time I came."

"No. I've been here just three months." She turned to Tucker. "No wheelchair today, young man. Doctor Holden has a surprise for you!" She wouldn't tell him what it was, but went away with a bright nod to Jim and a gay little laugh for Tucker. "Wait and see, Tucker Todd!"

Jim stared after her, and Tucker pulled at his hand. "Sit down, Jim! What do you s'pose my surprise will be?"

"Guess you'll have to wait and find out, fella. What's her name?"

"What's whose—oh, Miss Lacey's? Why—Miss Lacey!"

"I mean her first name," he asked.

"I don't know. Why not ask her?"

An odd little smile tugged at Jim's mouth. "Maybe I will—someday!"

Then suddenly there was Doctor Holden, his gray head towering over Miss Lacey's. "Well, young man! And Jim! How are you?" They shook hands, and then Jim's eyes clouded anxiously as the covers were folded back from Tucker's legs. The little blanket spread over his chest and tummy made a little hill for Tucker to peer over.

". . . and daily massages and exercises," Doctor Holden was saying, "until now I think we've some pretty good legs here!" He tweaked Tucker's ear. "Think you can make 'em work?"

All the laughter left Tucker's face as he looked up at them. Oh, they couldn't! They couldn't mean they wanted him to walk! And he swallowed hard as he realized that this was the big surprise. Jim's face glowed as if a light burned behind it. "Tuck!" he breathed, and Tucker, suddenly ill, turned his face away. He clenched his fists under the blanket. He couldn't walk! He knew he couldn't! He hadn't prayed like Miss Lacey told him to, so how could he? They didn't know he hadn't prayed. . . .

He lived through the long hours of that day somehow, trying not to remember that this was the day he had looked forward to for so long. Now it had come—and gone.

"I don't care!" he told himself, lying awake in the lonely night. "I don't care!" But he knew deep down that he did care, for he knew for sure now that he couldn't walk. And Jim knew it, too. Jim!

Tucker had tried to tell them. "Please, Doctor Holden—I can't!"

"Sure you can, Tucker! Come on now!"

Jim, too. Jim's eyes burned in his white face. "Tuck! Just one step over here fella—then back home."

So Tuck, his eyes fastened on his father's face, had set out into that gulf of space between them. Just one step—but he never made it. Miss Lacey's arms caught him as he fell, and he heard her cry!

"Oh, please! Don't do this to him!"

They put him very gently back into bed, and Tucker heard Jim's whisper: "Doctor!"

"Now, now, Jim! Just be patient." Doctor Holden's voice was tired. "I can't understand it. Those legs are in fine shape! Well— we'll just have to keep on . . ."

Tucker shuddered there in the dark, remembering. He had known it would be like that. And he had let Jim down. He turned over, and a long quivering sigh escaped him.

"Tucker!"

He held his breath, but Brenda's whisper came again. "Don't cry, Tucker."

"I'm not crying! I wouldn't! Where's Miss Dawson?" He didn't want her to hear!

"She went in the other room with the baby. Don't feel bad, Tucker. You'll walk again one day."

"No, I won't!" he cried out fiercely. "I never will 'cause—"

"'Cause why?"

Suddenly he had to tell her. He couldn't tell Jim, or the doctor, or even Miss Lacey, but he could tell Brenda. "'Cause—'cause I didn't pray!"

"Well, why don't you?"

"It wouldn't do any good. I've prayed for—for other things and never got 'em."

Brenda sat up in bed and stared over at him. "Maybe you prayed for the wrong things. We never get what isn't good for us."

He thought that over for a minute; then he asked fearfully, "Do you think it's wrong to pray for—a mother?"

"Oh." There was a little pause. "No, it isn't wrong, but you know you can't get a mother, Tucker. Not a real one. I asked my mama once, and she said that you can only have one real mother. You can have stepmothers and adopted mothers, but only the one who has the same blood you have can be your real mother."

When he didn't answer, she lay back down again. He pretended he was asleep, but the tears pressed tightly against his eyelids, and it was all he could do to hold them back. He hated Brenda! She had shown him once and for all that praying wasn't ever going to bring him a mother. A real one—and Tucker Todd only wanted a real one. One with the same blood as his.

And he knew that he'd never say another prayer. Never . . .

Everyone was very good to him after that awful morning. His days fell into their old pattern, except that Jim stayed on with him. They weren't busy at the farm, he said.

He was a little late one afternoon, and he smiled as he sat down. "I found out her name."

"Whose name?"

"Miss Lacey's. It's Anne." Jim looked a little embarrassed. "I—I just happened to be at the front steps when she came out, and we walked a little way."

"Oh." Tucker's attention wandered across the aisle. "Look, Jim. Brenda's mama brought her that little dollhouse. Cute, huh? For a girl!" he added hastily.

"Hm-m." Jim surveyed Brenda's table, piled high with a riotous array of toys. He looked back at Tucker's table, empty except for bits of grubby modeling clay and broken and stunted crayons that clearly showed long hours of hard usage. "Hm-m-m," said Jim again. He was quiet for quite a while; then he stood up. "Look, Tuck, I've got to go out awhile. I just remembered something. I won't be gone long." His footsteps echoed away.

Tucker lay watching Brenda play with the dollhouse. Her mother was knitting; his eyes were fascinated by the needles as they dipped in and out of the blue yarn, and his eyelids began to droop.

The next thing he knew, Jim was back—a happy, laughing Jim. Miss Lacey was with him. "Surprise, Tucker Todd!"

"Oh, Jim! Are they—mine?"

"All yours, Skipper."

"Oh, man!" He reached eagerly, and Jim very carefully put the glass bowl into his waiting hands. It was a small bowl, but it was large enough for the three fish that swam distractedly about in it. There was a tiny little castle and some green moss, too. Tucker had never seen anything quite so beautiful! "All my very own!" He blinked rapidly. "I never had anything like this!"

"We'll put them on your table where you can watch them," Miss Lacey said, "and you can feed them yourself every day."

"I'm going to name them for the Wynken, Blynken, and Nod Miss Lacey sings about." Tucker looked up, and he didn't know why she turned away, nor why Jim cleared his throat as he said, quite simply, "Thank you—so much!"

After that Tucker was never lonely. His small world centered around his goldfish, and everyone who came in the ward—doctors, nurses, visitors—all stopped to admire as Tucker, beaming with pride of ownership, told them, "My dad gave them to me!"

From across the aisle, Brenda watched; her toys lay neglected on her table. Tucker tried to hold the fish so she could see better, but he almost spilled them and never tried it again.

"I wish I had some!" she said wistfully one night as her mother was leaving.

"For heaven's sake, Brenda!"

"Please, Mama!"

"Now listen, Brenda. You're going home tomorrow, and I'm not going to bother with any smelly fish!"

Tucker's eyes blazed. Smelly! His fish?

Brenda was still crying long after the lights were out, in spite of Miss Dawson's efforts to comfort her. Tucker stood it as long as he could; then he sat up. "Hey, Brenda! Shut up, can't you?" He took a deep breath and said quickly, "You can borrow Wynken, Blynken, and Nod!"

Her sobs suddenly stopped, and she looked through swollen eyes. "Now?"

"Yes, now—only stop bawling!"

So a place was cleared on Brenda's table by stacking things in a pile, and the bowl was transferred across the aisle. Tucker's eyes followed them. He had a funny feeling in his tummy, but it was too late to back out. He wished that he'd let Brenda bawl her head off! He could see a flash of gold once in a while, and his gaze was still fixed on the shining bowl when he finally drifted off.

Hours later he awoke with a start, wondering what had wakened him. He listened, but he couldn't hear Miss Dawson anyplace. She must have gone to night lunch. The nurse from the next division would peek in occasionally, but he knew how long it was between peeks. He sat up and knew in a flash what had aroused him. The high stack of Brenda's toys had collapsed and—oh! He stared at the overturned bowl, the moss and water on the floor, and at the three bright spots slithering on the hardwood.

A strangled cry choked him. His fish! His precious fish! He tried to call Brenda, but he couldn't utter a sound. Terror held his voice.

Then he felt words on his lips—new words formed soundlessly, words that were dragged from his heart where he had kept them hidden. "Please, God! Oh, please, God—" He pushed back the covers and was out of bed. "Please, God! I've got to! Help me, please!"

His head felt queer and light, and his legs had needles jabbing at them—but they moved! He jerked along as if he were on stilts—stilts that hurt and were stiff and burned him—but they moved. Through his dizziness and his gasping breath, he heard a funny, whimpering little voice that said over and over, "Help me, God! Oh—please—help—"

Somehow he stooped over and picked up three bright, quivering things, and then he turned slowly, painfully back. His whirling brain and his groping fingers searched frantically. His water glass. His—water glass! Where was it? The stilts soared through his dizziness and held him in space, but they still moved. . . .

His fingers closed around the water glass, and he dropped the three bright things and heard them plop into the water. It would do until—until—where was his bed? Things were spinning so! "And—thank You, God!"

The stilts gave way, and Tucker clutched wildly at nothing.

Then there was a sharp, hard pain as something struck his head, and Tucker Todd lay very still.

Someone was crying. Crying deeply and not caring. Tucker opened his eyes. Why, it was Jim! Doctor Holden was there, too, and Miss Hemstreet. The sun was shining! There was a bandage on his head, and the inside of his arm hurt.

"Jim?"

"Right here, Skipper!"

"Did I hurt me, Jim?"

"You've a bad gash on your head, fella, but it's all sewed up now. You're okay." He choked suddenly. "Tucker! Oh, Tucker! You—you walked!"

So that was why Jim was crying—because he was happy! Tuck sighed, and happiness flowed over him. Even if he did feel queer, he felt like he could fly, too. He'd done it. He'd prayed—and he could walk!

A light step came down the aisle, and Jim's voice fairly sang, "Anne!"

Then came Doctor Holden's voice. "What are you doing here? I thought I told you to stay off duty for a while, young lady?"

"Off duty? I should say not! I feel fine. How is he?"

"He'll be right as rain in a few days, thanks to you. He lost a lot of blood, but the transfusion picked him right up. It's a blessing you're the same type and were so close by." He took a deep breath. "Well, I'll be on my way now . . ." His voice trailed off. Miss Hemstreet followed after him.

"Jim."

"Yes, Tuck?"

"My arm hurts."

"That's where the needle went in, Skipper. You have a pint of new blood to make up for last night's performance. And Tuck, listen—" Jim's voice shook. "There's something else. How—how would you like to have—a mother?"

Tucker lay quite still, with his eyes closed. He knew Jim meant Miss Lacey. Well, he loved Miss Lacey more than anyone, outside of Jim, but having her wouldn't be having a real mother—not like one with the same blood.

She bent over him, her face pink and her eyes shining. "He's trying to tell you, Tucker Todd, that I've always wanted a little boy like you."

He looked up into the gray eyes, and suddenly all his doubts faded at what he saw there. His arms went around her neck. "Oh, Miss Lacey—Anne! I do love you so very much!" It was then that he saw the white gauze on the inside of her elbow. "Your arm!"

"Never mind that, Tucker. It's just where they took the blood. It doesn't hurt. You have the same blood that I have now, young man, so—why, Tucker!" She stopped at the look of incredulous joy that swept over his face. A look so near to awe that she was startled. "What on earth—!"

"Oh!" Tucker sobbed as he pulled her down to him. "He heard me. Oh, He did hear me! And you're—*real!*"

And Tucker Todd, age seven, broke down and cried like a man.

THE GOLDEN
CHAIN

Josephine DeFord Terrill

There comes a time in our life when our parents' work is done and a teacher's begins. It is no exaggeration to say that second only to the impact made by the parents is that made by Christian teachers who help bridge the gap from childhood or adolescence to adult self-sufficiency. Blessed are they who have had at least one such mentor—someone like Professor Eman—to light the way.

*P*hyllis sat down on the long, oak bench that stood across the end of the hall near the letter rack just outside the Dean of Women's door. The handwriting on her letter aroused her curiosity; she must read it before she went down to supper. It read:

> *Dear Phyllis,*
>
> *You have been chosen from the group of girls in college this year to become a member of a club which is being formed at this time. Until we can have our first meeting to discuss the details more fully, we think it would be better if the existence of the club is unknown to the general student body.*

Phyllis flipped the page over to find the signature. Margaret Eman, the lovable psychology teacher! Phyllis's eyes shone with excitement as she devoured the rest of the letter.

> *In the meantime, we have outlined some definite work to be done by the members. The requirements for this week are as follows:*
>
> *First, please memorize these words: "I expect to pass through this life but once. If, therefore, there be any kindness I can show or any good thing I can do to any fellow being, let me do it now and not defer or neglect it, as I shall not pass this way again."*
>
> *Second, please find time for a short get-acquainted conversation with ten freshman girls and keep a list of their names where no one will see it. Your purse will make a perfect hiding place.*
>
> *If you feel that you do not care to join our club, please see me in my classroom not later than tomorrow afternoon. Otherwise*

we shall consider you one of us. Remember, we shall depend upon you not to discuss this letter or the plans of the club with anyone.

Be diligent! Be true!

Very sincerely yours,
Margaret Eman

Phyllis read the letter through twice before she thrust it into her pocket and went down to supper. A sudden elation filled her. The words were tingling in her brain: *"You* have been chosen." "A club which is being formed." Was she being rewarded for some unremembered act of friendliness, to be chosen from among all the girls at Wilbur College? Hardly knowing what she was doing, she chose her tray of food at the cafeteria counter and walked into the dining room. There was a scattering of students there. Two freshman girls were sitting alone at a table over in one corner. Instantly Phyllis realized that here was her first opportunity to begin work for the club.

"Do you mind if I sit with you?" she asked, her voice vibrant with emotion.

The girls looked up in surprise and murmured something in unison, while Phyllis removed the food from her tray and sat down.

"I hope I'm not interrupting a private chat," she began.

"Not at all," assured one of the girls.

"We just stick together because we don't know anybody else," giggled the other.

Phyllis smiled. "Are you roommates?"

"Yes, we are," replied the first student, her voice warm and courteous.

"Is this your first year?" A useless but complimentary remark.

"Yes, we're freshmen," laughed the second one again.

Phyllis liked them both at once, the one with her infectious sense of humor and the other, whose manners were so lovely. They ate in silence for a moment; then a question was asked, and Phyllis soon found herself expanding garrulously, her new interest in philanthropy luring her on. She told them useful details of dining-room procedure to which both girls listened eagerly. After they had finished eating, Phyllis asked if they would like to walk around the campus as everyone did while waiting for the bell to call them in to worship. The girls readily agreed. As they passed groups of wistful-eyed freshmen, Phyllis imagined that they looked enviously at the two of their number who had grown so chummy with a sophomore.

As soon as worship was over, Phyllis hurried to her room and, snatching a piece of paper, wrote two names and thrust them into her purse.

After breakfast the next morning, before her seven-thirty class began, Phyllis saw a girl standing beside the banister on the first floor of the administration building. Hildreth was one figure in the Freshman Class who could not fail to attract attention, for she was probably the tallest person in the entire school. Phyllis sauntered down the stairs and stopped two steps from the bottom, which put her on a level with the girl's face. "We are both early birds," she remarked, to open the conversation.

Relieved by the sense of ease it gave her to be on a level with the one to whom she was speaking, Hildreth smiled, her finely wrought face lighting up eagerly. "Then we should be lucky all day," she answered, her voice low and very musical.

Something in the girl's face touched Phyllis's heart. "If there be any kindness I can show . . ." Surely these first days in a new place must be hard for a girl as conspicuous as Hildreth, for there is always the inevitable joker whose lack of heart matches his lack of wit, always new faces to stare with faintly concealed amusement or curiosity at anything unusual. Seeing the fine edge of defiance in the girl's eyes, Phyllis resolved suddenly that she would come here a little early every morning to stand on the steps and talk with her.

"What class are you waiting for?" Phyllis asked.

"I'm taking psychology from Miss Eman."

"Isn't she marvelous?" exclaimed Phyllis.

"I think she is very charming and unusually capable as a teacher."

"Everyone adores her. I had her last year."

"Are you a junior?"

"No, a sophomore."

When Phyllis went to her room for a moment just before chapel, she did not forget to slip a new name into her purse, and with a heart pounding with joy, she repeated the already special verse: "I expect to pass through this life but once. If, therefore . . ."

Every day Phyllis watched for a letter announcing the meeting of the new club. Exactly one week from the day the first letter came, another lay in her compartment of the letter rack. Eagerly she opened it.

> *Dear Club Member,*
>
> *By now you have begun to understand the meaning and the purpose of our organization. I want to thank you for the way you have responded to the work asked of you. Already we seem to have achieved our aim, which is "Not a lonely girl in Wilbur College."*

That corroding loneliness which destroys the happiness of the usual freshman's first weeks in school is not so evident this year, thanks to the work of our society. A friend with a smile and a cheery greeting is worth more at the beginning of the year than any number of friends at the end of the year. Those girls whom you have befriended this week will never forget you. I know because I was once a college freshman.

We find that we must postpone our meeting until a little later, but in the meantime we want you to continue getting acquainted with freshman girls. Keep your list as you did last week. And please learn these words: "Happiness is a perfume which you cannot give to others without spilling a few drops upon yourself."

If you should feel the urge to discuss our club with one of your friends, turn to Matthew 6 and read the first six verses.

Be diligent! Be true!

Sincerely yours,
Margaret Eman

At the end of the third week, the third letter came.

Dear Club Member,

We have decided to postpone our meeting until you have had an opportunity to meet every girl in the Freshman Class. So do not grow weary of well-doing.

Have you found the friend you have always dreamed of finding someday? Perhaps she is a member of this year's Freshman Class.

Somewhere there waiteth in this world of ours
For one lone soul, another lonely soul;

Each chasing each through all the weary hours
And meeting strangely at one sudden goal.

I shall write you each week.
Be diligent! Be true!

Sincerely yours,
Margaret Eman

Phyllis had little time anymore for her own special friends, and though she missed them, yet the happiness she found in making new friends eclipsed the pleasure she had known in her old group.

She began to feel that she knew everyone in school, and she was constantly busy waving or smiling greetings as she went about her daily schedule. At the end of six weeks she had the name of every girl in the Freshman Class in her purse. Only a very few of them had not responded to her offers of friendship, but she determined to undermine their misanthropic tendencies bit by bit as the year progressed.

She knew that she had given happiness to many, yet she realized that she herself had received more than any of them. Her own ability to offer and accept friendship had increased a thousandfold, her powers of sympathy and understanding had deepened beyond measure, and her poise and manner had gained in grace. The "spilled drops" of the perfume of happiness that had fallen to her made her feel that she must be the happiest girl in all Wilbur College. She often wondered which of the other girls were members of the society, but there was no evidence of a planned campaign of friendship, except, perhaps, the entire lack of cliques and the unusual intermingling of freshmen and sophomores.

A week before the Christmas holidays, a special meeting of the Sophomore Class was called in the chapel one evening after worship. A short business session was conducted first, and the boys were dismissed to return to their rooms for their evening study period. The faculty adviser made a few remarks and then turned the girls over to the special speaker, the psychology teacher, Miss Eman.

"We have come here for a double purpose tonight, girls," she began, her eyes smiling in their personal way. "I hope you won't feel that we have played too many tricks on you when we explain."

A faint suspicion began to brew in Phyllis's mind. She leaned forward in her seat.

"Last fall, your Dean and I decided to form a club comprising certain sophomore girls. We wrote you letters asking that you join and perform certain duties, which you have done whole-heartedly. I think that all the members of that club are here tonight, so we are going to reveal ourselves. Will those girls who belong to this club please stand?"

There was a moment of hesitancy as if the girls were reluctant to disclose Miss Eman's partiality. Then, here and there, the shuffling of seats. A moment of breathtaking silence. Then a storm of laughter broke out, and wave after wave swept back and forth across the chapel. Every girl in the room was on her feet!

When the laughter had subsided, the teacher spoke. "I was sure you would be surprised to learn that our club consists of the entire class. I simply could not decide which of you to leave out, so I chose every one of you. But I was afraid that if you knew that you were working as a class, you would not feel that same enthusiasm as if you worked independently."

Phyllis nodded her head, realizing the truth in that.

"I should like to tell you," began Miss Eman, composing her features for a long, serious talk, "just what started the idea of our club. Last fall, as I sat in chapel watching the freshman girls take their places for their first assembly, I wondered how many of them were suffering from homesickness. In spite of all that is done during the first days of school by the Dean of Women, the administration, the teachers, and the older students, we still find way too much real distress among our new students.

"So I began to study the situation and decided that if we had an organization the specific duty of which was to make friends with these girls, we could prevent much of this homesickness. We all realize that there is no particular character-building value in the agony of loneliness. It is true that we need to learn independence, to stand on our own feet, to know the value of solitude, but all these things can be learned much better when the mind is free.

"Out of the slough of loneliness sometimes grow rare and beautiful characters, but more often that slough produces only blighted and bitter personalities. In most cases here in school, that early depression passes away with the finding of friends, but in the meantime there is much needless heartache. Far too often friendships are not formed until near the end of the year, whereas had they been made at the beginning, much happiness and benefit might have been realized.

"This year, by the help of my faithful crew of sophomore girls, we have had less homesickness than in any other year I have ever known. Innumerable fine friendships have formed already. School spirit and general cooperation have improved unbelievably."

As the tears gathered in her eyes, Phyllis knew the taste of real happiness. She recalled her struggles with Doreen, who at first was so unresponsive, so uncaring. Pauline had been contemptuous of the simple ways of their school; Harriet had not understood why rules must be obeyed.

Miss Eman continued. "The first week of school I talked personally with every one of the freshman girls. The second week I found time for a moment with every sophomore girl. I asked many of them how they felt this year in comparison to the way they felt at that time last year. Their answers convinced me that among them I should find the helpers we needed. We teach many subjects here at Wilbur College, but to me the most important thing to learn is the art of being kind. And to be kind in this case means to be friendly. There was a little book published a few years ago titled *The New Thing in Her Heart.* It was the story of a secret that an elderly woman whispered into the ear of a young girl. The secret was this: *Everybody is lonesome!* If we could always remember that, I am sure that we would always be kind."

There was a sudden trembling in the speaker's voice. She paused a moment. Then she said, "Let us repeat our first memory verse in unison."

Slowly, with subdued emotion, they began: "I expect to pass through this life but once. If, therefore, there be any kindness I can show or any good thing I can do to any fellow being, let me do it now and not defer or neglect it, as I shall not pass this way again."

"Now our aim."

"Not a lonely girl in Wilbur College!"

"Our motto."

"Kindness is the golden chain by which society is held together."

"Thank you, girls. And now may I tell you how much we appreciate your work this fall. The faculty of Wilbur College is proud of its class of sophomore girls. You have solved many problems for us, and you have prevented many more problems from developing.

We shall always be grateful to you. And now that you have done your work so well, we feel that there is no longer a need for our society to continue. Our first meeting is also our last. I am sure that each of you has learned enough about the joy of making friends to lead you to continue this delightful hobby throughout your entire life. You will always remember that we pass our way but once. Opportunities lost do not come again."

There was a moment's pause; then she continued: "Our experiment this year has been abundantly successful. Whether we shall try it again next year, we do not know. For the present, our work is done. Shall we feel free now to discuss our society and its methods? I shall leave that to the personal judgment of each girl. It seems to me, however, that we shall realize a more lingering satisfaction if we do not publish it abroad—at least until this present year is over. We do not want our freshman sisters," she laughed, "to think that we have gained their friendship by the aid of conspiracy."

"I believe that it is time now to return to your study period. Shall we stand and repeat for the first and last time, in unison, the last verse we learned?"

The girls rose and with hushed voices repeated, "Make it a rule and pray God to help you keep it, never to lie down at night without being able to say, 'I have made one human being a little wiser, or a little happier, or at least a little better this day.'"

Margaret Eman's eyes were shining. "And now may I say good night to the grandest group of sophomore girls in any college in the world."

Josephine DeFord Terrill

Josephine DeFord Terrill was a well-known writer of Judeo-Christian stories during the first third of the twentieth century.

"KETCHED"

Ida Alexander

*I*f only Mother didn't say ketched, mused Esther, then she'd feel comfortable asking her sophisticated roommate home during the summer! Well, it wasn't to be helped, she sighed.

*E*sther Shaw ran up to her room and locked the door before she opened her mother's letter. It was the last letter she would receive before going home for vacation. A feeling of relief came to her at the thought.

It had not always been easy to screen the letters from observation. So often one of the girls ran in before she had finished the letter; many times Lola Reid, her roommate, had watched her with questioning eyes. She had learned to be very careful of them after a time. Hungry as she always was for the dear home news, she usually waited till she was secure from interruption.

"I'm a little—beast!" she said as she reached the end of the letter. "And Mother is dear—*dear*. I oughtn't to mind a bit."

She glanced through the letter again with shining eyes. It was full of loving plans for the coming vacation. Esther's heart was tender as she read. But she put it down at last with a half sigh.

"If only Mother wouldn't say *ketched,*" she said to herself. "I'd be perfectly happy, I believe."

After a moment she put the letter away with the others. There were many of them. Mother was a faithful correspondent. And the letters were full of the little home happenings so dear to the exile's heart. Even the news that Roy had "ketched" two linnets was welcome.

"You've had a letter!" Lola cried when she came in. "I know it by your eyes. They're all soft and shining after you've heard from home."

"Yes." Esther smiled. "I had a letter from Mother—the dearest letter, full of vacation plans and home news. My brother Roy has caught two linnets, beautiful singers. He is taming them. By and by they'll eat out of his hand. And the bossy cow has a little speckled calf to show me when I go home."

"Lucky girl," sighed Lola, "with a farm waiting to welcome

you! I've always loved country life, though I've never had any of it—just trips now and then."

"I like it," said Esther. "I can hardly wait to get home and see all of them. It will seem strange at first to be at home. But after a day or so, I'll forget I've ever been away."

"Yes, I know how it is. I guess it's the same with everybody. Think of there being only two days more! Then we're off for home. It seems too good to be true."

"How are you going to spend your vacation, Lola? Are you going away?"

"The first two or three weeks we're going touring in the auto. I don't know what will come afterward. But good times of some sort. Mother is perfectly wonderful. She gets up the nicest things. And they're always to please me. Oh, she's the most wonderful mother! I couldn't tell you in a hundred years all that she is, all that she has been to me."

She paused.

"I know," agreed Esther. "I know by my own mother. I guess all mothers are wonderful." She half sighed as she said it. What would Lola think if she knew her mother said *ketched?*

"This automobile trip," Lola went on, "is because of my love of the country. Father and Mother planned for it the very first thing on account of me. I know, though they didn't say so. I wish we could live in the country as you do. Father and Mother would like it, too. But we have to live in the city on account of Father's business. I wish you were coming with us on the trip. We'll have a fine time. *Couldn't* you come?" Lola spoke eagerly.

Esther would have liked to go and could have gone, except for the return invitation which would be in order. She put the thought away in a fraction of a second.

"No, I couldn't go, much as I'd like to," she answered laughing.

"They'd never in the world spare me for three days, let alone three weeks. The boys have about a thousand things to show me. And the girls will be clamoring for every other minute. Between Mother and Father and the rest of them, I expect I'll not have much idle time. But it is dear of you to want me."

Long after Lola was asleep that night, Esther lay wide-eyed, worrying that she could not ask her to spend at least part of her vacation at the farm. She would like to have her. Mother, Father, all would like it and make her royally welcome. And yet she could not bring herself to give the invitation. Thoughts of her mother had stopped it whenever it trembled on her lips. She reddened in the darkness about the unworthy feeling. She hated herself for it.

If—only—Mother—would—not—say—ketched, was her last waking thought.

There were many things besides that—many, many things. But Esther found that she did not mind them, now that she was at home, away from the school where such things were so much emphasized. A sweeter, saner viewpoint came to her before she had been at home a day. And when her mother bade her come and see the linnets Roy had "ketched," she laughed in sheer delight, scarcely hearing or heeding the unlovely word.

The first few days were busy ones. Esther followed the others from grainfield to orchard, from orchard to meadow, down to the spring. There were so many new things to see, so many old ones to claim her attention once more.

And always there was the quiet talk with her mother and father after the others were in bed.

Lola's name came up many times.

"She must be a dear girl," said the mother. "I like everything I heard told about her. Why didn't you ask her to come an' stop with us a spell, Daughter, seein' she loves the country so, an' all?"

Esther's cheeks flared a sudden red, but in the glow of the firelight neither Mother nor Father noticed.

"Well, they had this automobile trip planned," she answered evasively, "so she couldn't come very well."

"But after it was over she could most likely come," persisted the mother. "An' we would of admired to have her. She'd be a sight o' company for you, too, Child."

"Company!" cried Esther. "Do I look as if I needed company, Mother? Why, I've forgotten what the word *lonely* means! When I wake up in the morning, I usually find Susie or Meg perched on the foot of the bed, waiting for me to open my eyes. And from that time on I'm seldom alone."

"I didn't know they did that. I must stop 'em. I'm afraid they pester you, Child."

"I love to have them," affirmed Esther. "I've been positively *hungry* for all of you, Mother; it's so nice to be home once more!"

The talk drifted away from Lola.

But it returned to her time and time again. The mother's hospitable soul yearned to bring the country lover to the country.

"You'd ought to ask her, Esther," she said more than once. "I hate to think of her missin' all these lovely days."

And Esther, seemingly assenting, diverted the talk into other channels.

Yet a strain of persistency in the mother refused to let the subject drop. There was no merrymaking at which she did not bewail the absence of the uninvited guest, few days when she did not say about one thing or another, "It's too bad Lola ain't here. She'd of liked this."

One night when she and Esther sat alone together, the mother eyed Esther shrewdly through her glasses. Suddenly she leaned forward and looked her daughter directly in the eyes. "I been thinkin'," she said. "An' at last I found out the real reason why you don't want Lola to come."

"No!" cried Esther.

"But I have. It come to me jest a few days ago. I spoke of it to Father. I been waitin' to speak of it to you."

Esther covered her face with her hands and said no word. *I'll never be happy again,* she thought dully. *And how can Mother forgive a thing like this? Most things could be overlooked or forgotten in time. But this will—hurt.*

"To think you wouldn't know your own mother better, after all these years! To think—"

"Mother!" cried Esther with a sob in her voice. "Mother, I . . ."

Her mother leaned over and patted Esther's knee with her work-worn hand.

"There! There!" she said. "I guess it ain't no crime, even if it's kinder gone out of fashion for girls to be careful of their mothers. But you'd oughter knowed me better. You'd really oughter, Esther. You don't need to ever think of that again. I'm plenty strong, an' with the help all of you give me, I can manage one more easy as—easy as makin' pies! 'Tis no more trouble to cook for eight or nine than 'tis for what I do for now."

Esther looked up. Relief was on her face, in her heart. In some miraculous fashion the real reason was still unguessed.

"You mean—," she faltered, her hand reaching out for her mother's.

"I mean I found you out," her mother continued fondly. "You

been trying to spare me. You been thinkin' Lola'd make too much work for me. An' that's why you wouldn't have her. For I knowed you wanted her from the first time you talked about her. I want her, too, Daughter. I want you to write an' invite her."

Esther could find no word to say. She sat and stared at her mother with troubled eyes.

It was some time before Mrs. Shaw understood what that dumb gaze meant. "That wasn't the real reason, after all?" she asked.

Esther shook her head. She could not trust herself to speak. Nor could she find shelter under a direct falsehood.

The mother sat awhile in silent thought. At last she brought forth the result of her musing but slowly, hesitatingly, as one not half-convinced of what she said. "It ain't—it ain't that you think she'd mind our plain way of livin', is it?" she asked.

"No, little Mother," cried Esther heartily. "It isn't that at all. The living is fit for a king. And there's not so good a cook as you in a dozen counties."

The mother beamed. She never had lost her pleasure in the praise of those she loved and toiled for. "I couldn't believe 'twas that." She smiled. "From your description of her I misdoubted she wasn't that kind of a girl. But her folks is well fixed, ain't they?"

"All the people whose daughters attend Miss Blakeley's school are well fixed, you extravagant mortal! No one but you would have sent me there when it costs as it does. And I'm not worth it, Mother; really, I'm not."

"I wanted you to have a good finishin'," said the mother. "Education's a great thing. An' Pa could afford it easy enough. We want our children to have the best there is. An' no best is too good for you, Esther."

"Don't think too well of me, Mother, or I'll cry," pleaded Esther, her head in her mother's lap.

"Well, I won't say what I think, if you don't like it. It's funny you don't. Fur my part, I always did enjoy a mite of praise."

"But you deserve it," said Esther soberly.

"No more'n you. Now this much I *will* say: A prettier or a sweeter girl than you ain't been raised, even if I say it, as I shouldn't. An' I calkilate Lola's a good deal like you, by you likin' her. 'Birds of a feather flock together' is a pretty true sayin'."

"Yes, Lola is sweet, Mother, sweet and dear. If you're sure she won't be a trouble to you, I'll write later and ask her to come."

"I'd admire to have her," said the mother. "I certainly would, an' no mistake. You write, Esther, right off, an' tell her to come an' stay jest as long as she's a mind to."

In her self-reproach, her shame, and her disgust at herself, Esther was eager to make amends. But the days slipped away, and the letter was unwritten—sometimes it would be recalled to mind by her mother; sometimes, as she watched the automobiles flying along the country road, it came to her in that way. Still the invitation was never written.

One day her mother sought her where she sat in the shade reading. She closed the book as her mother drew near and made room in the hammock for her.

"Sit beside me and rest awhile," Esther invited. "I was coming to you as soon as I'd finished the chapter. But I'm glad you came out."

"I came 'cause I've a s'prise for you," her mother said.

"Tell me." Esther smiled. "Ginger cookies?"

Her mother shook her head. "Miles off."

"Strawberry shortcake again?"

"No, 'tain't strawberry shortcake. But it's somethin' jest as sweet."

Esther guessed and guessed but gave it up at last. "I've guessed everything you've ever cooked, I believe," she laughed.

"I didn't say 'twas nothin' I was cookin'."

"Well, you always make us guess what you have for dinner. So I thought that was it."

"It's nicer than cookin'."

The eyes behind her glasses twinkled in their pleasure in the coming surprise. But Esther would guess no longer.

"Tell me! Tell me!" she cried eagerly as a child.

"I waited an' waited for you to write to Lola. An' you kept puttin' it off. So I up an' writ myself."

"You did?"

"I writ to her myself, so there wouldn't be no mistake. I got the address out of your desk. An' I writ my name in the corner an' said for it to be returned if 'twasn't delivered in four days."

Esther hugged her mother to her and kissed the eager face.

"I writ for 'em all to come an' stay a spell if they could manage it," she went on. "The spare room's nice an' ready, an' Lola kin sleep with you. Now that's off my mind, I kin kind of settle to things. I ain't felt jest myself with that hangin' over me."

After her mother had gone happily away, Esther sat and thought it all out. "If only she hadn't asked the mother and father!" she cried to herself. "Oh! I don't think I can bear it."

That was the thought that hurt. She could not bear to think of the contrast the two mothers would be. She scourged herself for the feeling as she had done at school. Quite unguessed, however, there lurked side by side with the smaller feeling a large one. And that one was love. It was love that would have protected her mother from the criticism of strangers.

But at the end of four days the letter was returned. Mrs. Shaw's face fell as one of the boys brought it in. "Then they ain't home yet," she said. She was so disappointed that Esther shared her disappointment, even though her own feeling was relief.

"Never mind, Mother," she cheered her. "I'll get another letter off in a few days, and they'll surely be home by then. It's a pleasure delayed, not lost."

"I was depending on 'em getting here by day after tomorrow at the latest. An' I've baked nearly everything I knowed how to. Now it will be wasted, like as not."

"If you think the food will go to waste," said Roy, "why don't you ask to supper those people whose car is broken down? They seem in a pretty bad fix; they've been tinkering for hours. And we're the nearest house."

He had spoken half in jest. But his mother's eyes lighted with hospitable eagerness. "Fetch 'em up! Fetch 'em up!" she cried. "How many air they? An' where is the car stuck?"

"There are two ladies and a man," Roy explained. "And they're stuck a piece up on the country road—about a quarter of a mile, I guess."

"Well, give 'em my compliments, an' ask 'em up. Dear knows but what they'll be glad. Thank goodness I got things fixed for a good supper."

Roy was not gone long. When he came back, the three strangers walked beside him up the long driveway that led to the house. The man was bundled up with rugs and carried tools. Roy and each of the women had a bundle or a bag.

Mrs. Shaw and Esther waited on the porch to welcome them. Suddenly, as they drew nearer, something vaguely familiar in one of the figures struck Esther. She looked more closely. "Mother!"

she cried. "It's Lola and her mother and father. Your visitors have come, after all."

Both ran down the steps to meet them. As Esther ran, her mind worked rapidly and not in the old groove. Her mother, her dear mother, no one must belittle her! Who was there like her? Let them give a slighting glance if they dared!

After the hasty introductions and congratulations on both sides, all walked back to the house.

"I was so glad to find 'twas you," the mother cried. "I writ a letter, invitin' you all to come. An' think o' you gettin' ketched almost at our very door!"

"The best luck we could o' had," Lola's mother answered. "This is the third time we got ketched on this trip, too."

For a moment, Esther thought Mrs. Reid had shown a finer courtesy than she ever had known. But the next words undeceived her.

"I says to Loly this mornin', says I, 'We ain't had a bit o' luck on this trip.' An' all the time this good luck was waitin' around the corner. It's the funniest thing I ever heerd tell of."

Ida Alexander

Ida Alexander was a prolific writer for inspirational magazines during the early 1900s.

A SANDPIPER TO
BRING YOU JOY

Mary Sherman Hilbert

*I*t's funny, isn't it? Some of the longest things one reads are the hardest to remember, and some of the shortest ones prove virtually impossible to forget. This short story is one of the latter. Quite simply, once you hear it, it will haunt you the rest of your days.

The characters are three: a winsome child, a wounded mother, and a pain-wracked daughter reeling from the suffering of her ailing mother. The setting: the sea.

These brief meetings were but wisps in the vast waving fields of time—yet out of them came six unforgettable words.

Several years ago, a neighbor related to me an experience that had happened to her one winter on a beach in Washington State. The incident stuck in my mind, and I took notes of what she said. Later at a writers' conference, the conversation came back to me, and I felt I had to set it down. Here is her story, as haunting to me now as when I first heard it.

She was six years old when I first met her on the beach near where I live. I drive to this beach, a distance of three or four miles, whenever the world begins to close in on me.

She was building a sand castle or something and looked up, her eyes as blue as the sea.

"Hello," she said.

I answered with a nod, not really in the mood to bother with a small child.

"I'm building," she said.

"I see that. What is it?" I asked, not caring.

"Oh, I don't know; I just like the feel of the sand."

That sounds good, I thought and slipped off my shoes. A sandpiper glided by.

"That's a joy," the child said.

"It's what?"

"It's a joy. My mama says sandpipers come to bring us joy."

The bird went glissading down the beach. "Good-bye, joy," I muttered to myself. "Hello, pain." I turned to walk on. I was depressed; my life seemed completely out of balance.

"What's your name?" She wouldn't give up.

"Ruth," I answered. "I'm Ruth Peterson."

"Mine's Wendy." It sounded like *Windy.* "And I'm six."

"Hi, Windy."

She giggled. "You're funny," she said. In spite of my gloom, I laughed, too, and walked on.

Her musical giggle followed me. "Come again, Mrs. P," she called. "We'll have another happy day."

The days and weeks that followed belonged to someone else: a group of unruly Boy Scouts, PTA meetings, an ailing mother.

The sun was shining one morning as I took my hands out of the dishwater. "I need a sandpiper," I said to myself, gathering up my coat.

The never-changing balm of the seashore awaited me. The breeze was chilly, but I strode along, trying to recapture the serenity I needed. I had forgotten the child and was startled when she appeared.

"Hello, Mrs. P," she said. "Do you want to play?"

"What did you have in mind?" I asked with a twinge of annoyance.

"I don't know. *You* say."

"How about charades?" I asked sarcastically.

The tinkling laughter burst forth again. "I don't know what that is."

"Then let's just walk." Looking at her, I noticed the delicate fairness of her face.

"Where do you live?" I asked.

"Over there." She pointed toward a row of summer cottages. *Strange,* I thought, *in winter.*

"Where do you go to school?"

"I don't go to school. Mommy says we're on vacation."

She chattered little-girl talk as we strolled up the beach, but my mind was on other things. When I left for home, Windy said it had been a happy day. Feeling surprisingly better, I smiled at her and agreed.

Three weeks later, I rushed to my beach in a state of near panic.

I was in no mood to even greet Windy. I thought I saw her mother on the porch and felt like demanding she keep her child at home.

"Look, if you don't mind," I said crossly when Windy caught up with me, "I'd rather be alone today." She seemed unusually pale and out of breath.

"Why?" she asked.

I turned on her and shouted, "Because my mother died!"—and thought, *Why am I saying this to a little child?*

"Oh," she said quietly, "then this is a bad day."

"Yes, and yesterday and the day before that and—oh, go away!"

"Did it hurt?"

"Did *what* hurt?" I was exasperated with her, with myself.

"When she died?"

"*Of course* it hurt!" I snapped, misunderstanding, wrapped up in myself. I strode off.

A month or so after that, when I next went to the beach, she wasn't there. Feeling guilty, ashamed, and admitting to myself I missed her, I went up to the cottage after my walk and knocked at the door. A drawn-looking young woman with honey-colored hair opened the door.

"Hello," I said. "I'm Ruth Peterson. I missed your little girl today and wondered where she was."

"Oh, yes, Mrs. Peterson, please come in."

"Wendy talked of you so much. I'm afraid I allowed her to bother you. If she was a nuisance, please accept my apologies."

"Not at all—she's a delightful child," I said, suddenly realizing that I meant it. "Where is she?"

"Wendy died last week, Mrs. Peterson. She had leukemia. Maybe she didn't tell you."

Struck dumb, I groped for a chair. My breath caught.

"She loved this beach; so when she asked to come, we couldn't say no. She seemed so much better here and had a lot of what she called happy days. But the last few weeks she declined rapidly. . . ." Her voice faltered. "She left something for you . . . if only I can find it. Could you wait a moment while I look?"

I nodded stupidly, my mind racing for something, anything, to say to this lovely young woman.

She handed me a smeared envelope with MRS. P printed in bold, childish letters.

Inside was a drawing in bright crayon hues—a yellow beach, a blue sea, a brown bird. Underneath was carefully printed:

A SANDPIPER
TO BRING YOU JOY

Tears welled up in my eyes, and a heart that had almost forgotten how to love opened wide. I took Wendy's mother in my arms. "I'm sorry, I'm sorry, I'm so sorry," I muttered over and over, and we wept together.

That precious little picture is framed now and hangs in my study. Six words—one for each year of her life—that speak to me of inner harmony, courage, undemanding love. A gift from a child with sea blue eyes and hair the color of sand—who taught me the gift of love.

Mary Sherman Hilbert

Mrs. Hilbert wrote this story a number of years ago for *Our Family*. Since then, *Reader's Digest* has taken it around the world, and it has gradually become one of the most cherished stories of our time. Mrs. Hilbert still freelances from her island home near Seattle.

HOUSES
AND HOMES

Martha F. Simmonds

*P*olly Moran was ashamed of the house, ashamed of the collie, ashamed of her brother, ashamed of her sisters, ashamed of her father—and ashamed of her mother. In fact, she was ashamed of just about everybody and everything.

If only she were rich! If only her family had money and class—as was true of her wealthy friend Isabelle Dunton.

Then unexpectedly Isabelle dropped in for a visit . . . and during the following several days, Polly learned some things about values, friends, brothers, sisters, fathers—and mothers.

*I*t was lovely, lovely weather, and the little town lay like a colorful picture in the valley between the snow-capped hills. Polly Moran looked down upon its red and green and slate gray roofs, glistening where the snow had so recently melted, at its twinkly windows shining rosily back as the sun sank out of sight, at the white spire of the little church, at the tall brown tower of the big one, and at the grove of pines that almost hid the school buildings.

Polly Moran was pleased with the village this afternoon and also pleased with herself. Tonight she would sing beneath that tall brown tower. And her voice was lovely. She knew it.

Briskly she went down the winding hillside path. The barberries were bright against the whiteness, and fat little gray birds winged a low and saucy flight in front of her. But Polly Moran did not see. She was thinking of—Polly Moran.

Into one of the green-roofed small houses she went—a house with rosy windows, too. She pulled off her slippers in the hall and hung up her hat and coat. Her hair was soft and yellow, her eyes large and gray, her mouth wide and sweet, and somehow she always managed to look so that everyone wanted to be friends with her at once. She opened the door into the living room.

The Morans' living room was large, but it did not have one extra foot of space! There was a big fireplace with an old leather davenport in front of it and two huge leather chairs nearby. There were bookcases and little tables and a big table, a piano, and more and more chairs. When Polly opened the door, she saw her father sitting in one big leather chair, reading under the rosy floor lamp. The twins were busy at the table, and Jimmie lay with his dog on the floor.

"Hi, Sis!" he shouted at her.

"I do wish you'd keep that dog outside, Jimmie. He gets hairs on everything!"

Jimmie hugged the dog tighter. "Mother said I might let him come in. He doesn't hurt anything."

"Tum thee my top, thither. It thpinth tho pretty."

"Yes, Doris, I see." Polly cast a glance at the table as she went by. Doris's chubby little face looked woebegone.

"Thither's pretty, too. I'd like tho much if the'd play with uth."

"She won't ever," answered Dorothy, the slim little twin, spinning her top vindictively.

Polly sat down at the piano and played a few experimental little notes. Then she began to thumb over the music.

"Nervous, Daughter?" asked her father kindly, looking over his newspaper.

"Oh, hardly," answered Polly.

Two long legs suddenly waved in the air above the top of the davenport. "I'm so used to singing. It never bothers me," came the obviously affected, obviously mocking, statement from the leather depths.

"Sarah! Why can't you sit up? Do you realize how unladylike you are?"

"Come down on the floor with me, Sal," invited Jimmie.

"Don't care if I do," drawled a careless voice, and a slim young form followed the legs into view.

In despair, Polly turned back to the piano. She played with precision and care; she sang clearly and well; but Father kept reading, and Jimmie and Sarah conversed in low tones all the while. As Polly finished the last notes, her mother spoke. "Here's your pie, honey. Or don't you want to eat before you sing?"

"Oh, Mother!" In dismay, Polly took the blue willowware plate with its thick wedge of coconut pie. She set it on the bench by her and swung around to gaze at the room. Her father ate pie and read the newspaper; the twins busily devoured forkfuls at the table; and on the floor, Jimmie and Sarah, one on each side of the dog, lay on their stomachs and ate—and ate.

"What's wrong, Daughter?"

Polly Moran pushed her hair back wearily. "I wish you wouldn't call me 'Daughter,' Mother. And why can't Sabbath evening lunches be confined to the dining room? It's so terribly messy and improper."

"But no one's here, Polly. And we don't want much. It's so much easier than setting the table."

"Sarah can set the table."

"Set it yourself! What's wrong with this, anyhow? I like to eat on the floor, and I get tired o' Sal havin' to do all the work." Jimmie glowered at her before opening his mouth for a huge bite of pie.

"Don't say 'Sal'! It's crude—it's positively vulgar. Mother, why don't you train the children differently? Must we always act as if we didn't have any manners? I get so tired of it!"

Mother's face was very tired, but Polly Moran did not notice. Jimmie spoke again.

"Aw, keep still! Turn around an' sing some more—that's all you care about anyhow!"

"Don't you see how impudent he is, Mother? And a lot of good it does to sing—no one in this whole town appreciates it, least of all my family!"

Gone was Polly's elation, her satisfaction. Gone, too, was the happiness of the family. Mother looked sorry—very sorry. She was about to speak, when suddenly there was a quick little knock at the door, and it was flung open with startling suddenness. Above a brown fur coat one could see a laughing mouth, flaming cheeks, black eyes, and black hair.

"Oh!—Oh!—Isabelle Dunton! Mother—Mother, it's Isabelle. I met her last summer at Aunt Evelyn's," Polly tried to explain. Isabelle had swung the door shut and met Polly by the table.

Isabelle stood away in a minute, breathless with the embrace she had received and given. "You must forgive me—but I get so lonely, and I wanted to see you. And I wanted to surprise you, so I'd see you as you are. Please don't introduce me, Polly, darling! I think I'll know—this is your mother!"

Hesitantly Isabelle Dunton crossed to the outstretched hand. A long time she looked at the lined sweet face, and tears came into her eyes. She bent and kissed the hand she held.

"I'm so glad—," she said, and then turned quickly. "And that's your father—" more brightly, "and—Doris and Dorothy—and Jimmie and Sarah—oh! Is that Ring?"

The fur coat came off and went over a chair, and the little hat followed. Down on the floor sat Isabelle Dunton in her pretty wool dress.

"Will you please like me, Laddie? Shall we be friends, Ring?"

She did not move, but just looked at him. And presently the collie lifted a slow paw and laid it on her knee. Then Isabelle put a hand on each side of his head and shook it a little and laughed.

"Say! You know how to treat a dog. Ring'll make friends—but he's not much on girls." Jimmie's voice was very admiring.

"Isn't he? Well, he's—Jimmie Moran! Where did you get that delicious wedge of pie? Do you suppose—"

"There's another whole one, Isabelle! I'll get you a piece." Sarah was on her feet quickly.

"May I have it served on the floor, Mother Moran?" asked Isabelle.

"Certainly, if you like, dear. Jimmie and Sally usually eat theirs that way."

"And Polly—aren't you going to eat some? Come right here by me."

"I—don't think I'd better," said Polly lamely. "I have to sing tonight."

"Oh, one piece of pie won't hurt you, honey! It's so early yet. Come on—sit down by me, anyhow."

Meekly, Polly sat down. The pie arrived, and Isabelle set a fork down through the crisp brown coconut, flaky meringue, and thick yellow sweetness, but she did not eat the bite.

Father had come to the fireplace to watch this new guest. "Lost your appetite?" he asked.

"No." Isabelle smiled at him. "But I feel sort of selfish to be getting it."

"Selfish—why should you?"

"Because—Samjoe drove me down and he's out in the cold and he likes coconut pie."

"Samjoe—who's he?" Jimmie was curious.

"My chauffeur."

"A man just to drive your car?"

"Yes."

"Why didn't some of your folks come along?"

Polly Moran frowned, but Isabelle answered quietly. "I haven't any folks, Jimmie—just a house."

There was a moment's dead silence, and then Sarah jumped to her feet. "I say, Dad! Aren't you going to have Mr. Samjoe come in?"

Father Moran sprang into action, and then everyone seemed to be busy at once. Samjoe, a shy little man of past middle age, came in and ate coconut pie awkwardly. And Mother made steaming hot cocoa and brought it presently with quickly made sand-wiches. Jimmie put Ring through all his tricks, and then Dorothy came carefully back to Isabelle Dunton.

"I have a top," she said uncertainly, almost in a whisper. But Isabelle's ears were quick. She turned, smiling.

"Indeed you have! Where do you spin it? On the table? May I try?"

Presently the twins' eyes were shining as Isabelle taught them to spin the top upside down, to spin it on a plate, to spin it down a table leaf.

To Polly Moran the whole thing was a nightmare. She had planned so carefully for Isabelle's visit. The house spick-and-span, the children out of sight as much as possible, flowers, music, the best china and glass and silver, shining linen, low lights, and everyone coached as to manners. She remembered Isabelle Dunton's precision. And here was Isabelle Dunton, eating pie on the floor, spinning tops, talking to Father about the hardware store.

"Well, I guess we'd better go." Isabelle rose reluctantly.

"Go? Why, you just came!" Jimmie's very tones were despairing. "Can't you stay overnight, anyhow? Must you go right back?"

"Well—" Isabelle paused uncertainly. "We have a week's vacation, but—I don't know."

"Stay two days, anyhow, won't you?" Jimmie pleaded.

"You'd be more than welcome to spend all the week, Isabelle," said Mother Moran warmly.

"Well—but I haven't any clothes."

"You can wear Polly's," spoke Sarah hopefully. "Or—" she stepped over near Isabelle suddenly—"why, you're more my size, but I haven't pretty clothes—like yours. I've sweaters and shirts and middies and things. One wool dress I sort of like—and a little party one—"

"I won't need the party one, dear—just a skirt and sweater. And—and until Thursday! Will you come for me then, Samjoe?"

"That I will, Miss."

Isabelle Dunton went to church and heard Polly sing and came home again. And in the three days she visited school with Polly, coasted and skated with Jimmie, made a snowman with the twins, wore Sarah's sweaters and skirts, made a huge cake under Mother Moran's directions, and went all over the store with Father. She popped corn at the fireplace and cracked nuts joyously on the back porch.

She made wee dresses for the twins' dolls and mended Jimmie's ball, and had long, long talks with Sarah—who was Sally to Isabelle.

On the last night she was there Isabelle crawled at last into bed, snuggled over close to Polly, put her hand on Polly's shoulder, and curled Polly's arm around her. "Hug me tight, Polly dear," she whispered.

And Polly hugged.

"Oh, aren't you happy and happy and happy?" asked Isabelle. "You have a real home, Polly—the kind I've always wanted! I think your father's just an old dear, and you have the loveliest mother! That beautiful white hair—and the kindest eyes and such a sweet voice! And her hands are so warm, Polly. Do you know, I can't even remember my mother?"

"I'm sorry." Polly hugged a little harder.

"And Polly—the twins are so cunning. I just love Doris's funny little lisp, and she's such a giving little thing. And Dorothy! And I think Sally is—well, she is a real girl, and I like her. I'm going to write to Sally. Of course I like Jimmie! It must be wonderful to have a brother, Polly."

Polly didn't know what to say. "Have you—really enjoyed being here?" she asked lamely.

"Oh, yes! More than anything in the world. Oh, Polly, if you'll just let me come back sometime—"

"Whenever you like, dear! But we have such a common house, and yours is so lovely and—"

"Oh, Polly! But yours is a *home!*"

When Polly came home from school alone the next evening, she was thinking of that very thing. Her steps quickened. Suddenly it seemed to her that she could not get home fast enough.

She opened the door, took off her things, and went on into the living room.

"Hello, Jimmie!" She patted the dog's head as she passed.

"Nice time, kiddies? My, that's a pretty little dress, Doris! Did Isabelle make that? Hello, Dad!"

And Polly went on through the door before she had time to notice the looks of amazement that followed her.

Her mother was singing softly in the pantry. She had not heard Polly come in. She never sang where Polly could hear anymore. There were reasons! But Polly now came in and put a hand against her hair.

"What lovely hair you have, Mother! It sounds so good to hear you sing, and I do love that old-time tune."

Her mother's hand poised in midair. She turned slowly, bewildered. "Polly, have you lost your senses?" But there was a look on her daughter's face that she could not misinterpret. Her eyes filled with tears. "Polly," she faltered, "will you say that again?"

But Polly just kissed her mother instead.

BILLY BRAD AND
THE BIG LIE

Author Unknown

*O*f all the stories I told my children when they were young, this—hands down—was their favorite! Now that they are grown, it is their favorite still.

More than any other story I know, it reveals the sad truth that all too often our discipline is based more on whim than on principle. In fact, we often appear to be more than a little bit irrational and inconsistent in our decrees, ultimatums, and punishments. So much so, in fact, that I cringe every time I read this old story.

And perhaps . . . just perhaps . . . that is why children love it so.

*B*illy Brad stood straight before his mother and told the lie. There were cake crumbs on his mouth and a smear of chocolate icing on the side of his nose, and yet he looked right into her eyes and uttered it. "And—and a big bear comed up on the porch—and—and it ringed the bell, and—and I said, 'Go 'way, bad bear! You can't have any of Mama's cake'—and it tooked its gun and it shooted me dead. And it eated the cake and I took the old bear's gun an'—and I maked it run away, I did."

It was a splendid effort. It was the first time in his life he had felt creative joy in its fullness. Other times he had told tales of the bear and the gun, but they had never fully satisfied him. Now he had woven a tale which had a foundation in fact. His big eyes looked larger than ever—they looked far away into the realms of bears that have guns. But his mother did not follow him. She only stood with tightly set lips and looked at him sadly.

"And—and a big old cow comed up on the porch, and—and I didn't let him in and he hooked the door down and—he tooked his so-ward and he killed me dead, and he went into the pantry and—and he eated my poor mama's cake, and—and he hooked the house all down."

"Billy Brad!"

Billy Brad hesitated.

"But I builded the house up again, and I tooked the old cow's so-ward and I killed him all to pieces!"

"Billy Brad, that is a big, big lie, and I shall tell your father!"

Billy Brad was not worried. He was not aware of having done anything wrong, and his conscience was at rest. He was willing to trust his father with the final fate of the tale he had told. As an appreciator of pure fiction of the big bear variety, his father had always been a better audience than his mother.

"Now, then," said Mr. William Bradley Smith Sr. when dinner was over and the three were in the living room, "let us have this story about Billy Brad and the big lie."

"Well, William, I really think you will have to punish Billy Brad. For I went out to the market and left Billy Brad alone in the house. I was not gone five minutes, and I left a cake on the lowest shelf of the pantry. I distinctly told Billy Brad not to touch it. And yet when I got home I found a large piece gone."

"Maybe the cat ate it."

"It was a big bear." Billy Brad brightened and sat up in his father's lap. "It—comed up on the porch and it ringed the doorbell and—it shooted me dead and it eated the cake."

"It is nonsense about the cat, William. And Billy Brad's mouth was smeared all over with crumbs, and his face was smeared with icing. Billy Brad ate the cake and then told a deliberate falsehood about it, Father."

Mr. Smith held his son at the end of his knee and looked at him. The two big eyes of the boy looked straight into his without a trace of guilt or deceit.

"Now, Billy Brad, Mother says that you have told her a lie. We can't have that. Do you know what a lie is?"

"No—and a big cow comed up on the porch and—he ringed our doorbell and he tooked his old so-ward and he killed me dead, and—and he went right into the pantry, and he eated my poor mama's cake."

"Now, stop! I want you to tell me who *did* eat the cake."

"Why—why a big old cow comed up on the porch—"

"No, it didn't."

"And a big old cow did not—comed up on the porch and ringed the doorbell?"

"No, it did not ring the doorbell."

Billy Brad looked at his father silently. "And it didn't hook the door down? How did the old cow come in then, Papa?"

"It did not come in. There was no cow. Who *did* eat the cake, Billy Brad?"

"Mother went away," said Billy Brad carefully, "and the cake was in the pantry—"

"That's right. Now, be careful."

"And a great big awful noss-er-ness flewed into the window—and—and it shooted me dead and it eated up the cake—"

"Stop there! In the first place, I told you not to say 'noss-er-ness.' Say *rhinoceros*. Say it!"

"Nosserness."

"Rhinoceros!"

"I-noss-er-ness."

"Well, there was no rhinoceros. A rhinoceros does not fly, and one couldn't get in at the window. I doubt if they like cake, and they don't have guns, and one couldn't shoot you if it wanted to, and you are not dead, and we can plainly see that the whole story is another lie. Didn't you eat that cake yourself, Billy Brad?"

"Yes," admitted Billy Brad cheerfully. "I eated it all up, and the old bear eated it all up. We all eated, and the old cow eated it all up. We all eated it all up, and there wasn't any cake left."

"The idea. There was lots left. He only ate a little, William."

His father sat him on the floor and arose. "Well, I don't know what to do. He has admitted that he ate the cake. I don't think he means to tell a willful lie. I don't believe he has any idea what a lie is. I might spank him for eating the cake when he was told not to do it. I might spank him for telling all that story about the bear and the cow. I'll do whatever you say. I am only afraid that if I spank him he will get the idea that he is being punished for telling us that he ate the cake." He turned to Billy Brad. "Son, if I spank you now, what will I be spanking you for?"

"For—for—because the big noss-er-ness cannot—fly."

"No, not for that. It is because you told what is not so. You ate the cake and when your mother asked you who ate the cake, you said a big cow and a bear ate it. That was not true. That was a lie. If you had told your mother you had eaten the cake and had said nothing about the bear and cow, that would have been the truth, and you would not have been telling a lie. Then you would have been spanked but once—for eating the cake. But now I shall have to spank you twice—once for the lie and once for taking the cake. Come with me."

After a spanking the only place for a boy to go is to bed—and Billy Brad went there. He lay between the cool sheets and sobbed until the sobs dwindled into little sighs, and then he lay still for a long time, looking into the darkness and listening to the voices of his parents in the living room below. He was still awake when they came up, and when his father tiptoed into the room to take a last look, Billy Brad looked up at him with bright eyes.

"Good night, old boy. We won't tell any more lies, will we?"

"No!" Billy Brad spoke heartily.

A few nights later his mother came to tuck him in snugly for the night, and she, too, threw her arms around him and kissed him. "Good night. But you shouldn't throw down the covers, little boy."

"No, Mama—I—didn't! A—a—great big angel comed right through the screen and—and it said 'Is it too hot?' and it tooked my covers off and it flewed away and—and—and nobody seed for—because nobody can't see no angels!"

APPLESAUCE
NEEDS SUGAR

Author Unknown

*W*ith the single exception of the Great Depression
of the 1930s, no other financial depression America
has ever experienced was worse than the Panic of
1896. It started when far-off India switched its coinage
of silver to gold, an act that sent Western mining stocks
and silver, especially, plunging. Within six months,
the silver dollar was worth only sixty cents, Treasury
gold reserves had dropped to a paltry 80 million dollars,
over six hundred banks were forced to close their doors,

seventy-four railroads collapsed and declared bankruptcy, and thousands of businesses failed.

It was in that bleak economic setting that this poignant story was born. Papa with no job, Mama with no food for their growing family, no government or state aid or food stamps—what was a mother to *do?*

The Hammonds were living in Texas when they had the sugar shortage back in '96. It was their own personal shortage, and they were short of everything, so they lived three weeks on cornmeal mush, but it was the sugar the children remembered best, because Mama prayed for sugar. She would never pray for anything she could get any other way, and she didn't mention bacon or fresh meat or milk or even a job for Papa, because the sugar meant something special. If the angels up in heaven didn't know what sugar was, they certainly must have been curious by the time Mama got through.

The family was really Canadian, but the panic had hit Papa while he was doing some building in Nebraska, and there weren't any relief offices then and no way to turn. He took to selling books and somehow got down to Texas with the children and couldn't get back. Then he got the Texas fever, and it hung on for almost a year, so he was simply beat and discouraged at the end, and no use talking to him.

The house they lived in was somewhere around Dallas. It wasn't in the city but outside where a man could get a shack for almost nothing, and nobody would bother to put him out when he couldn't pay rent. Mama had grown a big garden, but it was all gone by fall, and she'd made crayon portraits and done some dressmaking. Mostly the neighbors were as bad off as she was, so all they gave her for pay was cornmeal. She didn't go away from the house anymore because of her condition. The children didn't know what that meant, but they supposed it was the same reason the older ones couldn't go to school and had their lessons at home.

It was Papa who talked about starvation after they'd got down to cornmeal mush. The children heard him in the night. "What are going to *do?*" He'd say it over and over, as if he hurt inside and was angry, too. "What are we going to do? We've got five children, if you remember, and there are two men out of work for every man working."

Mama answered low and quiet, "We've got to have faith, Papa. People are given their brains so they'll look after themselves as best they can. Then, when we go as far as we can, we'll get help."

Papa hollered worse than ever. "You can't eat faith! Don't talk that way! We've got to have food! Something to eat, not faith!"

"Hush, the children will hear you."

"They might as well know that people are starving all over the country, and there's nothing to keep us from it." But after she talked to him awhile, he got his voice quieter, so everybody could go to sleep. The older ones dreamed of cakes and doughnuts all night, but they'd wake up just when they got their hands on the food.

In the morning, Mama banged pots and pans around on the stove the way she did when she didn't want to talk. There was cornmeal mush for breakfast, but no milk or sugar. Papa hadn't clipped off his mustache for a long time. It hung down straggly on his thin face, and his eyes were sort of red and hot. He pushed back his plate. "What are your plans for today?"

Mama was feeding little Bruce his mush, and she didn't look up. "There's a rig stopping at the gate, Papa."

He looked out the window. "Now, by George, if that Jim Ranney thinks he can collect anything on that grocery bill—" He banged the door after him, and everybody crowded around the window. Mama wouldn't let them go pushing outside to stare when people came, but they could look through the window, because they were only human and she didn't expect them to behave like flowerpots on a shelf.

It was Mr. Ranney's rig, all right, with his white horse and the wagon covered with a round top painted black, with gold letters saying RANNEY GROCERIES. Mr. Ranney sat on the seat. He was a thin man with a big mustache and a wide-brimmed hat. He hardly ever smiled.

"Is he bringing something to eat?" John asked. Mama shook her head without even looking. Ranney wasn't a soft man. He had let the Hammonds have credit for a long time while Papa was sick, but when Papa never did get a job, Mr. Ranney said there were too many in the same fix and he couldn't do anything more. Mama had a kind of shamed look, and she wouldn't go to the window. She was used to having all her debts paid, and this one was staring her in the face pretty hard.

Mr. Ranney said something to Papa, waved with his whip across the railroad track, and drove away. Papa came back, dragging his heel.

"Apples! What good are they? No, not a word about the bill. I'll say that much for him. Just apples. What will we do with apples?"

"Where?" John and Allie asked.

He sat down in the old chair with the carpet seat that was almost worn out with his sitting. "That old orchard beyond the tracks. Grown up to weeds. Warty and warped, and nobody will buy them or bother to pick them. So he gives them to us. And everybody has been helping themselves anyway."

They had, but they didn't know *he* knew it. He'd have spanked them for stealing, but they just had to have something besides mush, and they were pretty good apples, although they didn't take the place of real eating. Now it turned out that it was Mr. Ranney's orchard, and they could have all they wanted to haul away.

Mama got up with a little sigh. "Now, Papa, this means we aren't at the end of our rope yet. You take the children and some gunnysacks and bring home apples."

It was fun getting them, and everybody carried some in a sack while Papa loaded several sacks on the little wagon. When they got home, Mama had the stove going and a lot of pots and pans she'd borrowed from the neighbors. She was moving around fast, the way she used to. The old beer barrels somebody had left back of the shed were on the porch now, soaking and smelling like beer.

By the time Papa got home—he stopped to rest and the others came on ahead—she had some applesauce cooking, and everybody had begun peeling apples like mad.

He fell into his chair. He used to sit down, but now he let go like a sack of potatoes and just dropped. "What's going on around here?" he asked in his discouraged voice. "What are the barrels for? And these pots and pans?"

"We are going to make apple butter," Mama said. "We'll ask Mr. Ranney to sell it for us at the store. And apple vinegar. I know how. I've done it at home in Ontario."

"Vinegar!" Papa roared. "And how do you propose to make vinegar?"

Well, of course, Mama was brought up on a farm, and she always knew how to make things other people had to buy in stores. Papa had lived in cities mostly, and he didn't know people made things like vinegar. Mama tucked Bruce up higher in her lap. A bee had stung him, and she was getting him to stop crying. "Vinegar is made from apple juice and a little sugar to make it work faster, and then it makes itself. Apple butter is just applesauce boiled down with sugar and some spice, and I've got a little spice left. It will be brown and thick and smell like perfume. We used to make it in an iron kettle in the yard back home."

Papa stamped to the door. He probably didn't see much scenery, because it was a lot of flat country and the neighbors' shacks and the road going by the gate, but he kept looking, with his back to the family.

"So it takes sugar! Where do we get the sugar, if you please? I notice Ranney isn't giving away sugar, and it doesn't grow on bushes. Not in this neighborhood, anyway. I grant you—" He sounded as if he had hiccups coming on. "I grant you that apple butter might possibly be sold, and vinegar is a stable commodity, but we can't make either of them without sugar, and we might as well wish for a gold mine to open up in the yard and be done with it."

When he talked in that tone, the children were all scared of him. Maybe Mama was, too, but she didn't show it.

"The apples have been provided," she said, continuing to peel. "We have barrels and wooden buckets and can get more. There is an old cider press out back of Sander's barn we can have if you get it working. I already asked about it, and we won't need the sugar until the other things are ready."

"Then what?"

"The sugar will be provided," Mama said. "Now, Papa, look at the cider press and see if you can fix it. . . . John, take the little wagon again, and Alexandra and Frances will help you bring more apples. Pick out the best you can find, without worm holes. . . . Millie, stay and help me peel apples. . . . Bruce, dear, you go with Papa to see the cider press. . . . And hold his hand, Papa, and don't let him walk fast."

Of course, Papa could fix the press all right. He could fix most things, and when he was working he didn't holler hardly at all. John and Allie and Frances came back with the little wagon loaded and went back for more, and Mama scrubbed barrels and peeled, and Millie peeled and got wood for the stove.

They had applesauce with their cornmeal mush at noon, but it isn't much good without sugar, and the smell gets tiresome when the place is full of apples cooking. For supper Mama made corn bread with some sour milk one of the neighbors was going to throw out. She found enough drippings to make gravy, and it was pretty good.

Papa sat awhile turning his pipe around in his hands. He hadn't smoked for months. He said, "My stomach is upset."

Mama took down the soda box. She always gave him soda when he had an upset stomach.

He saw her scraping around with the spoon, and he reached over for the box. "So we need soda too! Five cents a pound, and we can't buy it. How can you make corn bread without soda? And how will we get any more cornmeal anyway? And what shall I have faith in?"

She lifted up the big Bible and pushed it into his hands. "We've got to read our chapter before the light goes. You read about Elijah and the ravens."

He read it.

"Now about the servants with the talents, and the one who didn't use the talent he was given."

He read that, too, and shut the Book and sat looking at her.

"Our way isn't shown very far ahead," Mama said, and the room seemed to quiet down to listen. "We've got apples, and we're going as far as we can. Then the Lord will take a hand."

Before he could answer, she started singing "How Firm a Foundation" and "Faith of Our Fathers," and she got them all off to bed without Papa doing any more talking. He went to bed, too, and groaned quite a lot, but he didn't holler.

Next morning they had family prayers again. The kitchen looked odd, with barrels of apple juice along the wall, ready for covers to be put on after the sugar was added so it could turn itself into vinegar. Pans and buckets and pots were full of applesauce, turning brown, partly cooked down, waiting for the sugar. And Mama had to push things back from the top of the stove so she could make mush.

This time she didn't ask Papa to read. She started praying. "Heavenly Father, we've gathered the apples You sent us, and the juice is ready and the applesauce boiling down. We will continue today, finishing the job as far as we can go. Now we need sugar. We could use it today, but first thing tomorrow morning will be just right. Brown sugar will do. It doesn't need to be white. We bring You this problem, Father. Amen."

They ate their mush and started to work again, hauling more apples and all. This time Papa didn't go. He watched Mama awhile, and then he poked into one of the pots that were boiling. Then he jammed his hat on his head.

"I can't stand any more," he said, and his hands were shaking. "You wait here for the sugar. I'll go off somewhere. Probably I'm a sinner, not having faith. Maybe it will come quicker if I'm not around." He looked around the kitchen with all the applesauce and clutter. "You left a two-hundred-acre farm to come with me. I can't see that you improved yourself."

"Harry!" Mama was almost crying. "You know if you hadn't been sick you'd have taken care of the family, and I always trust you to do it, and we'll probably have ten children, because I come from a family that has lots of children, and I'll never need anybody but you to take care of us all. You don't think it is because I don't trust you that I have to pray, do you, Harry?"

He said, "Keep on praying. Maybe there'll be a miracle."

He turned down the road toward the city, walking slowly but not once turning back.

Mama watched after him until he was out of sight, and her hands twisted in her apron. Then she turned back and spoke sharply for the first time. "Now everybody get to work."

They hauled more apples and got more barrels and borrowed more wooden buckets. They peeled and put wood in the stove and pumped water, and the minute one of them quit, Mama was saying, "Back to work. No slacking." Even little Bruce, hardly more than two, had to help carry sticks.

It was a long day. Some of the neighbor women drifted in, thin and droopy, with their snuff sticks stuck under their lips. They asked, "What you all doing?" Mama didn't explain much, but she borrowed another pan or two, and if the girls asked about sugar and how it would probably come, she started singing a hymn. She kept watching down the road, but she wouldn't answer any questions.

So they had supper again, and it was still mush and applesauce. And Mama read "The Lord is my Shepherd," and they went to bed. It must have been the middle of the night when Papa came home. He moved quietly and didn't say a word. Mama asked him something in a low tone, but he sort of moaned and they didn't talk anymore.

It isn't easy to sleep with an unsatisfied feeling inside, so they all got up when it was daylight. The children felt kind of queer. If anything was going to happen, it would have to be pretty soon now. They moved around quietly, the way they did Christmas morning before it was time to get presents, not wanting to ask right out, and afraid maybe this time there might not be anything, but at the same time sure there would be. The girls kept little Bruce quiet, and John washed his face without even being told. Mama's mouth was tight, and she dished up the rest of the mush.

Mama asked the blessing, only it wasn't a blessing. She said, "Father, the applesauce is ready and past its prime, and the juice is turning. We have gone as far as we can, each of us, and even the baby is working. Now we need sugar in about an hour. Father, we have faith."

They ate their mush and scraped the dishes clean and just sat there not knowing what to do. The smell of apples was everywhere, sweetish and sourish. As soon as the day warmed up, everything would spoil.

The train whistled off near Dallas, and John said, "That's seven o'clock," for their clock had been sold long ago.

Papa pushed back his chair. "The grocery store will be open soon," he said, his mouth almost shut tight. "I'll step along and see if your sugar has come."

Mama went a little pale. "Now, Papa, you stay right here."

He said, looking around the table at all of them, "I figured this thing out. We do all we can, clear up to the end. But now we need sugar. You pray for sugar. Now this is the time we need the sugar, isn't it?" He didn't wait for an answer. "Well, suppose the Lord means us to have sugar. In this country it comes in bags from the factory. It's loaded into freight cars and shipped to the warehouse in Dallas, and the grocers go with their delivery wagons and haul it to their stores, so we get it from a grocery store. Unless you want me to wreck a train?"

"Harry! Don't talk so wild!"

"Then the natural way for the Lord to get the sugar to us," he said carefully, "will be from Jim Ranney's store. I figure nobody will go around the block to do a job when there's a straight path. The Lord has plenty to do in the universe, and this is only a little job for Him. So, since Ranney is the only grocer who knows us, I figure he either has our sugar there waiting right now or we are on the wrong road. I propose to go and find out.

"So," he said, standing straighter than he had stood in a long, long, time, "you trim my hair and brush my suit as best you can, and I'll shave and look my best and go down and ask Jim Ranney. Now that is my last word."

Mama didn't know what else to do when it was set down in front of her like that. Ranney would never give out the sugar. She got hot water in the basin and set out his shaving things. There was only a little drop of soap in a cup, left over from what she'd made, and Papa made a face at it, but he used it as best he could. He was thin, of course, and his eyes were sort of burning, and he cut himself twice, but he went right on getting ready. When he was finished, he had his head lifted up and his jaw shut tight. He looked hard and a little dangerous.

"Now Mama," he said, with his hat in his hand, "you actually expect this sugar?"

She looked him in the eye, covering her hands with her apron. "I do with my soul."

His teeth showed, but he wasn't smiling. "Then pray for Jim Ranney."

"Don't you do anything desperate!" Mama ran after him, but he banged the gate shut and strode off fast. Now the tears came rolling down Mama's cheeks. "Maybe I've driven him too far," she said almost despairingly. She put her hands up before her face. "Father, keep Thy hand over my husband. He is desperate, and a man can't help what he does when his children are hungry. Lord, he's a good man, and I've pushed him too far."

She saw all of them staring, and she wiped her eyes. "My goodness, children, let's clean up here. . . . John, bury the rest of those peelings before all the flies in the country get here. . . . Allie, wash the dishes and be sure to wipe the table. . . . Millie and Frances, you make the beds and pull the covers straight, one of you on each side, the way I showed you. . . . Bruce, honey, you come to Mama. We've got to give you a bath. . . . John, when you've finished the peelings, dear, get the rake and straighten up the yard a bit."

She fixed Bruce and brushed his hair over her finger in a curl on top of his head. Everybody was working fast. Things had to be spick-and-span. Mama stood and studied the stove a long time. She kept wiping her eyes. Then she said, "Yes, I'll carry on clear to the last. . . . John, dear, bring some more wood, so the applesauce can keep on boiling. . . . Girls, get your clean aprons on and brush each other's hair. You look so nice when you're all brushed up."

They did, and there they were again, waiting and nobody saying anything. Then they heard a rig coming. This time they all went out into the yard, and Mama didn't say to come back inside. Sure enough, it was Ranney's rig coming, with the white horse walking and Ranney alone in the front seat. Mama went slowly down to meet him, and the children followed: John, a big boy for nine years, and Allie and Frances and Millie, and Bruce only two. Mama wasn't very old, either, with her little brown curl on her neck at the back and the skin on her throat as soft as Bruce's.

Mr. Ranney twisted the reins around the whip and got down over the wheel. "Mrs. Hammond, I came to see your kitchen."

She looked at him, surprised, and he looked straight back. She said, "Certainly," the way she spoke to strangers, and turned toward the house. Ranney looked in the door and saw the applesauce boiling and the juice waiting and the place clean. He grunted and came back and looked at the children, one by one. They were clean and their hair was brushed and the yard raked.

He stopped by Mama and said, "Five children so far, isn't it?"

She got a little pink, but she looked him right in the eye. "We expect to have a large family, Mr. Ranney. My husband can take care of us all, as soon as he gets his strength."

Ranney took off his hat slowly, and his head was almost bald. That was funny, because his mustache was so big and bristly. "Ma'am, this morning I saw a miracle. Your husband came walking in, clean and shaved and straight up like a man. 'Ranney,' he says, 'we need sugar. Four sacks will do for a start.'

"'Hey!' I says. 'What's that again?'"

"He grinned at me then," Ranney said. "The first time I've seen the man smile since he came to this neighborhood. He said to me, 'Ranney, my wife has been praying for sugar, because she's making apple butter to sell this fall and winter. It will be the thick, brown, sweet kind that smells like perfume, the way they make it back in Ontario. And she needs sugar.'"

"Where is he?" Mama said.

"'And vinegar, too,'" Ranney went on. "'Apple vinegar, the best in the world,' he told me. 'My wife knows how to do these things, and she is working on them at home in the kitchen this minute, and they'll be good.'

"And I said—excuse me, ma'am—but I said, 'Well, brother, I can't help you. I've gone as far as I can, and this wildcat business of yours won't get me my money.' So he pulls a notebook out of his pocket, and he looks me in the eye in a way he never did before and says, 'Ranney, I spent yesterday in the city, going from store to store. Here is a list of stores that will sell our apple butter.' He shoved his notebook at me, and he had taken dozens of orders which were for more apple butter than I ever saw. I says, 'Are these really orders, Hammond?'

"'Not exactly,' he says, speaking the truth like a man. 'I offered them apple butter on speculation, to sell the first batch. Now I have faith, Ranney,' he says. 'My wife makes good apple butter. That stuff will sell. And on this page they'll take vinegar. And we want four sacks of sugar right now.'"

"Where is he?" She came close to him, sort of ruffling up. He moved out through the gate, and Mama followed. "What have you done with him?"

Ranney put his hat on, finishing his story. "Now, ma'am, I'm near to the end of my own rope, what with so many owing me, and four sacks of sugar ain't such a small item. So I stood a minute thinking how maybe there'd be a job among people I know in Dallas for a man like that, when he says, like a crazy one, 'If I don't get it with your permission, I'll take it without.' Then he tries to pick up a sack of sugar, and he sort of folds at the knees and flops right down on the floor in a faint."

Mama gave a low cry. "He hasn't eaten since yesterday! Now, Mr. Ranney, if you've put him in jail or anything, you'll—you'll have *me* to deal with! He's desperate, and the babies are hungry—"

His mustache moved and rippled, and his eyes wrinkled up. Mama realized that he was smiling. "Oh," she said, gasping, and was around behind the wagon like a flash. There inside was Papa, pulling and tugging at a big box of groceries that was blocked in behind the sacks of sugar.

"Harry!" she said. "Harry!"

He came down out of the wagon and put his arms around her and patted her back. The children had forgotten how he looked when he smiled. "The Lord picked a pretty feeble delivery boy," he said. "Plenty of faith, but the works aren't so good. . . . No, Ranney, if you please. You've done enough." He reached up and pushed his hat on tighter, so it sort of cocked over one eye, and he looked as if he could handle anything. "Jane," he said, "do you think I can carry in a sack of sugar, now it is delivered to the gate?"

"Harry, you can do *anything!*"

He picked up the sugar and went toward the house, not even staggering.

THEIR FATHER'S
WIFE

Priscilla Hovey

The twins—the Pretty Twin and the Quiet Twin—
composed a masterpiece of a letter to Daddy, warning
him that they would treat their new stepmother with the
courtesy due a guest—but that would be all. Then they
mailed it.

Then she came . . . and nothing happened as expected.
It was exasperating, it was frustrating, it was reason
enough to take a drastic step.

*R*osamond wrote the letter and Rhoda dictated it. The division of labor was equitable in every respect, because Rosamond could write more plainly than Rhoda, and Rhoda could think more quickly than Rosamond.

"Now read it as far as we've gone," commanded Rhoda, tossing her short blonde curls as she sat on the window seat. The Pretty Twin, Rhoda had always been called.

Rosamond turned in her chair at the spinet desk and raised a pair of sober, wide brown eyes that matched her soft, straight brown hair.

"Don't you think it's just a bit strong?" The Quiet Twin, Rosamond had always been.

"We've got to be strong," declared Rhoda majestically, "and firm. Now read it. We've got to have a good sentence at the end. Miss Edwards told us in English, you know, to have our conclusions gripping and conclusive."

Rosamond coughed a little and began:

"Dear Daddy,

"We received the news of your marriage last week to a Miss Anne Murdock and were greatly shocked. Of course, you know your own business best, but it doesn't seem to us that a wife is necessary when you have us and Tanty and Squills.

"You say you're going to bring her home. It's your house and we can't say anything, but we think it is only fair to warn you that—"

She stopped and looked inquiringly and admiringly at Rhoda, who sat with her chin cupped in her small slender hands, a thoughtful frown on her face.

"We think it is only fair to warn you," Rhoda repeated, picking up the threads of her dictation, "that although we shall treat her with the courtesy due a guest—" Rosamond's sweatered right arm went through the approved motions of penmanship—"our policy on the whole will be that of ig*nor*ance!"

"But, Rhoda." Rosamond looked up, pen poised in midair. "Is there such a word? Of course there's *ignorance*. But is there ig*nor*ance?"

"Why not?" Rhoda was irritated. "Ig*nore*—ig*nor*ance. There must be. Now don't you go looking it up in the dictionary, Rosamond Farnsworth," she exclaimed as the latter reached for *Webster's*. "It takes you an age to find anything, and we've got to get this off in the afternoon mail so Daddy will surely have it before he leaves New York. I know there's such a word— ig*nor*ance—ig*nor*ance—I've heard it time and time again."

"All right," yielded Rosamond. "But I'll put a dash on top of it so they won't make any mistake, or else put a line underneath. What would you do, Rhoda?"

"Come, we must hurry," said Rhoda, looking at the tiny watch on her wrist.

As they went downstairs arm in arm, a plump, middle-aged, gray-haired woman came out of the kitchen, a sprinkling bottle in one hand and a frilly organdy dress in the other—Mrs. Stanley, or Tanty as she had been christened by the twins when they were babies.

"Where are you going?" she asked.

"Just down the street," replied Rhoda.

"Well, come back in time to do your lessons." Tanty, ever a mild mentor, went on. "And I think you'd better tidy up your room a bit."

"It's tidy enough now." Rhoda, looking at herself in the hall mirror, adjusted a blonde curl over each ear.

"But there's your new ma coming soon, and we want to have everything extra special."

Rosamond gave a long drawn-out "O-o-o-o-h," and Rhoda was frozen at the hall mirror.

"Tanty!" she said tensely. "You are never to call her that again!"

The good Tanty's mouth was agape. "And what is she, I'd like to know, if she's not that?"

"She's Mrs. Farnsworth, our father's wife," announced Rhoda with dignity, and Rosamond bobbed her head in agreement.

Mirth seized upon the plump figure of the housekeeper and shook it. To her, the twins, although now thirteen, were but the adorable, tyrannical babies they had been when she had come to them twelve years ago after the death of their mother. She never thought of them as distinct individualities. Single, they were twins; plural, twinses.

"If that don't beat everything," she chuckled. "She's not your ma; she's your pa's wife!"

"You just wait," prophesied Rhoda. "She'll boss you. She'll tell you just what puddings you can make and what you can't. You won't be laughing then!"

"Your pa's one of the best men God ever made," Tanty declared solemnly, "and he wouldn't bring any woman into the house unless she'd be decent to me. I've served him for twelve years and taken care of you girls and done things that nobody else would do. Many's the night I've gone without sleep when you two had the mumps and who knows what. And when Rosamond put a bean in her ear—"

"Tanty!" pleaded Rosamond.

"But I'd willingly be bossed, as you say," continued Tanty darkly, "if your pa'd only bring somebody who'd know what to do with you two young ladies who are so saucy they ought to be turned up and—"

A slam reverberated through the house.

"I thought for a minute we'd have Tanty on our side," said Rhoda as the two sped on their way down the street to the Post Office. "It would be fine then. She could have refused to cook things or else cook them something terrible, until Daddy said what a mistake he'd made and had the marriage—I don't mean erased—what is it when people have their marriage crossed out? It's not a divorce—"

"Annulled, I think," said the more accurate Rosamond. "I guess Tanty won't be on our side, though."

"She makes me sick!" sniffed Rhoda. "Always bringing up what she's done for us. As if we asked her to nurse us when we were sick!"

"I know it!" breathed Rosamond fervently.

They went to mail the letter, applying to it with much vigor a Special Delivery stamp.

"There!" Rhoda watched it drop into the slot with satisfaction. "That ought to make him think."

"I hope it doesn't make him cross." Rosamond's brown eyes were troubled. "He's so delightful when he's home from a trip. Do you suppose he'll take us to the park and to the city for dinner again, same's he did last time?"

"He'll take his wife to places now." Rhoda was merciless.

"But—but he will us, once in a while?"

"Maybe once in a *very great* while."

"Do you suppose she'll be homely?"

"Daddy wouldn't pick out anybody that was homely." Rhoda was positive. "I have an idea she'll be good-looking enough, but not beautiful like our mother. Naturally she'll be old, for Daddy's forty his next birthday, and she'll have to be pretty near as old as that. I don't see why he had to have her, though. I think it was horrid of him—" A catch came to Rhoda's voice, and she blinked her lashes furiously to keep back the tears.

By the following forenoon the news of David Farnsworth's marriage, thanks to Tanty, had circulated through most of West Kempton. The twins met all inquiries and exclamations in regard to the report with heroic stolidity.

But then they sought refuge under the apple tree in their own backyard and heard through the open window of the Cartwright house next door the shrill, penetrating voice of Mrs. Cartwright engaged in conversation over the telephone: "Yes, I say it's a good thing, too! Those girls need a mother over them. Not that Mrs. Stanley has not been capable and conscientious, but they need someone with a restraining and guiding hand."

"Restraining and guiding hand!" Rhoda reached up and yanked off a sprig of apple blossoms.

"Old gossip!" pouted Rosamond.

"It just shows you what people think," said Rhoda savagely. "Everybody in this old town is tickled to think Daddy's got a wife."

"I hope she won't be cross." The sensitive Rosamond shuddered.

"She won't be nasty mean, and she won't be gooey sweet," Rhoda declared thoughtfully. "She'll be just plain meddlesome, telling us when to wear galoshes and all that. And we've got to make it so—er—uncomfortable for her that she'll be glad enough to leave!"

At supper that night Tanty announced brightly, "A telegram came from your pa this afternoon. The bride and groom."

"Goodness!" protested Rosamond. "Don't talk about bride and groom when they're both as old as forty!"

"Well, whatever they are, Miss Smarty, they're coming tomorrow morning, so they'll be here when you get home from school. Think of that!"

The twins thought—and made faces.

The next day at school, the twins could do little work. Even the conscientious Rosamond found she could study only by exerting great moral pressure upon herself. Rhoda flagrantly shirked. At noon they walked home arm in arm, alternately hurrying and loitering.

"I suppose *she's* there now," Rhoda hissed.

"I suppose so," gulped Rosamond.

"Remember our policy—ignorance!"

"I know. But I still wish I had looked it up in the—"

"Hush up!" commanded Rhoda.

They opened the front door and went in almost stealthily. Nobody was in sight. This was so different from the usual homecomings. Then Daddy had always been at the door, often hiding behind it, ready to jump out with a whoop. They had flung themselves on him with an answering shout, Squills had barked, Tanty had exclaimed, "Horrors, there'll be nothing left of your poor father, I declare!"

Tears were in Rosamond's eyes, but Rhoda, who was made of sterner stuff, coughed and called up the stairs, "Is anybody up there?"

"Rather!" Daddy's voice came down. "Come right up!"

Daddy seemed glad, but he didn't *sound* the same. The twins held hands as they went upstairs. It was comforting, somehow.

"To your right!" directed Daddy jovially.

On tiptoe they went to the big front room that, whenever he was home, was Daddy's. He was standing on the threshold, smiling and handsome as ever. They kissed and they hugged, the three of them; they squeezed and squealed, but it wasn't very satisfying. *She* was watching them as she sat in a chair by the window.

She was pretty, too, and stylish; smaller than Daddy, of course, but not *too* small. The twins liked their heroines tall and vigorous rather than clinging.

"And now come and meet your—my wife," said Daddy in a matter-of-fact voice. For a moment he looked stern as if he were about to scold, then thought of something and tucked his tongue in his cheek instead. He marshaled them to the window. *She* stood up. The twins stiffened as if they were to face a firing squad.

"When she kisses you," Rhoda had instructed Rosamond on the way home, "just think of yourself as a barbed-wire fence. And when she says something about 'my little girls,' cross your fingers."

"How do you do?" *she* said cordially but casually, extending a hand first to Rhoda and then to Rosamond.

"How do you do?" stammered the twins.

This was not right, not a bit! She ought to have *tried* to kiss them or at least say something slushy. Instead she had spoken to them as if they were strangers.

"Stuck up, isn't she?" sniffed Rhoda after they had gone to their room. Conversation about school, weather, Squills, and so on, had died. "After all, we're her husband's daughters."

"I like her eyes," said Rosamond dreamily. "And I like the way she does her hair. It's not all perfect as if it were frosting squirted out of a tube, but it's natural and wavy."

"Rosamond Farnsworth!" Rhoda gripped her twin fiercely by the shoulders. "Don't you dare weaken!"

"Why, of course I'm not going to weaken," protested Rosamond.

But it was hard to be firm and relentless in the carrying out of a perfectly good policy when there was such fascinating newness about the house in the days that followed. It was exciting to come home from school and have four people at the table. And *she* fixed the table so pretty, too. Tanty never used anything but tablecloths and then put the food on them efficiently and energetically.

Rhoda was not generally troubled with curiosity as a rule, but she found herself listening eagerly to talks at the table or about the house between Daddy and *her*. On previous homecomings Daddy had talked wholly with herself and Rosamond. Oh, he still asked about school, told jokes and stories, but he seemed to prefer, thought Rhoda jealously, to talk to that wife of his. They went off on long rides and walks together. Sometimes in the afternoon the twins went too, and one evening all four went out to dinner, but it wasn't the joyous excursion of old. Daddy apparently did not notice any difference. Of course *she* didn't. But the twins felt uncomfortably cut off and left by themselves.

"I don't believe we needed to have worried about being bossed," said Rosamond from her bed one night to Rhoda in hers. "She doesn't pay any attention to us."

"Just wait!" Rhoda's voice was hopeful. "She's letting us alone now because Daddy's here, but he goes off again next week, and then she'll start in on us. You'll see."

"Do you suppose he got that letter?" queried Rosamond.

"Must have. I'd like to ask him, but I don't quite dare."

Daddy went and *she* stayed, but she did not concern herself anymore with the twins than she had when he was at home. She did not notice whether they went to school, came home, did their lessons, had any clothes to wear, or in fact, existed at all. Rosamond and Rhoda were puzzled. Why, she was as stiff and standoffish as Miss Wainwright, the school principal, only more so, because Miss

Wainwright did spy around to see that you didn't leave fruit in your desk or wet towels in your shower locker.

She didn't care what you did, for one day the twins opened their bureau drawers at haphazard angles, left clothes upon the floor and the beds unmade, and *she* didn't say a thing. The room was in the same chaos at night as it had been in the morning, and rather disgruntled, they put it to rights. They went off without breakfast, wore sweaters when they should have worn coats, and on a rainy morning elected to venture forth with satin slippers and no galoshes. What did they accomplish? Empty stomachs, chills, and wet feet!

And there was no use in talking matters over with Tanty, for the latter had entirely capitulated to the charms of the new mistress. Moreover, after twelve years of anxious clucking service, she suddenly thrust the twins from under her wings. No longer did she stand at the door to give advice about the length of skirts, the adjustment of sweaters, and the smoothing of hair. She stopped scolding, and she stopped caressing.

"You'd think that after all the years Tanty's been with us, she'd continue to be the same," mourned Rosamond.

"Oh, I don't know," Rhoda sighed. "The longer I live the more I wonder whether there's any true affection in the world or not. Daddy used to love us, and now he's just nice, same as an uncle or a grandfather might be; Tanty doesn't care about us anymore, and this—*this wife* acts as if we weren't around. I want her to mind her own business, but, after all, as Daddy's wife, she's got some duties here."

The days grew more and more melancholy for the twins. Tanty was strangely unsatisfying, and so was Squills. They actually began to waste away, growing daily a little more quiet, wide of eye, and pale of cheek, until the subject of the mother-and-daughter picnic was suddenly thrust before them. They had completely forgotten about that annual event, which had long ago become a village tradition.

Aileen Henderson caught up with the twins one day on the way home from school. "Won't it be great?" she exclaimed breathlessly. "You can have a mother this year, too. And she's so good-looking! Can she play tennis? I'm sure she and you, Rhoda, could beat Grace Tilton and her mother."

The twins were noncommittal, but that night at supper they could not eat. Tanty spoke of their lack of appetite, and even *she* was jogged out of customary indifference, but *she* spoke of summoning the doctor.

"We don't need a doctor," said Rhoda almost rudely, pushing her chair away from the table.

That night in the darkness of the room Rosamond reached one shy, trembling hand and caught Rhoda's hot, twitching one. "What will we do?"

Rhoda, the daring, the defiant, was temporarily beaten. "I don't know," she confessed. "Of course, we ought not to ask *her,* because that would mean we accept her. But we might stretch a point just for the sake of convention. I'd say we might as well ask her, only—" Rhoda had difficulty in swallowing—"she wouldn't come. She doesn't care a nickel about us, not even two cents." Slowly but surely the rate of exchange declined. "She doesn't like us. She likes everybody in this old town but us. She wouldn't go. She'd laugh at us!"

"Maybe she'd stretch a point, too," offered Rosamond helpfully, "just for the sake of convention. Maybe she *would* go."

"I wouldn't want her to go then." Rhoda's voice became firm and final. "If she didn't go because she liked to go and liked us, I wouldn't want her to go."

"Rhoda Farnsworth! I believe you like her!"

"Of course I do," sobbed Rhoda into her pillow.

They decided their course the very next day. Rather, Rhoda decided it, and Rosamond agreed to it.

"But I don't *want* to go," sniffed the latter as she neatly folded dresses into her suitcase. "I want to finish the year. I'm positively certain I'd get an A in history."

"What's an A in history when the turning point of your life has come!" demanded Rhoda. "You can stay if you like, but I can't remain another moment in this house!"

"Maybe she'd come if we asked."

"No. She just simply dee-spises us. It's perfectly evident. She'll be glad to think we're gone. I've always heard that no home is big enough to hold two women, and there are four of us here. Even Squills is female."

"I wish we could take Squills."

"Good grief! Another mouth to feed!"

They left on the afternoon train. Circumstances for flight were propitious. Tanty was visiting her sister in a neighboring village, and *she* had gone shopping. Financially, they were girt up with four five-dollar gold pieces, past birthday and Christmas presents; physically, with two heavy suitcases and a bag of sandwiches; morally, with the vow never to return to the home where they were not wanted.

On the powder puff on their dressing table—they had no pin-cushion—they left a note: "We've gone to the city to earn our living. Don't bother to find us. Rhoda and Rosamond."

"Daddy'll feel sorry." Rosamond mopped her eyes as the train left West Kempton for the city some thirty miles away.

"He brought it on himself," the hard-eyed Rhoda said.

It was about six o'clock when they reached the city. The twins went at once to the only hotel they knew, the one Daddy always took them to when they had dinner.

"A room for the night, please," requested Rhoda with the briskness of a businesswoman. "A bath isn't necessary." After all, four five-dollar gold pieces wouldn't last forever! "Misses Jane and Joanna Brown of Boston."

The clerk looked over the top of his glasses at the hotel's newest guests. He was a middle-aged man with a family at home, daughters as well as sons.

"Er—um, yes," he murmured, and at the same time lifted an eyebrow significantly in the direction of a quiet-mannered man a short distance away. The quiet-mannered man nodded in return, and a few moments later the twins, in a little room with the quiet-mannered man and a woman who was something or other, were telling who they were. They really *had* to tell, because the detective—the twins suspected he was such—although perfectly polite, asked questions in such a way that you found yourself giving the answers, in spite of everything.

"So you're David Farnsworth's girls," he observed conversationally. "I thought I had seen you here before. Well, I guess we'd better telephone your daddy. Don't you think so?" He patted Rosamond's head.

"He's not there," said Rhoda in a low voice. "You'll have to—you'll have to call our . . . mother. . . ."

No one noticed that Rhoda had to swallow after that last word as if her throat were sore, but the woman saw how white and frightened she was and patted her hand soothingly.

The detective telephoned and came back with the message. "Your ma'll be in on the next train. And you're to have a room, have supper in it, and wait for her. There's no train back to West Kempton tonight, so she'll stay."

When they heard the door click two hours later, the twins, who had sat supperless in two straight-backed chairs, sprang to their feet. If only she would be cross, awfully, awfully cross. But quite plainly she was going to be just as she had always been, as cold—as cold—as cold—Watching as *she* silently took off her coat and hat, the twins shivered. Then *she* faced them and said simply, "Well?"

Rosamond succumbed on the spot. "I didn't want to run away," she whimpered. "I didn't want to be a nursemaid. If a baby had the colic I wouldn't know what to do!"

Anne Farnsworth came to her and put an arm about her. "You don't have to be a nursemaid unless you wish to, Rosamond."

Rhoda, the daring, the defiant, stood alone; but not for long. Because she was the stronger of the two, her surrender was the more complete. "I didn't want to go either," she said huskily. "But we had to or else ask you to go to the mother-and-daughter picnic with us. We'd have asked you, but we knew you wouldn't want to go. I don't blame you for not liking us. You married Daddy, not us. We're sort of in the way. But we'd have asked you because we—" she gripped the back of the chair for support—"we really love you."

"Why, little Rhoda!"

And suddenly there was another arm being used, warm and comforting.

After an interval Anne Farnsworth blew her nose and observed with a smile, "I've heard of heavy rainfalls before, but I don't believe there's ever been one the equal of this! Now while you two are deciding about shopping and things for tomorrow—we might as well take the day and make a party of it—I'll go downstairs. There's a message I want to send to Daddy."

"Foe yields just bad case of nose out of joint poor policy that won't work both ways. Anne."

Upstairs, Rhoda greeted her. "Mother!" It was delicious to say the word now. It didn't smart a bit. "Did you see the letter we wrote Daddy right after you were married?"

Anne nodded.

"I'd like to get hold of that letter." Rhoda flushed. "I'd tear it into a million billion pieces!"

"I think that letter will be carefully preserved for posterity," said Anne. "It's rather masterly in spots."

"Was there such a word?" Rosamond demanded.

"As what, darling?"

"Ig*nor*ance."

"Not in the dictionary." Anne shook her head.

"There, Rhoda Farnsworth. What did I tell you!"

But Rhoda only shook her blonde curls as she retorted happily, "Shucks! Who cares?"

BETH MARTIN'S
PRETTY MOTHER

Francis Bowman

$\mathcal{W}$ork. *Unrelenting work . . . drives one into the ground as if bludgeoned in by a pile driver. And it prematurely ages one as well.*

So it was with Beth Martin's mother—old before her time; so Beth determined to do something about it. Surely Dr. Wood, the family doctor, would know what to do.

*B*eth Martin could tell the very day and hour and minute when the desire came to her to transform her plain, old-fashioned mother into a pretty mother. It was on the ninth day of July, just the day before the big musical entertainment when Beth was to show the people of Maybrook what a fine musician she was getting to be. It happened this way: Beth was lying in the hammock, out of sight behind the tall hedge, when she heard voices. She instantly recognized them as her mother's old friends. One of the ladies was saying:

"How plain and old-looking she is! She never goes anywhere. Why, I can remember when Mrs. Martin was called very handsome, but that was before Mr. Martin died and left her to pay off the mortgage on the farm and educate Beth and—"

The voices were left in the distance, and suddenly Beth sat up with a jerk as a new idea lodged in her ever-active brain. She'd like her mother to be pretty. She wondered why she had not thought of it before. There were so many pretty mothers nowadays. "I'll do it," she whispered to herself. "I'll make her over into a pretty mother. I'll just make her."

Beth had a way of "making" Mother do things, and now she was going to make this plain, businesslike, old-fashioned mother over into a "pretty mother."

I'll fix her hair and make her get some white-and-lavender gowns instead of those old black ones, was her mental comment a half hour later when she stood in the little sewing room and took note of her mother's fine brown eyes, heavy gray hair, and slender figure, now a little stooped from years of hard work. "Oh, Mother," she cried, "put away that dress you are sewing on. I'm going to wear my white one to the musicale, and I want you to fix up something pretty for yourself to wear, and—"

"I can't go," interrupted Mrs. Martin. "You hadn't ought to think I would."

"Now, Mother," began Beth, her face flushing with annoyance, "don't say 'hadn't ought,' and don't say 'ain't.' And don't, please don't pull your hair back so tight from your face; and you sit all stooped over as though you were a hundred years old. We've got some money. You work like a slave. I'm going to see to it that you have it easy this summer, Mother."

Mrs. Martin's face went white as she looked helplessly at her big, strong, attractive daughter. She wondered what Beth had in her mind to do. She was honestly afraid of this assertive yet lovely girl who had found so much fault, of late years, with everything she did.

As Beth stood a moment studying her mother's face and figure, a new thought came to her. She believed her mother ought to have some medicine. Her face was thin. She would consult old Dr. Wood. Perhaps if he prescribed a rest and some medicine for her mother, she could more easily carry out her plans of making her pretty.

As Beth acted expeditiously in her plans, a half hour later found her in old Dr. Wood's office.

"Well, well, well," began the doctor. "So you've come back to Maybrook a full-fledged musician. My, but we shall be proud of you! I suppose after the concert you'll be besieged with music pupils. There is no music teacher here now."

"Why—I hadn't thought of teaching," answered Beth in surprise. "I'm going to travel a bit next year. See the country and—"

"How do you like traveling out to feed your mother's chickens? They're a fine-looking lot, aren't they?"

"Why, really, I haven't seen them," answered Beth. "I came to ask you about—"

"What? Haven't you seen those handsome white leghorns? I suppose, though, that you are busy looking after the farm. That new barn is a dandy, isn't it?"

"I—I—I haven't been out to the farm yet," stammered Beth. "You see, Mother always looks after those things. I came to ask you about—"

"Oh, I might have known you'd be busy with the housework! I venture your mother enjoys your cooking all right."

"But I don't cook," laughed Beth, her face flushing under the doctor's queer questioning. "I came to ask you about—about Mother," she stammered out. "I think she needs a tonic. She looks too thin and old and—and—and I'd like to have her spruce up and be pretty."

"Oh, so you'd like to have a pretty mother!" retorted the doctor. "I can remember when she was handsome, but paying off ten-thousand-dollar mortgages, running a big farm, keeping hens, doing housework, and later sewing to send a daughter to school hasn't somehow developed Mrs. Martin's beauty. I see—I see—I—suppose you call tonight and I'll have a prescription for you. Your mother does need a tonic."

Beth felt a bit uncomfortable as she thought over the doctor's strange questions. She felt so annoyed that she walked straight home and on out to the henhouse and looked at the white leghorns. Then she walked slowly back to the house. "I wonder what he was getting at," she muttered to herself as she sat down on the porch and was soon deeply absorbed in a recent novel.

Six o'clock that afternoon found Beth again in the doctor's office. "I do hope the prescription will help Mother's complexion and make her look rested and young," she remarked as she took the rather bulky envelope the doctor handed her and paid her office fee.

Dr. Wood stood in the window and watched Beth hurrying down the street. *If she's got any heart and any sense, she'll help me carry out the prescription,* he said to himself shrewdly. *I'd like to see her when she reads it. If her eyes don't snap fire, then I miss my guess; but I had to do it.*

Before reaching the drugstore, Beth stopped to look at the prescription. She was astonished to find a long, closely typewritten list of directions with the date and day carefully marked out. It began with the following day:

Thursday, July 10: A few words of appreciation are the best things in the world for a mother's complexion. Begin by telling her that she's pretty. She may make the effort to live up to your opinion. Persuade her to go to the musical entertainment with you. See that she wears a pretty dress and has a seat where she can see her accomplished daughter when she plays. Don't go to paying out a lot of money for her new dress. It would worry her. She earned everything you have in too hard a way to spend it recklessly. Drop a hint that you may start up a class in music. A businesswoman like your mother would appreciate a daughter who could earn money.

Friday, July 11: Start out to get some music pupils. Talk it over with your mother and see if she does not think it would be a good idea for you to begin to earn some money to pay for your musical education.

Saturday, July 12: Take your mother to the milliner's shop and get her a new hat. Then call on the new minister's wife.

Sunday, July 13: Insist on your mother's going to church with you. Kiss her twice today and tell her that she is the dearest and best mother in all the world. Better take her arm as you walk along the village street. Mothers sometimes like to lean on their strong young daughters.

Monday, July 14: Get up early and see that the washing is well under way before your mother awakens.

Tuesday, July 15: Convince yourself and your mother that you want to learn how to take care of the chickens. Then take care of them.

Wednesday, July 16: Drive out and spend the day at the farm. Learn all you can about the place: what rent the man pays, how much stock is on the farm, how high the taxes are, and if it is well insured.

Thursday, July 17: Today the county grange meets here. Take your mother to the meeting. She'll appreciate the speeches, and it will help you to assist her in running the farm.

Friday, July 18: Persuade your mother to give up sewing for other people. Your music pupils ought to more than make up for the money she would earn with the needle.

Saturday, July 19: Take your mother on an excursion to the beach. Let people see that she is truly a companion for you.

Sunday, July 20: Kiss your mother three times today. Tell her she grows prettier every day. Take her to church and out for a walk in the afternoon.

Monday, July 21: Invite your mother's best friends in for a little afternoon tea party. Play your choicest selections for them, and serve your tea on the front porch. Call at my office sometime during the day and tell me how your mother improves under my prescription, and perhaps I can suggest some medicine if she needs it.

Beth's face was very grave as she carefully reread the peculiar prescription. For the first time in her life she faced the fact that she had never appreciated her mother. Her mother was a wonderful woman, and Beth had always criticized her and found fault with her. She suddenly saw herself from her own selfish point of view, and she set about carrying out the doctor's prescription.

The next morning Beth began to plan what her mother would wear to the musicale. "I think your black silk, with a little fixing over and with pretty, dainty white lace at the neck and sleeves, would be very nice," suggested Beth.

"What? For me!" answered Mrs. Martin. "You didn't think I'd go to the musicale, did you?"

"Certainly. Do you think I would go without you?" replied Beth. "You gave me my musical education, and I want you to see if you are pleased with it and with me."

That night when Mrs. Martin was dressed for the musicale, she scarcely recognized the little lady who smiled out at her from the looking glass. The black silk dress with its handsome lace collar and dainty white lace at the neck and sleeves looked new and stylish. Her cheeks were flushed with excitement, and her eyes were shining. Her hair, which had been combed in a becoming way by Beth's clever fingers, softened the outline of her face till she actually looked pretty. A tiny red rose was half hidden in the folds of her waist. "There," said Beth, giving her mother an affectionate little squeeze, "if people don't think you are the prettiest mother there, I miss my guess; and when the folks hear me play, they'll want me to give their children music lessons, and then I'll begin to earn some money."

Tears sprang to Mrs. Martin's eyes. She could not trust herself to speak. But over and over as she sat in a prominent place in the big hall, the words "You're the prettiest mother" came to her, and she felt repaid for all the long years of hard work. As for Beth, she had never played better.

As the week passed, each day's prescription was faithfully carried out, and when Beth told her mother of the ten music pupils who were going to begin taking lessons, and they drove out to the farm, and Beth set about with the air of a businesswoman to learn all about its every detail, Mrs. Martin's cup was full to over-flowing.

"I declare," she remarked to Dr. Wood, who chanced to stop by the porch where Mrs. Martin was sitting, reading, "I thought a week ago I was going to die, and I didn't care much if I did. But now that Beth takes care of the hens and does so much work and looks after the farm, I feel like a different person. She's even got me a new white dress and a hat with pale lavender flowers on it." Then she added with pardonable pride, "She's going to pay for them with the first money she earns giving music lessons."

One afternoon a few weeks later, Beth Martin knocked softly on the door of Dr. Wood's office. "I came to thank you for the prescription," she said. "It worked like a charm. What Mother needed was appreciation, and she's growing prettier every day. When we walk along the street, people say, 'There go Beth Martin and her pretty mother.'"

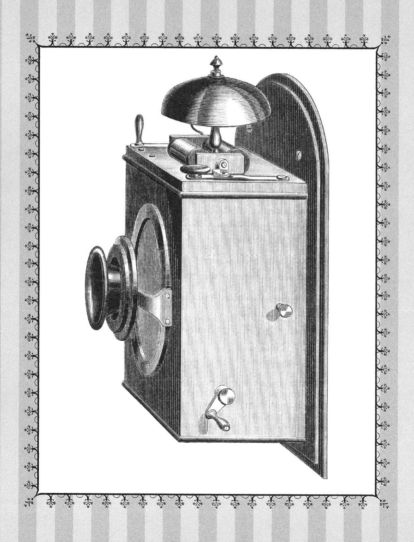

INFORMATION
PLEASE

Paul Villiard

*F*ewer and fewer Americans can remember back to
the days when the phone operator had real personhood
and, more important, was a local resident. In this story,
the operator was much more than just a source of tele-
phone-number information—for the author/narrator,
she was a surrogate mother.

*W*hen I was quite young, my family had one of the first telephones in our neighborhood. I remember well the polished oak case fastened to the wall on the lower-stair landing. The shiny receiver hung on the side of the box. I even remember the number—105. I was too little to reach the telephone but used to listen with fascination when my mother talked to it. Once she lifted me up to speak to my father who was away on business. Magic!

Then I discovered that somewhere inside that wonderful device lived an amazing person—her name was Information Please, and there was nothing she did not know. My mother could ask her for anybody's number; when our clock ran down, Information Please immediately supplied the correct time.

My first personal experience with the genie-in-the-receiver came one day while my mother was visiting a neighbor. Amusing myself at the tool bench in the basement, I whacked my finger with a hammer. The pain was terrible, but there didn't seem to be much use crying because there was no one home to offer sympathy. I walked around the house sucking my throbbing finger, finally arriving at the stairway. The telephone. Quickly I ran for the footstool in the parlor and brought it to the landing. Climbing up, I unhooked the receiver and held it to my ear. "Information, please," I said into the mouthpiece just above my head.

A click or two and a small, clear voice spoke into my ear. "Information."

"I hurt my finger-r-r," I wailed into the phone. The tears came readily enough, now that I had an audience.

"Isn't your mother home?" came the question.

"Nobody's home but me," I blubbered.

"Are you bleeding?"

"No," I replied. "I hit it with the hammer and it hurts."

"Can you open your icebox?" she asked. I said I could. "Then chip off a little piece of ice and hold it on your finger. That will stop the hurt. Be careful when you use the ice pick," she admonished. "And don't cry. You'll be all right."

After that, I called Information Please for everything. I asked her for help with my geography, and she told me where Philadelphia was and the Orinoco—the romantic river I was going to explore when I grew up. She helped me with my arithmetic, and she told me that my pet chipmunk—I had caught him in the park just the day before—would eat fruit and nuts.

And there was the time that Petey our pet canary died. I called Information Please and told her the sad story. She listened, then said the usual things grown-ups say to soothe a child. But I was unconsoled. Why was it that birds should sing so beautifully and bring joy to whole families, only to end as a heap of feathers, feet up, on the bottom of a cage?

She must have sensed my deep concern, for she said quietly, "Paul, always remember that there are other worlds to sing in."

Somehow I felt better.

Another day I was at the telephone. "Information," said the now familiar voice.

"How you spell *fix?*" I asked.

"Fix something? F-i-x."

At that instant my sister, who took unholy joy in scaring me, jumped off the stairs at me with a banshee shriek.

"Yaaaaaaaaaa!"

I fell off the stool, pulling the receiver out of the box by its roots. We were both terrified—Information Please was no longer there, and I was not at all sure that I hadn't hurt her when I pulled the receiver out.

Minutes later there was a man on the porch. "I'm a telephone repairman," he said. "I was working down the street, and the operator said there might be some trouble at this number." He reached for the receiver in my hand. "What happened?"

I told him.

"Well, we can fix that in a minute or two." He opened the telephone box, exposing a maze of wires and coils, and fiddled for a while with the end of the receiver cord, tightening things with a small screwdriver. He jiggled the hook up and down a few times, then spoke into the phone. "Hi, this is Pete. Everything's under control at 105. The kid's sister scared him, and he pulled the cord out of the box."

He hung up, smiled, gave me a pat on the head, and walked out the door.

All this took place in a small town in the Pacific Northwest. Then when I was nine years old, we moved across the country to Boston—and I missed my mentor acutely. Information Please belonged in that old wooden box back home, and I somehow never thought of trying the tall, skinny new phone that sat on a small table in the hall.

Yet as I grew into my teens, the memories of those childhood conversations never left me; often in moments of doubt and perplexity I would recall the serene sense of security I had had when I knew that I could call Information Please and get the right answer. I appreciated now how very patient, understanding, and kind she was to have wasted her time on a little boy.

A few years later on my way west to college, my plane put down in Seattle. I had about half an hour between plane connections, and I spent fifteen minutes or so on the phone with my sister who lived there now, happily mellowed by marriage and motherhood. Then, really without thinking what I was doing, I dialed my hometown operator and said, "Information, please."

Miraculously, I heard again the small, clear voice I knew so well: "Information."

I hadn't planned this, but I heard myself saying, "Could you tell me, please, how to spell the word *fix?*"

There was a long pause. Then came the softly spoken answer. "I guess," said Information Please, "that your finger must have healed by now."

I laughed. "So it's really still you. I wonder if you have any idea how much you meant to me during all that time."

"I wonder," she replied, "if you know how much you meant to me. I never had any children, and I used to look forward to your calls. Silly, wasn't it?"

It didn't seem silly, but I didn't say so. Instead, I told her how often I had thought of her over the years, and I asked if I could call her again when I came back to visit my sister after the first semester was over.

"Please do. Just ask for Sally."

"Good-bye, Sally." It sounded strange for Information Please to have a name. "If I run into any chipmunks, I'll tell them to eat fruit and nuts."

"Do that," she said. "And I expect some of these days you'll be off for the Orinoco. Well, good-bye."

Just three months later I was back again at the Seattle airport. A different voice answered, "Information," and I asked for Sally.

"Are you a friend?"

"Yes," I said. "An old friend."

"Then I'm sorry to have to tell you. Sally had only been working part-time in the last few years because she was ill. She died five weeks ago." But before I could hang up, she said, "Wait a minute. Did you say your name was Villiard?"

"Yes."

"Well, Sally left a message for you. She wrote it down."

"What was it?" I asked, almost knowing in advance what it would be.

"Here it is, I'll read it—'Tell him I still say there are other worlds to sing in. He'll know what I mean.'"

I thanked her and hung up. I *did* know what Sally meant.

Paul Villiard

This *Reader's Digest* award-winning story by Paul Villiard means even more to me since it was read at the funeral of one of my cherished aunts, Ruby Hamilton, of Turlock, California. Aunt Ruby's entire life embodied the caring love of "Information Please."

MOM AND THE
TALKING BEARS

Doris Elaine Fell

*M*ore and more often today, parenting represents a new kind of role, one unprecedented in human history. The average adult today may expect to spend more years caring for the needs of an aged parent than for any one child.

This incredible reversal of parent-child roles represents one of the most traumatic experiences each of us will face in life.

I never thought Mother would grow old.

To me, Mother stood for living and laughter. Vibrance and enthusiasm. A five-foot-one-inch retired schoolteacher with shiny brown hair and hazel eyes that sparkled with life.

She had her flaws. Sometimes she was stubborn and shortsighted. Sometimes spunky or passively resistant. Yet she flourished on friends and parties, travel and new experiences—an ordinary woman who loved her church and her God. She was too busy to grow old and wrinkled.

I remember well the day in England when I noticed the first threat of her aging. We were on the last day of a three-week, ten-country whirlwind European tour. I couldn't budge—I had hit mileage exhaustion. But my then seventy-two-year-old mother hovered over me fully dressed, a list of the day's activities already mapped out.

As she prodded me to wakefulness, the sun pierced the London fog and stole through the window of our mediocre hotel—its filtered beams highlighting flecks of gray in Mother's hair. "Mother," I stammered incredulously, "you've got gray hair."

She gave me a hand-to-hip stance, her amused expression ageless. "I'm old enough," she announced.

Even then I laughed her old age away, deluded into thinking that she was invincible, eons away from frailty.

Three weeks shy of her eighty-sixth birthday, she was still traveling, planning more trips, active in a handbell choir, and contemplating her next birthday party. Then cerebral strokes hit her like an eighteen-wheeler splintering a wooden barricade, thrusting ill health and old age on her. Her illness hurled her back in time to other days, other memories. She fought back with everything within her—groping for recall, clutching at normalcy, refusing to quit.

In the days following that first ministroke, I cried all the way to work and all the way home, a thirty-mile round-trip of tears. I was blinded to the thousands of others bearing a similar pain and was haunted by my long-standing promise to the Lord to always take care of my mother.

As Mother became more dependent, my freedom dwindled. I went from full-time registered nurse at a hospital to full-time caregiver at home. Soon two of us were living Mother's life; no one was living mine. My frustration mounted. *Counting it all joy* never entered my thought process.

I was splintered from the same block. I had Mom's creativity and integrity, her stubbornness and tenacity. But I was explosive in my personality. We seemed always to be two iron wills locking, grating against each other. But we were fiercely loyal. Somehow, we'd survive.

For Mother, life's dignities dropped slowly, one by one. She described herself well, saying, "Here I come just scuffing along—sheer grit, dogged determination." Then she whispered, "It's so sad. Nine-tenths of it is nothing but old age. I'm growing old, and I can't do anything about it. It's happening so fast."

Even though she was failing, I determined that she would keep the dignity of looking nice—hair permed, clothes neat, and matching shoes shined. I focused on the outward appearance, forgetting her heart cries. Then one day as she shuffled into the kitchen, gripping her walker, she said, "Steer me over to the sink, Doris. I may not be much good anymore, but I can still dry dishes."

My throat tightened. Had I robbed her of the dignity of being needed? From then on, as long as she was able, she dried dishes—at times only one or two.

Somewhere along those early days of her illness, the reversal of roles slipped in unannounced. I became like the mother, she like the child. I tried to shield her from rejection when friends stopped visiting and the phone ceased ringing. I read Bible passages and sang hymns to her at bedtime. As the years slipped by, I cringed at the sight of blenderized vegetables, fumed at spilt juices, and scowled at missing buttons. But when she stumbled and fell, over and over, I lifted her to her feet and gently helped her take those first halting steps again.

Mom constantly resisted mother-sitters, but she found joy at the home of a friend—a home alive with five toddlers, two grandmothers, and two poodle dogs. And she always marched off proudly to the Garden Grove Day Care Center ("school" as she called it). I framed her artwork from the center and tucked her loving, witty sayings in my heart and in my journal.

In these lonely, painful days of my single parenting, she pressed me with questions about dying, innocent and childlike in their intensity: Will I be afraid? How long does it take to get to heaven? Will my mom and dad know me?

Yes, her parents would know her. But I was still earthbound. I balked when she forgot my name, sometimes calling me Helen, Bella, or Marion. I felt like *my* identity was slipping until she said sadly, "All those names I've known for years, I keep forgetting them. One moment they're here. The next they're gone."

After that, I conceived ways to help her remember names. We took frequent hand-treks through the old-fashioned family album with pictures dating back one hundred years or more. We sorted through the snapshots of her seven siblings, her children, and grandchildren. And then, in the third year of her illness, we stumbled upon the most effective way of all to help her remember. A friend gave Mother a cuddly stuffed bear with a lavender ribbon around its neck. Mother laughed and hugged the bear. We named it Elmira for her mother. After that, friends and family—even Mother's hairdresser—showered her with thirty bears of every shape and personality. We named each one for a family member.

The biggest bear of all—brown, floppy, and lovable—was named Alonzo for the dad she so dearly loved. The one with the anchor cap for Harold, the retired rear admiral in the family. And the smallest bear, Ryan, for her handsome, dark-eyed great-grandson.

It was easy for me to go from hugging the stuffed bears to frequently reaching out and bear-hugging Mother. One day when her spirits seemed low, I picked up the biggest bear and went to her. Pretending to speak for the bear, I said, "Hello, Edith. I'm Alonzo Cotton. Do you remember me?"

Her eyes misted. "Oh, yes. You're my pop."

"Do you remember walking down that dusty trail with me to meet Jesus?" the bear asked.

"Yes," she said clearly. "When I was seventeen."

I nudged the bear's face closer to her own. "Edith, you're my only child not in heaven."

"The only one?"

"The only one."

"My brothers? Harold . . . Ed . . . Alex?"

"They're all here with Mother and me. And someday Jesus is going to call you to heaven, too, Edith. Then we'll all be together again."

She nodded, her face so full of understanding. "And I'll be ready to go," she answered softly. "I'm so very tired now."

I pressed the bear into her arms and she hugged it, a hug that must have reached clear to heaven.

Sometimes, however, heaven seemed distant to me as the days of Mother's painful journey toward eternity stretched on. I was angry with everyone, including God. From the beginning, it had been an almost insurmountable emotional journey. But even more, it was spiritual warfare: a battle to maintain *faith, hope, and love*.

Once in my frustration, I cried out, "Why am I taking care of you? What did you ever do for me?"

She looked so vulnerable when she answered, "I have always loved you, Doris."

I noted these things that Mother said and did in my journal. Her love and faith kept shining through. I began to see beyond her deteriorating body and catch glimmerings of that person tucked inside. Her body was dying, but her soul that would live forever was sparked with victory. God had not forgotten Mother or me. He was still holding our hands, walking with us, sheltering us in His love, carrying us over the rough spots, and bottling up our tears in eternity.

I gathered these truths like bouquets of flowers. Now I saw them as tiny delicate rosebuds of her love, His love. In Mother's frailty, God allowed me to see her inner strengths. Through Mother, He awakened me to the nearness of heaven.

One such truth stands like a rose, taller than the rest. I was leaning against the kitchen sink one day, my hands thrust deep in the dishwater. Agonizing self-pity pricked my soul. I was arguing with God—putting limitations on my six-year-old impossible burden. I confessed that I was botching the job. I couldn't make it one more day. The room was midnight-still, but inside I was half screaming, begging for a way out. I turned suddenly. Mother stood framed in the narrow hallway, gripping her walker for balance. Her hazel eyes held mine. For a fleeting moment I wondered how long she had watched me. In a fragile whisper she said, "Someday, Doris, you'll be glad you took care of me."

Amazingly, she who bore me knew me better than I knew myself. I caught the fragrance of her love like a rose in bloom as I crossed the room to her and buried my chin in her salt-and-pepper waves. "I'm already glad I'm caring for you," I said sincerely.

On January 19 we celebrated Mother's ninety-second birthday. As her thin, vein-rippled hands tugged at the birthday wrappings, I realized again that Mother had never intended to grow old or ill or helpless. Our eyes met; she smiled happily. Watching her joy, I was keenly aware of my goodly heritage.

Mother would not leave me houses and lands, padded bank accounts, or sparkling diamonds. But she would leave me her strength of character as a living legacy. That tremendous capacity to love and forgive. Her amazing fairness. Her spiritual wisdom. Her humor. Her unquestionable integrity. Her ability to sometimes melt my impatience and cutting remarks with a trusting smile. And her confident unswerving conviction that *the Lord was her Shepherd.*

I crossed the room to the one entrusted to my care, and Mom stretched her thin, frail hands toward me, her expression warm and loving.

Deep within me I sensed God's garment of praise for my spirit of heaviness.

As I reached Mom and gave her a bear hug, I was unaware that our six-year journey was almost over. I had only one more promise to keep. Mother would have the dignity of dying in her own home.

In February, Mother suffered two major strokes. For the first time in her long illness, she was confined to bed, too weak to be up and dressed in the pretty clothes she loved to wear.

Toward midnight, February 15, I knew Mom's death was imminent. For the last hour and a half of her life, I pillowed her head in my hand. She slipped her fingers gently around my other hand, her gaze intent on me.

"Mom, I love you," I said. "I'll miss you." Then, my voice still calm, I continued. "Mom, you're almost home. In just a few minutes you're going to see Jesus. . . ."

Moments later, she went, unafraid, to her Shepherd-Savior, her frail fingers still wrapped lovingly around mine. My mom had broken the shackles of illness and old age, stepping sprightly from the bondage of her bed and wheelchair into eternal life.

In the quiet hush of her room, I could almost hear Mother shouting, "Oh, Doris, I'm going on a trip now, you know. I'm going home!"

Doris Elaine Fell

Doris Elaine Fell, a freelance author and editor, originally wrote this story for *Focus on the Family* magazine. She had previously been a teacher with Wycliffe Bible Translators and later became a nurse. Miss Fell is the author of the Seasons of Intrigue fiction series by Crossway Books.

THE DIPLOMACY
OF GRANDMA

Author Unknown

Few people have greater impact upon our lives than do our grandparents. They have time to spend when parents do not. They are the ones who pass on family traditions, family wisdom.

Stephen's teachers had given up on him. Even Stephen's parents had given up on him.

That left only . . . Grandma.

*G*randma was a person of decided character. From the first, Stephen Ward had been her favorite grandchild, and she had never taken any pains to conceal her partiality for the sturdy lad. His sister Eleanor was by far the prettier baby, the more attractive child, and the greater credit to the family during her teens; but Stephen, although he was slow to discover the fact, had found the somewhat difficult way to his grandmother's loyal heart. By the time Stephen was seventeen, there was a curious bond of friendship between the bright old lady and the awkward boy.

It was this sympathetic grandmother who caught Stephen preparing to smoke his first—and last—pipe. Wisely refraining from any reproaches, the astute old lady showed him how to pack the tobacco into the bowl, heroically sat beside him in the reeking atmosphere of the barn (where the episode took place), and remained with him to the bitter end. How bitter the end was, only Stephen and his grandmother ever knew. From that time forth, Stephen trusted his grandmother with secrets that another boy would have kept securely locked within his own heart.

Stephen loved the woods and the water to an unusual degree. He knew the habits of the birds; he could swim like a fish in the waters of Lake Superior; he could distinguish between spruce and balsam, hemlock and jack pine, soft maple and hard maple.

Moreover, he was honest, sweet tempered, and obliging. But in spite of these good traits, his parents and his teachers found him a difficult problem.

Stephen hated school. His young sister easily overtook him, jogged along beside him for a week or two, and then left him far behind on the path of knowledge.

"Stephen's only ambition," one of his teachers reported, "is to escape with the others at four o'clock. When he isn't looking out of the window, he is watching the clock or drawing maps of the lumber roads north of the town."

"Isn't there a single study that he takes a little interest in?" asked Mrs. Ward anxiously.

"It is possible he might shine in the kindergarten department," was the teacher's reply, "for I found twenty-seven kinds of leaves in his desk the other day. But seriously, Mrs. Ward, I'm afraid Stephen will never get out of the freshman class. He seems to be anchored right there. It's a wonder to me that he ever got that far. His spelling is really atrocious, and his algebra—"

"He was promoted by special arrangement," said Mrs. Ward. "Professor Perkins thought it might be better for him to skip the eighth grade and make it up later. Perhaps he'll be more interested when he gets to the botany class."

"He'll never get there," said the discouraged teacher. "There are too many other things that come before botany."

Besides being slow, Stephen was easily the biggest boy in his grade. He grew sensitive as well as tall, and finally he announced that he would not go to school another day.

"I'll do anything else you want me to," said Stephen, sitting in solemn conclave with his disappointed parents. "I'll go to the copper country and work in the mines, or I'll stay here and work up from the bottom in one of the iron mines. I'll fire an engine or go into the powder mills, or I'll work on a farm—but no more school for me!"

"But Stephen," urged his mother, "you can't do any of these things successfully without an education."

"Captain Banks did."

"Do you want to be like Captain Banks?"

"Well, not *just* like him," Stephen admitted. "I don't intend to drink or to bluster around the way he does, but he makes piles of money. He boasts that he never went to school a day in his life."

"Well," agreed Mrs. Ward, "no one who had ever listened for five minutes to his conversation would think of disbelieving him."

His mother coaxed, his father scolded, and Eleanor upbraided him, but all to no purpose. Stephen would start out (ostensibly for school, to keep peace in the family), but in reality, he spent all school hours in the woods, as he frankly confessed when he returned at night.

His parents did not know what to do. Stephen was too old for corporal punishment, and he would not listen to reason.

It was at this juncture that Grandma Ward rose to the occasion. "Let the boy alone," said she. "You're not using the right sort of bait. He's got a streak of his Grandfather Ward in him. His grandfather was so obstinate that he would have planted his apple trees upside down if anybody had told him not to. It took me fifteen years to learn to manage Alonzo Ward, but when I once learn a thing, I don't forget. Leave that boy to me for a month; but whatever you do, don't let him suspect that I'm paying any extra attention to him."

Grandma Ward's room was on the ground floor of the rambling, old-fashioned house. She was too stout to climb stairs easily, and her thoughtful daughter-in-law had made the large room a very comfortable spot.

The elder Mrs. Ward never objected to Stephen's "trash," as his mother called the curiously shaped bits of fungi, the specimens of mineral, the agates, and the insects the boy was constantly collecting. He never felt that his own room was entirely safe from invasion. The housemaid's devastating broom had more than once played havoc with his hoard, but he had implicit confidence in his grandmother. His choicest treasures occupied the shelf over her grate, and no one knew how frequently she was obliged to disentangle her knitting from the ribs of his precious but evil-smelling skeletonized trout.

Stephen, with no schoolwork to do, fell into the habit of spending many of his evenings on his grandmother's hearth rug. It was almost dark by five o'clock, and the boy usually reached home at that hour. He had always been an obliging youth, except in the one matter of going to school. When his grandmother, whose eyes seemed suddenly to have failed, asked him one evening to write some important business letters for her, incompetent Stephen complied with the utmost cheerfulness.

The concern with the outside world that his grandmother seemed all at once to possess came as something of a surprise to Stephen. He had had no idea that the enterprising old lady had so many and such varied interests.

Stephen was required to order seeds from the catalogue, to inquire into the details of various projects advertised in the magazines, to write for information regarding certain stocks, bonds, and parcels of land that existed only in his grandmother's fertile imagination. The unsuspicious boy never knew how many of the laboriously written letters were mailed, to quote Grandma Ward's quaint phrase, "up the chimney to Santa Claus." Stephen wrote them all in good faith. He patiently and conscientiously added up long columns of figures, looked up in the dictionary the words he was unable to spell—their number was truly appalling!—and began, just as Grandma Ward intended he should, to realize his limitations. Up to this point she had said little, but finding her unsuspicious pupil in a receptive mood one day, she confided some of her troubles to him.

"You see," she said apologetically, "I'd write those letters myself, but it isn't only my eyes that trouble me; it's my lack of learning. Business letters have to be done sort of particular. My writing's terribly poor, I don't always know how to spell, I'm not sure of my grammar, and I never could figure well enough to come within a dozen rows of apple trees of being right. I didn't have a chance to learn those things when I was young, and nobody knows what a difference it has made all through my life.

"A body that can't figure can't do anything. It's surprising, when you come to think about it, what a quantity of figuring there is in everything. Then there's grammar. If you don't feel sure of your grammar, there are times when you don't dare open your mouth for fear of shocking your relatives. Many's the time I've kept my mouth shut when I was just bursting to say something, but didn't have the grammar to say it with.

"If your father hadn't had to leave school when he did," continued the wise old lady, "'twould have been dollars in his pocket. He had to learn things when he was a grown man that most ten-year-old boys know nowadays.

"I've lost friends that I'd have been glad to keep, only I was afraid they'd find out I wasn't educated if I wrote to them. I had a letter from Horace Greeley once when I was a girl, and I couldn't read it. I used to know him well, and I would have answered that letter, but I didn't know how. I couldn't spell much more than my own name in those days."

Stephen thought of his own spelling and blushed.

"Did Stephen write this?" asked Mr. Ward, holding up a sheet of paper that he had found on his mother's table one day, as he was looking for a magazine.

"Yes," said Grandma Ward.

"Why, that's a better business letter than I can write today. His teachers must have been mistaken about him."

"Oh, no, they weren't," said Grandma Ward with a twinkle in her eye. "He's improved lately. He is now my private secretary."

"Your *what?*" gasped Mr. Ward.

"My private secretary. I've started a business college for his benefit."

"You?"

"Yes, Robert. Common sense makes up for the lack of education sometimes, although I wouldn't admit that to Stephen."

"He ought to be in school," grumbled Mr. Ward.

"Never you mind about that," said Grandma Ward. "You won't be able to keep him out of school by this time next year. Letter writing isn't the only thing I'm teaching him."

"I won't interfere," promised Mr. Ward, "but I have my doubts about his ever liking school."

There were times when Grandma Ward, too, had doubts. If Stephen had not been genuinely fond of his grandmother, the good woman, shrewd as she was, would have failed in her curious undertaking. As it was, Stephen swelled with pride when he noted how indispensable he was to his poor, dependent grandmother. No one else had ever made him feel that he was indispensable, and he thoroughly enjoyed the novel sensation.

Grandma Ward continued to lie awake at night to concoct business for Stephen to attend to in the daytime. She saw with delight that when a particularly knotty problem came up, Stephen turned, as a last resort, to his hated textbooks for the solution to the difficulty.

With rare tact she made him feel at every turn how poorly he was equipped for any sort of business career.

"Grandma," said Stephen, looking up from the dictionary one winter night, "you can keep a secret, I know, for you never told anyone about that awful pipe. Don't say a word about this to the others until I'm safe out of the house, but I've made up my mind to go back to school in the morning. There are a lot of things I've just got to know more about. I believe some part of my brain has been taking a nap. Things seem more interesting than they used to. I believe I could catch up with the class if I tried."

And he caught up before the next term ended.

THE REVOLT
OF MOTHER

Mary E. Wilkins Freeman

*W*henever I want to communicate to my students the
seismic changes that have taken place during the past
century—especially where women are concerned—chances
are I will read this story to them.

It reveals a world as foreign to ours as that we depict
in science fiction, a world where men were dominant
and women were mere chattels, a world where the comfort
of farm animals was valued more than the comfort of the
farmer's wife and children.

It also reveals . . . well, perhaps I'll let you find out for
yourself. . . .

*F*ather!"

"What is it?"

"What are them men diggin' over there in the field for?"

There was a sudden dropping and enlarging of the lower part of the old man's face, as if some heavy weight had settled therein; he shut his mouth tight and went on harnessing the great bay mare. He hustled the collar onto her neck with a jerk.

"Father!"

The old man slapped the saddle upon the mare's back.

"Look here, Father, I want to know what them men are diggin' over in the field for, an' I'm goin' to know."

"I wish you'd go into the house, Mother, an' 'tend to your own affairs," the old man said then. He ran his words together, and his speech was almost as inarticulate as a growl.

But the woman understood; it was her most native tongue. "I ain't goin' into the house till you tell me what them men are doin' over there in the field," said she.

Then she stood waiting. She was a small woman, short and straight-waisted like a child in her brown cotton gown. Her forehead was mild and benevolent between the smooth curves of gray hair; there were meek downward lines about her nose and mouth; but her eyes, fixed upon the old man, looked as if the meekness had been the result of her own will, never of the will of another.

They were in the barn, standing before the wide-open doors. The spring air, full of the smell of growing grass and unseen blossoms, came in their faces. The deep yard in front was littered with farm wagons and piles of wood; on the edges, close to the fence and the house, the grass was a vivid green, and there were some dandelions.

The old man glanced doggedly at his wife as he tightened the last buckles on the harness. She looked as immovable to him as one of the rocks in his pastureland, bound to the earth with generations of blackberry vines. He slapped the reins over the horse and started forth from the barn.

"Father!" said she.

The old man pulled up. "What is it?"

"I want to know what them men are diggin' over there in that field for."

"They're diggin' a cellar, I s'pose, if you've got to know."

"A cellar for what?"

"A barn."

"A barn? You ain't goin' to build a barn over there where we was goin' to have a house, Father?"

The old man said not another word. He hurriedly hitched the horse to the farm wagon and clattered out of the yard, jouncing as sturdily on his seat as a boy.

The woman stood a moment looking after him; then she went out of the barn across a corner of the yard to the house. The house, standing at right angles with the great barn and a long reach of sheds and outbuildings, was infinitesimal compared with them. It was scarcely as commodious for people as the little boxes under the barn eaves were for doves.

A pretty girl's face, pink and delicate as a flower, was looking out of one of the house windows. She was watching three men who were digging over in the field which bounded the yard near the road line. She turned quietly when the woman entered.

"What are they digging for, Mother?" said she. "Did he tell you?"

"They're diggin' for—a cellar for a new barn."

"Oh, Mother, he ain't going to build another barn?"

"That's what he says."

A boy stood before the kitchen glass combing his hair. He combed slowly and painstakingly, arranging his brown hair in a smooth hillock over his forehead. He did not seem to pay any attention to the conversation.

"Sammy, did you know Father was going to build a new barn?" asked the girl.

The boy combed assiduously.

"Sammy!"

He turned and showed a face like his father's under his smooth crest of hair. "Yes, I s'pose I did," he said reluctantly.

"How long have you known it?" asked his mother.

"'Bout three months, I guess."

"Why didn't you tell of it?"

"Didn't think 'twould do no good."

"I don't see what Father wants another barn for," said the girl in her sweet, slow voice. She turned again to the window and stared out at the digging men in the field. Her tender, sweet face was full of a gentle distress. Her forehead was as bald and innocent as a baby's, with the light hair strained back from it in a row of curlpapers. She was quite tall, but her soft curves did not look as if they covered muscles.

Her mother looked sternly at the boy. "Is he goin' to buy more cows?" said she.

The boy did not reply; he was tying his shoes.

"Sammy, I want you to tell me if he's goin' to buy more cows."

"I s'pose he is."

"How many?"

"Four, I guess."

His mother said nothing more. She went into the pantry, and there was a clatter of dishes. The boy got his cap from a nail behind the door, took an old arithmetic from the shelf, and started for school. He was lightly built but clumsy. He went out of the yard with a curious spring in his hips that made his loose homemade jacket tilt up in the rear.

The girl went to the sink and began to wash the dishes that were piled up there. Her mother came promptly out of the pantry and shoved her aside. "You wipe 'em," said she; "I'll wash. There's a good many this mornin'."

The mother plunged her hands vigorously into the water; the girl wiped the plates slowly and dreamily. "Mother," said she, "don't you think it's too bad Father's going to build that new barn, much as we need a decent house to live in?"

Her mother scrubbed a dish fiercely. "You ain't found out yet we're womenfolks, Nanny Penn," said she. "You ain't seen enough of menfolks yet to. One of these days you'll find it out, an' then you'll know that we know only what menfolks think we do, so far as any use of it goes, an' how we'd ought to reckon menfolks in with Providence, an' not complain of what they do anymore than we do of the weather."

"I don't care; I don't believe George is anything like that, anyhow," said Nanny. Her delicate face flushed pink; her lips pouted softly as if she were going to cry.

"You wait an' see. I guess George Eastman ain't no better than other men. You hadn't ought to judge Father, though. He can't help it 'cause he don't look at things jest the way we do. An' we've been pretty comfortable here, after all. The roof don't leak—ain't never but once—that's one thing. Father's kept it shingled right up."

"I do wish we had a parlor."

"I guess it won't hurt George Eastman any to come to see you in a nice clean kitchen. I guess a good many girls don't have as good a place as this. Nobody's ever heard me complain."

"I ain't complained either, Mother."

"Well, I don't think you'd better, a good father an' a good home as you've got. S'pose your father made you go out an' work for your livin'? Lots of girls have to that ain't no stronger an' better able to than you be."

Sarah Penn washed the frying pan with a conclusive air. She scrubbed the outside of it as faithfully as the inside. She was a masterly keeper of her box of a house. Her one living room never seemed to have in it any of the dust which the friction of life with inanimate matter produces. She swept, and there seemed to be no dirt to go before the broom; she cleaned, and one could see no difference. She was like an artist so perfect that he apparently has no art. Today she got out a mixing bowl and a board, and rolled some pies, and there was no more flour upon her than upon her daughter who was doing finer work. Nanny was to be married in the fall, and she was sewing on some white cambric and embroidery. She sewed industriously while her mother cooked, her soft milk white hands and wrists showed whiter than her delicate work.

"We must have the stove moved out in the shed before long," said Mrs. Penn. "Talk about not havin' things, it's been a real blessin' to be able to put a stove up in that shed in hot weather. Father did one good thing when he fixed that stovepipe out there."

Sarah Penn's face as she rolled her pies had that expression of meek vigor which might have characterized one of the New Testament saints. She was making mince pies. Her husband, Adoniram Penn, liked them better than any other kind. She baked twice a week. Adoniram often liked a piece of pie between meals. She hurried this morning. It had been later than usual when she began, and she wanted to have a pie baked for dinner. However deep a resentment she might be forced to hold against her husband, she would never fail in sedulous attention to his wants.

Nobility of character manifests itself at loopholes when it is not provided with large doors. Sarah Penn's showed itself today in flaky dishes of pastry. So she made the pies faithfully, while across the table she could see, when she glanced up from her work, the sight that rankled in her patient and steadfast soul—the digging of the cellar of the new barn in the place where Adoniram forty years ago had promised her their new house should stand.

The pies were done for dinner. Adoniram and Sammy were home a few minutes after twelve o'clock. The dinner was eaten with serious haste. There was never much conversation at the table in the Penn family. Adoniram asked a blessing, and they ate promptly, then rose up and went about their work.

Sammy went back to school, taking soft sly lopes out of the yard like a rabbit. He wanted a game of marbles before school and feared his father would give him some chores to do. Adoniram hastened to the door and called after him, but he was out of sight.

"I don't see what you let him go for, Mother," said he. "I wanted him to help me unload that wood."

Adoniram went to work out in the yard unloading wood from the wagon. Sarah put away the dinner dishes, while Nanny took down her curlpapers and changed her dress. She was going down to the store to buy some more embroidery and thread.

When Nanny was gone, Mrs. Penn went to the door. "Father!" she called.

"Well, what is it?"

"I want to see you jest a minute, Father."

"I can't leave this wood nohow. I've got to git it unloaded an' go for a load of gravel afore two o'clock. Sammy had ought to helped me. You hadn't ought to let him go to school so early."

"I want to see you jest a minute."

"I tell ye I can't, nohow, Mother."

"Father, *you come here.*" Sarah Penn stood in the door like a queen; she held her head as if it bore a crown; there was that patience which makes authority royal in her voice. Adoniram went.

Mrs. Penn led the way into the kitchen and pointed to a chair. "Sit down, Father," said she; "I've got somethin' I want to say to you."

He sat down heavily; his face was quite stolid, but he looked at her with restive eyes. "Well, what is it, Mother?"

"I want to know what you're buildin' that new barn for, Father."

"I ain't got nothin' to say about it."

"It can't be you think you need another barn?"

"I tell ye I ain't got nothin' to say about it, Mother; an' I ain't goin' to say nothin'."

"Be you goin' to buy more cows?"

Adoniram did not reply; he shut his mouth tight.

"I know you be, as well as if you said so. Now, Father, look here—" Sarah Penn had not sat down; she stood before her husband in the humble fashion of a Scripture woman—"I'm goin' to talk real plain to you; I never have sence I married you, but I'm goin' to now. I ain't never complained, an' I ain't goin' to complain now, but I'm goin' to talk plain.

"You see this room here, Father; you look at it well. You see there ain't no carpet on the floor, an' you see the paper is all dirty an' droppin' off the walls. We ain't had no new paper on it for ten year, an' then I put it on myself, an' it didn't cost but ninepence a roll. You see this room, Father; it's all the one I've had to work in an' eat in an' sit in sence we was married. There ain't another woman in the whole town whose husband ain't got half the means you have but what's got better. It's all the room Nanny's got to have her company in; an' there ain't one of her mates but what's got better an' their fathers not so able as hers is. It's all the room she'll have to be married in. What would you have thought, Father, if we had had our weddin' in a room no better than this? I was married in my mother's parlor, with a carpet on the floor an' stuffed furniture an' a mahogany card table. An' this is all the room my daughter will have to be married in. Look here, Father!"

Sarah Penn went across the room as though it were a tragic stage. She flung open a door and disclosed a tiny bedroom, only large enough for a bed and bureau, with a path between. "There, Father," said she, "there's all the room I've had to sleep in forty year. All my children were born there—the two that died an' the two that's livin'. I was sick with a fever there."

She stepped to another door and opened it. It led into the small, ill-lighted pantry. "Here," said she, "is all the buttery I've got—every place I've got for my dishes, to set away my victuals in, an' to keep my milk pans in. Father, I've been takin' care of the milk of six cows in this place, an' now you're goin' to build a new barn an' keep more cows an' give me more to do in it."

She threw open another door. A narrow crooked flight of stairs wound upward from it. "There, Father," said she, "I want you to look at the stairs that go up to them two unfinished chambers that are all the places our son an' daughter have had to sleep in all their lives. There ain't a prettier girl in town nor a more ladylike one than Nanny, an' that's the place she has to sleep in. It ain't so good as your horse's stall; it ain't so warm an' tight."

Sarah Penn went back and stood before her husband. "Now, Father," said she, "I want to know if you think you're doin' right an' accordin' to what you profess. Here when we was married forty year ago, you promised me faithful that we should have a new house built in that lot over in the field before the year was out. You said you had money enough, an' you wouldn't ask me to live in no such place as this. It is forty year now, an' you've been makin' more money, an' I've been savin' of it for you ever since, an' you ain't built no house yet. You've built sheds an' cow houses an' one new barn, an' now you're goin' to build another. Father, I want to know if you think it's right. You're lodgin' your dumb beasts better than you are your own flesh an' blood. I want to know if you think it's right."

"I ain't got nothin' to say."

"You can't say nothin' without ownin' it ain't right, Father. An' there's another thing—I ain't complained; I've got along forty year, an' I s'pose I should forty more, if it wa'n't for that— if we don't have another house. Nanny she can't live with us after she's married. She'll have to go somewheres else to live away from us, an' it don't seem as if I could have it so, noways, Father. She wa'n't ever strong. She's got considerable color, but there wa'n't never any backbone to her. I've always took the heft of everything off her, an' she ain't fit to keep house an' do every-thing herself. She'll be all worn out inside of a year. Think of her doin' all the washin' an' ironin' an' bakin' with them soft white hands an' arms, an' sweepin'! I can't have it so, noways, Father."

Mrs. Penn's face was burning; her mild eyes gleamed. She had pleaded her little cause like a Webster; she had ranged from severity to pathos; but her opponent employed that obstinate silence which makes eloquence futile with mocking echoes. Adoniram arose clumsily.

"Father, ain't you got nothin' to say?" said Mrs. Penn.

"I've got to go off after that load of gravel. I can't stan' here talkin' all day."

"Father, won't you think it over an' have a house built there instead of a barn?"

"I ain't got nothin' to say."

Adoniram shuffled out. Mrs. Penn went into her bedroom. When she came out, her eyes were red. She had a roll of unbleached cotton cloth. She spread it out on the kitchen table and began cutting out some shirts for her husband. The men over in the field had a team to help them this afternoon; she could hear their halloos. She had a scanty pattern for the shirts; she had to plan and piece the sleeve.

Nanny came home with her embroidery and sat down with her needlework. She had taken down her curlpapers, and there was a soft roll of fair hair like an aureole over her forehead; her face was as delicately fine and clear as porcelain. Suddenly she looked up, and the tender red flamed all over her face and neck. "Mother," said she.

"What say?"

"I've been thinking—I don't see how we're goin' to have any—wedding in this room. I'd be ashamed to have his folks come if we didn't have anybody else."

"Mebbe we can have some new paper before then; I can put it on. I guess you won't have no call to be ashamed of your belongin's."

"We might have the wedding in the new barn," said Nanny with gentle pettishness. "Why, Mother, what makes you look so?"

Mrs. Penn started and was staring at her with a curious expression. She turned again to her work and spread out a pattern carefully on the cloth. "Nothin'," she said.

Presently Adoniram clattered out of the yard in his two-wheeled dump cart, standing as proudly upright as a Roman charioteer. Mrs. Penn opened the door and stood there a minute looking out; the halloos of the men sounded louder.

It seemed to her all through the spring months that she heard nothing but the halloos and the noises of saws and hammers. The new barn grew fast. It was a fine edifice for this little village. Men came on pleasant Sundays in their meeting suits and clean shirt bosoms and stood around it admiringly. Mrs. Penn did not speak of it, and Adoniram did not mention it to her, although sometimes, upon a return from inspecting it, he bore himself with injured dignity.

"It's a strange thing how your mother feels about a new barn," he said confidentially to Sammy one day.

Sammy only grunted after an odd fashion for a boy; he had learned it from his father.

The barn was all completed ready for use by the third week in July. Adoniram had planned to move his stock in on Wednesday; on Tuesday he received a letter which changed his plans. He came in with it early in the morning. "Sammy's been to the Post Office," said he, "an' I've got a letter from Hiram." Hiram was Mrs. Penn's brother, who lived in Vermont.

"Well," said Mrs. Penn, "what does he say about the folks?"

"I guess they're all right. He said he thinks if I come up country right off there's a chance to buy jest the kind of horse I want." He stared reflectively out of the window at the new barn.

Mrs. Penn was making pies. She went on clapping the rolling

pin into the crust, although she was very pale, and her heart beat loudly.

"I don' know but what I'd better go," said Adoniram. "I hate to go off jest now, right in the midst of hayin', but the ten-acre lot's cut, an' I guess Rufus an' the others can git along without me three or four days. I can't get a horse round here to suit me, nohow, an' I've got to have another for all that wood haulin' in the fall. I told Hiram to watch out, an' if he got wind of a good horse to let me know. I guess I'd better go."

"I'll get out your clean shirt an' collar," said Mrs. Penn calmly.

She laid out Adoniram's Sunday suit and his clean clothes on the bed in the little bedroom. She got his shaving water and razor ready. At last she buttoned on his collar and fastened his black cravat.

Adoniram never wore his collar and cravat except on special occasions. He held his head high with a rasped dignity. When he was all ready, with his coat and hat brushed and a lunch of pie and cheese in a paper bag, he hesitated on the threshold of the door. He looked at his wife, and his manner was defiantly unapologetic. "*If* them cows come today, Sammy can drive 'em into the new barn," said he, "an' when they bring the hay up, they can pitch it in there."

"Well," replied Mrs. Penn.

Adoniram set his shaven face ahead and started. When he had cleared the doorstep, he turned and looked back with a kind of nervous solemnity. "I shall be back by Saturday if nothin' happens," said he.

"Do be careful, Father," returned his wife.

She stood in the door with Nanny at her elbow and watched him out of sight. Her eyes had a strange, doubtful expression in them; her peaceful forehead was contracted. She went in and about her baking again. Nanny sat sewing. Her wedding day was drawing nearer, and she was getting pale and thin with her steady sewing. Her mother kept glancing at her.

"Have you got that pain in your side this mornin'?" she asked.

"A little."

Mrs. Penn's face changed as she worked; her perplexed forehead smoothed, her eyes were steady, her lips firmly set. She formed a maxim for herself, although incoherently, with her unlettered thoughts. "Unsolicited opportunities are the guideposts of the Lord to the new roads of life," she repeated in effect, and she made up her mind to her course of action.

"S'posin' I *had* wrote to Hiram," she muttered once when she was in the pantry. "S'posin' I had wrote an' asked him if he knew of any horse? But I didn't, an' Father's goin' wa'n't none of my doin'. It looks like a providence." Her voice rang out quite loud at the last.

"What you talkin' about, Mother?" called Nanny.

"Nothin'."

Mrs. Penn hurried her baking; at eleven o'clock it was all done. The load of hay from the west field came slowly down the cart track and drew up at the new barn. Mrs. Penn ran out. "Stop!" she screamed. "Stop!"

The men stopped and looked; Sammy upreared from the top of the load and stared at his mother.

"Stop!" she cried out again. "Don't you put the hay in that barn; put it in the old one."

"Why, he said to put it in here," returned one of the haymakers wonderingly. He was a young man, a neighbor's son, whom Adoniram hired by the year to help on the farm.

"Don't you put the hay in the new barn; there's room enough in the old one, ain't there?" said Mrs. Penn.

"Room enough," returned the hired man in his thick, rustic tones. "Didn't need the new barn, nohow, far as room's concerned. Well, I s'pose he changed his mind." He took hold of the horses' bridles.

Mrs. Penn went back to the house. Soon the kitchen windows were darkened, and a fragrance like warm honey came into the room.

Nanny laid down her work. "I thought Father wanted them to put the hay into the new barn," she said wonderingly.

"It's all right," replied her mother.

Sammy slid down from the load of hay and came in to see if dinner was ready.

"I ain't goin' to get a regular dinner today as long as Father's gone," said his mother. "I've let the fire go out. You can have some bread an' milk an' pie. I thought we could get along." She set out some bowls of milk, some bread, and a pie on the kitchen table. "You'd better eat your dinner now," she said. "You might jest as well get through with it. I want you to help me afterward."

Nanny and Sammy stared at each other. There was something strange in their mother's manner. Mrs. Penn did not eat anything herself. She went into the pantry, and they heard her moving dishes while they ate. Presently she came out with a pile of plates. She got the clothes basket out of the shed and packed them in it. Nanny and Sammy watched. She brought out cups and saucers and put them in with the plates.

"What you goin' to do, Mother?" inquired Nanny in a timid voice. A sense of something unusual made her tremble, as if it were a ghost. Sammy rolled his eyes over his pie.

"You'll see what I'm goin' to do," replied Mrs. Penn. "If you're through, Nanny, I want you to go upstairs an' pack up your things;

an' I want you, Sammy, to help me take down the bed in the bed-room."

"Oh, Mother, what for?" gasped Nanny.

"You'll see."

During the next few hours a feat was performed by this simple, pious New England mother which was equal in its way to Wolfe's storming of the Heights of Abraham. It took no more genius, audacity, or bravery for Wolfe to cheer his wondering soldiers up those steep precipices under the sleeping eyes of the enemy, than for Sarah Penn, at the head of her children, to move all their household goods into the new barn while her husband was away.

Nanny and Sammy followed their mother's instructions with-out a murmur; indeed, they were overawed. There is a certain uncanny and superhuman quality about all such purely original undertakings as their mother's was to them. Nanny went back and forth with her light loads, and Sammy tugged and hauled with sober energy.

At five o'clock in the afternoon the little house in which the Penns had lived for forty years had emptied itself into the new barn.

Every builder builds somewhat for unknown purposes and is in a measure a prophet. The architect of Adoniram Penn's barn, while he designed it for the comfort of four-footed animals, had planned better than he knew for the comfort of humans. Sarah Penn saw at a glance its possibilities. Those great box stalls, with quilts hung before them, would make better bedrooms than the one she had occupied for forty years, and there was a tight car-riage room. The harness room, with its chimney and shelves, would make a kitchen of her dreams. The great middle space would make a parlor, by and by, fit for a palace. Upstairs there was as much room as down. With partitions and windows, what a house there would be! Sarah looked at the row of stanchions before the allotted space for cows and reflected that she would have her front entry there.

At six o'clock the stove was up in the harness room, the kettle was boiling, and the table set for tea. It looked almost as homelike as the abandoned house across the yard had ever done. The young hired man milked, and Sarah directed him calmly to bring the milk to the new barn. He came gaping, dropping little blots of foam from the brimming pails on the grass. Before the next morning he had spread the story of Adoniram Penn's wife moving into the new barn all over the little village. Men assembled in the store and talked it over; women with shawls over their heads scuttled into each other's houses before their work was done. Any deviation from the ordinary course of life in this quiet town was enough to stop all progress in it. Everybody paused to look at the staid, independent figure on the side track. There was a difference of opinion with regard to her. Some held her to be insane; some, of a lawless and rebellious spirit.

Friday the minister went to see her. It was in the forenoon, and she was at the barn door shelling peas for dinner. She looked up and returned his salutation with dignity; then she went on with her work. She did not invite him in. The saintly expression of her face remained fixed, but there was an angry flush over it.

The minister stood awkwardly before her and talked. She handled the peas as if they were bullets. At last she looked up, and her eyes showed the spirit that her meek front had covered for a lifetime.

"There ain't no use talkin', Mr. Hersey," said she. "I've thought it all over an' over, an' I believe I'm doin' what's right.

I've made it the subject of prayer, an' it's betwixt me an' the Lord an' Adoniram. There ain't no call for nobody else to worry about it."

"Well, of course, if you have brought it to the Lord in prayer and feel satisfied that you are doing right, Mrs. Penn," said the minister helplessly. His thin gray-bearded face was pathetic. He was a sickly man; his youthful confidence had cooled; he had to scourge himself up to some of his pastoral duties as relentlessly as an ascetic, and then he was prostrated by the sting.

"I think it's right jest as much as I think it was right for our forefathers to come over from the old country 'cause they didn't have what belonged to 'em," said Mrs. Penn. She arose. The barn threshold might have been Plymouth Rock from her bearing. "I don't doubt you mean well, Mr. Hersey," said she, "but there are things people hadn't ought to interfere with. I've been a member of the church for over forty year. I've got my own mind an' my own feet, an' I'm goin' to think my own thoughts an' go my own ways, an' nobody but the Lord is goin' to dictate to me unless I've a mind to have him. Won't you come in an' set down? How is Mis' Hersey?"

"She is well, I thank you," replied the minister. He added some more perplexed apologetic remarks; then he retreated.

He could expound the intricacies of every character study in the Scriptures, and he was competent to grasp the Pilgrim Fathers and all historical innovators, but Sarah Penn was beyond him. He could deal with primal cases, but parallel ones worsted him. But, after all, although it was aside from his province, he wondered more how Adoniram Penn would deal with his wife than how the Lord would. Everybody shared the wonder. When Adoniram's four new cows arrived, Sarah ordered three to be put in the old barn, the other in the house shed where the cookstove had stood. That added to the excitement. It was whispered that all four cows were domiciled in the house.

Towards sunset on Saturday, when Adoniram was expected home, there was a knot of men in the road near the new barn. The hired man had milked, but he still hung around the premises. Sarah Penn had supper all ready. There were brown bread and baked beans and a custard pie; it was the supper that Adoniram loved on a Saturday night. She had on a clean calico, and she bore herself imperturbably. Nanny and Sammy kept close at her heels. Their eyes were large, and Nanny was full of nervous tremors. Still there was to them more pleasant excitement than anything else. An inborn confidence in their mother over their father asserted itself.

Sammy looked out of the harness room window. "There he is," he announced in an awed whisper. He and Nanny peeped around the casing. Mrs. Penn kept on about her work. The children watched Adoniram leave the new horse standing in the drive while he went to the house door. It was fastened. Then he went around to the shed. That door was seldom locked, even when the family was away. The thought how her father would be confronted by the cow flashed upon Nanny. There was a hysterical sob in her throat. Adoniram emerged from the shed and stood looking about in a dazed fashion. His lips moved; he was saying something, but they could not hear what it was. The hired man was peeping around a corner of the old barn, but nobody saw him.

Adoniram took the new horse by the bridle and led him across the yard to the new barn. Nanny and Sammy slunk close to their mother. The barn doors rolled back, and there stood Adoniram, with the long mild face of the great Canadian farm horse looking over his shoulder.

Nanny kept behind her mother, but Sammy stepped suddenly forward and stood in front of her.

Adoniram stared at the group. "What on airth you all down here for?" said he. "What's the matter over to the house?"

"We've come here to live, Father," said Sammy. His shrill voice quavered out bravely.

"What—!" Adoniram sniffed. "What is it smells like cookin'?" said he. He stepped forward and looked in the open door of the harness room. Then he turned to his wife. His old bristling face was pale and frightened. "What on airth does this mean, Mother?" he gasped.

"You come in here, Father," said Sarah. She led the way into the harness room and shut the door. "Now, Father," said she, "you needn't be scared. I ain't crazy. There ain't nothin' to be upset over. But we've come here to live, an' we're goin' to live here. We've got jest as good a right here as new horses an' cows. The house wa'n't fit for us to live in any longer, an' I made up my mind I wa'n't goin' to stay there. I've done my duty by you forty year, an' I'm goin' to do it now; but I'm goin' to live here. You've got to put in some windows and partitions; an' you'll have to buy some furniture."

"Why, Mother!" the old man gasped.

"You'd better take your coat off an' get washed—there's the washbasin—an' then we'll have supper."

"Why, Mother!"

Sammy went past the window, leading the new horse to the old barn. The old man saw him and shook his head speechlessly. He tried to take off his coat, but his arms seemed to lack the power. His wife helped him. She poured some water into the tin basin and put in a piece of soap. She got the comb and brush and smoothed his thin gray hair after he had washed. Then she put the beans, hot bread, and tea on the table. Sammy came in, and the family drew up. Adoniram sat looking dazedly at his plate, and they waited.

"Ain't you goin' to ask a blessin', Father?" said Sarah.

And the old man bent his head and mumbled.

All through the meal he stopped eating at intervals and stared furtively at his wife; but he ate well. The home food tasted good to him, and his old frame was too sturdily healthy to be affected by his mind. But after supper he went out and sat down on the step of the smaller door at the right of the barn, through which he had meant his Jerseys to pass in stately file, but which Sarah designed for her front house door, and he leaned his head on his hands.

After the supper dishes were cleared away and the milk pans washed, Sarah went out to him. The twilight was deepening. There was a clear green glow in the sky. Before them stretched the smooth level of field; in the distance was a cluster of haystacks like the huts of a village; the air was very cool and calm and sweet. The landscape might have been an ideal one of peace.

Sarah bent over and touched her husband on one of his thin, sinewy shoulders. "Father!"

The old man's shoulders heaved; he was weeping.

"Why, don't do so, Father," said Sarah.

"I'll—put up the—partitions, an'—everything you—want, Mother."

Sarah put her apron up to her face; she was overcome by her own triumph.

Adoniram was like a fortress whose walls had no active resistance and went down the instant the right besieging tools were used. "Why, Mother," he said hoarsely, "I had no idee you was so set on't as all this comes to."

Mary E. Wilkins Freeman
(1852–1930)

Mary E. Wilkins Freeman, a New England realist, was well known in the late nineteenth and early twentieth centuries. Then her star almost disappeared. Today, however, as women search for their roots, she has come roaring back. Of her stories in *A Humble Romance* and *A New England Nun,* F. O. Mathiesen observed:

> In them, she revealed a profound insight into the tragic aspects of life. . . . The struggle of the heart to live by its own strength alone is her constant theme, and the sudden revolt of a spirit that will endure no more from circumstance provides her most stirring dramas.

WHEN MA ROGERS
BROKE LOOSE

Author Unknown

How passing strange it is that the more a parent does for a child, the less the parent is appreciated. It took an exasperated friend to awaken Ma Rogers to the true state of affairs under her own roof.

Since halfhearted measures patently wouldn't work, Ma Rogers went on the warpath.

*I*t was a hot smothery July morning. Heat waves shimmered above the thick white dust of the country road, and the sun broiled down upon the vegetable patch beside it with fierce intensity.

As Ma Rogers stood in the kitchen doorway, a huge tin pan in one hand and a sunbonnet in the other, she sighed a meek little sigh, for she was tired. She had been at work many hours already, and the prospect of gathering peas in that pitiless heat was not an inviting one. But the sigh was followed by a smile as she put on her sunbonnet and hurried down the path, saying to herself, "Oh, well, I ought to be glad I have any peas to gather."

Ma Rogers had what might be termed an "oh, well" disposition. If she wanted to go anywhere and was disappointed, she said to herself, "Oh, well, I hadn't anything to wear"; and if sometimes she wished she had a new dress, she said, "Oh, well, I don't go many places to wear it."

She had made herself a slave to her husband and to her boy and girl, and, as is often the way with families, they had let her do it. They never noticed that she was wearing out, that she was always tired and always shabby.

The sun was still broiling down on the vegetable patch, and the July morning was an hour older when Eliza Bonner came up the front path and scowled darkly at the picture of Susan Rogers lolling in the hammock, reading a novel. Eliza had a sharp face, a spare frame, a shrewd mind, and a big, kind heart which she went to all sorts of trouble to conceal.

"Susan, where's your ma?"

"What ye say? Oh, Ma! I dunno. I guess she's down in the garden." As Eliza reached the back steps, Ma Rogers came wavering up from the garden. She had pushed her bonnet back to get air; her face was purple, and perspiration streamed from every pore. The swollen veins on her forehead and neck throbbed visibly. She smiled bravely and sank down in a little heap on the step in the shade of the arbor.

"My! It's hot, ain't it? But the peas are done! My! Seems as if I'd never cool off." And Ma Rogers wiped her dripping face with her apron.

"Why didn't you get Susan to help you?"

"Oh, well, she's readin' a story, an' I hated to ask her."

"Why didn't John Rogers or Joe pick 'em las' night afore sundown?"

"Why, you know, they like 'em right fresh picked, and seems as if they do taste better."

All of a sudden Eliza boiled over.

"The trouble with you is, you're too pleasant, Jane Rogers, an' your family jest tromps over you. If your bein' pleasant done anybody any good, I wouldn't say a word, but it don't. It don't do any good to you, that's certain, fer everybody just naturally puts on you because you ain't got gumption enough to object; and it don't do them any good, fer they're turnin' into the laziest, selfishest lot o' lumps I ever set eyes on."

"I've tried so hard to bring 'em up right."

"I know you've tried, but you ain't succeeded, because you ain't gone about it right. If you want folks to be o' some use in the world, don't wait on 'em hand and foot. Make 'em wait on you.

"Look at that fat son o' your'n in front o' the fire winter days, with his feet propped up an' a book in his hand, yellin', 'Ma, the fire needs attention,' an' never even lookin' up with a word o' thanks when you come staggerin' in with both arms full o' logs an' stirrin' up the fire to keep him warm.

"Look at that big lummox of a husband o' your'n! You on your knees after a hard day's washin', takin' off his shoes an' puttin' on his slippers fer 'im.

"Look at that saucy snub of a daughter. Instead o' her hustlin' roun' to get breakfast fer you, she lays abed an' lets you bring 'er milk an' rolls in the morning, because she read about it in a book once!

"An' what good's it goin' to do 'em? When you die, nobody's goin' to do things fer 'em, fer nobody'll like 'em well enough. They're growin' too hateful an' selfish.

"I hope I ain't spoke too plain—but it's all Gawspel truth. What you want to do is to break loose some o' these days an' scare the wits out of 'em. Then maybe they'll sit up an' take notice.

"Well, I must be goin'. Good-bye, Jane, an' don't let yourself get overhet like this again—if—if you kin help it."

Ma Rogers was stunned. Was it true? Was she making the children so nobody would like them? She had never thought of anything except that she loved them so dearly that she wanted to make everything easier for them. Eliza had said that they were hateful and selfish. They weren't hateful, but then, of course, she never crossed them. Selfish! Now that she thought of it, they never *did* try to do anything for her—or for *anybody*.

Finally, with a funny mixture of fright and resolution on her face, she got up and went around the side of the house.

"Susan, I wish you'd help me shell the peas. I'm afraid dinner'll be late."

"Oh, Ma, I can't. I'm just in the middle of this book."

Ma Rogers went back to the kitchen step and just stood there.

Yes, there was no doubt of it. Susan was selfish, and nothing mild mannered would cure her of it. She had tried politeness; now she'd have to "break loose," as Eliza had told her. Suddenly she whirled about, rushed around to the hammock, and snatched the book out of Susan's hand.

"Now, you hike around there and shell them peas as fast as you kin shell! An' what's more, you don't git a peek in this book until you've done a day's work. After you've helped with the meals an' washed the dishes an' cleaned up, you kin think about readin'."

Ma Rogers had hard work to retain the look of stern command throughout this long speech, for Susan looked so funny and got out of the hammock so fast that it was as much as Ma Rogers could do to keep from looking astonished herself.

As Susan went out of sight, Ma Rogers suddenly sat down in the hammock. Then she got to thinking it all over again, and as she thought, she swung gently back and forth. It was pleasant there, cool and shady, and a little breeze fanned her as she swung. Then she wondered how it would feel to lie down and swing. She wondered what people would say.

The miracle had happened. Ma Rogers was asleep in the hammock in the middle of the day.

Finally she opened her eyes on the awestruck face of Susan standing beside the hammock.

"I've shelled the peas an' pared the potatoes, but I dunno what else to do, an' Pa an' Joe are just comin' over the hill."

Ma Rogers flew up in a panic. Pa and Joe! And dinner couldn't be on time, and they always fussed so if it was five minutes late. She scrambled out of the hammock and rushed back to the kitchen. Breathlessly she put on the water for the vegetables and ran here and there after the meat and milk and butter; and then in they came.

"My, but I'm hungry," growled Joe. "Ain't dinner ready, Ma?"

Pa Rogers walked over to the fire and grumbled, "Why don't

ye put some wood in this fire? Looks to me's if dinner won't be ready fer an hour."

A violent trembling fit took possession of Ma Rogers, and her hand shook so that she dropped the butter dish, butter and all.

"No, and what's more, it won't ever be ready without'n you two big lazy things git out there in the woodshed an' chop some wood. Do you think I'm goin' to work my fingers to the bone doin' two or three women's work an' then do men's work besides? Not much, I ain't! You git out there an' hustle in that wood. No wood, no dinner. Quick, now! Don't stand starin'."

Silently, in a dazed sort of way, the two men passed on out to the woodshed.

Ma Rogers, watching through the crack of the door, rocked back and forth with suppressed laughter; their faces were so unutterably funny, and they walked along so meekly.

At the table, they all looked so subdued she could hardly keep her face straight. She looked at her plate to hide the mischievous look in her eyes, and then she said, "Susan, I want you should learn to make cake. Two weeks from tomorrow is the church picnic. I'm goin', so we'll need two cakes. I'll make one, an' you—kin make the other."

Three mouths hung wide open in amazement. For years Ma Rogers had made the good things for the rest of them to take to the picnic, but she had always stayed home. She had always said she had nothing to wear, and Pa Rogers remembered that.

"Why, Ma, you ain't got nothin' to wear."

"I said I was goin' to the picnic, an' I meant I was goin' to the picnic. As fer havin' noth'n to wear, John Rogers, it's about time I *did* have somethin' to wear, an' you kin have till tomorrow to get me ten dollars to buy somethin' with, an' then I'll have two weeks to make it in. Jest because I've been a fool an' a fright all my life ain't no reason why I should *always* be a fool an' a fright. Now, then! An' fer goodnes' sake, shut your mouths. You look like I dunno what, that way."

For two weeks the dazed look never left the faces of Pa Rogers and Joe and Susan. They were at the beck and call of Ma Rogers, who scolded and complained and commanded. Everything went like clockwork, and Ma Rogers grew less and less tired and sewed secretly on her new clothes with a feeling of lawlessness and wild abandon. The only thing that troubled her was the sensation of distress at the thought of how the others must feel and what they must think of her.

The day of the picnic arrived. With Susan's help the baskets had been packed with a delicious lunch, and Ma Rogers had gone upstairs to dress. Somehow she could not get rid of the feeling that the rest of the family would not enjoy the picnic—they seemed so depressed and meek and quiet. However, when she finally put on her new dress, she forgot everything else in the elation of that moment. Then she donned a silver gray hat, and the effect was such that she pinched herself to see if she was awake.

With her gray silk gloves swinging in one hand, she almost ran downstairs, and from the hall she could see John Rogers sitting by the kitchen window. She stopped and caught her breath, and then she raised her head high and entered the room with an air such as she always thought she would have if she ever had the clothes to bear it out.

John stood up, and his paper went fluttering to the floor. "Why, Janie," he said softly, breathlessly. "Why, Janie!"

"Well, John, how do I look?"

John reached out both hands and took her gently by the shoulders. "You look like a peach blossom in the sun," he said wonderingly.

Ma Rogers swallowed hard several times. "My! I do hope I ain't agoin' to mess myself all up cryin', but seems's if I do feel terrible queer. There's somethin' I've got to git off my mind before this picnic. Here come the children, an' I'll tell you all at once."

Without giving them time to express their astonishment at her appearance, she started right in to tell them how somebody had opened her eyes to what she was doing to them and how she had resolved to change things. Ever since, she had been scolding and ordering until she herself was in danger of becoming a tyrant, so she thought it was time to talk things over and come to some sort of an agreement whereby they might all help one another and all be happy and pleasant.

"Seems's if I just couldn't go to this picnic with you all thinkin' me so disagreeable."

WHEN QUEENS
RIDE BY

Agnes Sligh Turnbull

When hen one thinks of mothering (of nurturing someone or
something from helplessness to self-sufficiency), it is natural
to conceptualize long-term processes involving many years.
Obviously, a mother mothers—or certainly ought to! Clearly,
a teacher or mentor can mother. But . . . could a complete
stranger—one never seen before and likely never to be seen
again—possibly be responsible for major life changes? The
kinds of seismic changes one associates with years of instruc-
tion, conditioning, and mentoring?

Well, that is what this story is about. I first read it some thirty
years ago, and it was old then. I include it in this collection for a
number of reasons. When this story was written, women were the
acknowledged mainstay of the American home. Since that time,
the two-paycheck family has become the norm rather than the
exception. As a natural result, the home environment has radically
changed—in some respects for the better and in some respects for
the worse. But the issue itself—the woman's role in the home—is
perhaps addressed better in this story than in any other I have ever
read.

*J*ennie Musgrave woke at the shrill rasp of the alarm clock,
as she always woke—with a shuddering start and a heavy
realization that the brief respite of the night's oblivion was
over. She had only time to glance through the dull light at the
cluttered, dusty room, before John's voice was saying sleepily as
he said every morning, "All right, let's go. It doesn't seem as if
we'd been in bed at all!"

Jennie dressed quickly in the clothes, none too clean, that,
exhausted, she had flung from her the night before. She hurried
down the back stairs, her coarse shoes clattering thickly upon the
bare boards. She kindled the fire in the range and then made a
hasty pretense at washing in the basin in the sink.

John strode through the kitchen and on out to the barn. There
were six cows to be milked and the great cans of milk to be taken
to the station for the morning train.

Jennie put coffee and bacon on the stove, and then, catching up
a pail from the porch, went after John. A golden red disk broke
the misty blue of the morning above the cow pasture. A sweet,

fragrant breath blew from the orchard. But Jennie neither saw nor felt the beauty about her.

She glanced at the sun and thought, *It's going to be a hot day*. She glanced at the orchard, and her brows knit. There it hung. All that fruit. Bushels of it going to waste. Maybe she could get time that day to make some more apple butter. But the tomatoes wouldn't wait. She must pick them and get them to town today, or that would be a dead loss. After all her work, well, it would only be in a piece with everything else if it did happen so. She and John had bad luck, and they might as well make up their minds to it.

She finished her part of the milking and hurried back again to the overcooked bacon and strong coffee. The children were down, clamorous, dirty, always underfoot. Jim, the eldest, was in his first term of school. She glanced at his spotted waist. He should have a clean one. But she couldn't help it. She couldn't get the washing done last week, and when she was to get a day for it this week she didn't know, with all the picking and the trips to town to make!

Breakfast was hurried and unpalatable, a sort of grudging concession to the demands of the body. Then John left in the milk wagon for the station, and Jennie packed little Jim's lunch basket with bread and apple butter and pie, left the two little children to their own devices in the backyard, and started toward the barn. There was no time to do anything in the house. The chickens and turkeys had to be attended to, and then she must get to the tomato patch before the sun got too hot. Behind her was the orchard with its rows and rows of laden apple trees. Maybe this afternoon—maybe tomorrow morning. There were the potatoes, too, to be lifted. Too hard work for a woman. But what were you going to do? Starve? John worked till dark in the fields.

She pushed her hair back with a quick, boyish sweep of her arm and went on scattering the grain to the fowls. She remembered

their eager plans when they were married, when they took over
the old farm—laden with its heavy mortgage—that had been
John's father's. John had been so straight of back then and so jolly.
Only seven years, yet now he was stooped a little, and his brows
were always drawn, as though to hide a look of ashamed failure.
They had planned to have a model farm someday: blooded stock, a
tractor, a new barn. And then such a home they were to make of
the old stone house! Jennie's hopes had flared higher even than
John's. A rug for the parlor, an overstuffed set like the one in the
mail-order catalogue, linoleum for the kitchen, electric lights!

They were young and, oh, so strong! There was nothing they
could not do if they only worked hard enough.

But that great faith had dwindled as the first year passed. John
worked later and later in the evenings. Jennie took more and
more of the heavy tasks upon her own shoulders. She often
thought with some pride that no woman in the countryside ever
helped her husband as she did. Even with the haying and riding
the reaper. Hard, coarsening work, but she was glad to do it for
John's sake.

The sad riddle of it all was that at the end of each year they
were no further on. The only difference from the year before was
another window shutter hanging from one hinge and another
crippled wagon in the barnyard which John never had time to
mend. They puzzled over it in a vague distress. And meanwhile
life degenerated into a straining, hopeless struggle. Sometimes
lately John had seemed a little listless, as though nothing mattered.
A little bitter when he spoke of Henry Davis.

Henry held the mortgage and had expected a payment on the
principle this year. He had come once and looked about with
something very like a sneer on his face. If he should decide someday to foreclose—that would be the final blow. They never would

get up after that. If John couldn't hold the old farm, he could never try to buy a new one. It would mean being renters all their lives. Poor renters at that!

She went to the tomato field. It had been her own idea to do some tracking along with the regular farm crops. But, like everything else, it had failed of her expectations. As she put the scarlet tomatoes, just a little overripe, into the basket, she glanced with a hard tightening of her lips toward a break in the trees a half mile away where a dark, glistening bit of road caught the sun. Across its polished surface twinkled an endless procession of shining, swift-moving objects. The State Highway.

Jennie hated it. In the first place, it was so tauntingly near and yet so hopelessly far from them. If it only ran by their door, as it did past Henry Davis's for instance, it would solve the whole problem of marketing the fruits and vegetables. Then they could set the baskets on the lawn, and people could stop for them. But as it was, nobody all summer long had paid the least attention to the sign John had put up at the end of the lane. And no wonder. Why should travelers drive their cars over the stony country byway, when a little farther along they would find the same fruit spread temptingly for them at the very roadside?

But there was another reason she hated that bit of sleek road showing between the trees. She hated it because it hurt her with its suggestion of all that passed her by in that endless procession twinkling in the sunshine. There they kept going, day after day, those happy, carefree women, riding in handsome limousines or in gay little roadsters. Some in plainer cars, too, but even those were, like the others, women who could have rest, pleasure, comfort for the asking. They were whirled along hour by hour to new pleasures, while she was weighted to the drudgery of the farm like one of the great rocks in the pasture field.

And—most bitter thought of all—they had pretty homes to go back to when the happy journey was over. That seemed to be the strange and cruel law about homes. The finer they were, the easier it was to leave them. The poorer they were, the more you were tied to them. Now with her—if she had the rug for the parlor and the stuffed furniture and linoleum for the kitchen, she shouldn't mind anything so much then; she had nothing, nothing, but hard slaving and bad luck. And the highway taunted her with it. Flung its impossible pleasures mockingly in her face as she bent over the vines or dragged the heavy baskets along the rows.

The sun grew hotter. Jennie put more strength into her task. She knew, at last, by the scorching heat overhead that it was nearing noon. She must have a bite of lunch ready for John when he came in. There wasn't time to prepare much. Just reheat the coffee and set down some bread and pie.

She started toward the house, giving a long yodeling call for the children as she went. They appeared from the orchard, tumbled and torn from experiments with the wire fence. Her heart smothered her at the sight of them. Among the other dreams that the years had crushed out were those of little rosy boys and girls in clean suits and fresh ruffled dresses. As it was, the children had just grown like farm weeds.

This was the part of all the drudgery that hurt most. That she had no time to care for her children, sew for them, teach them things that other children knew. Sometimes it seemed as if she had no real love for them at all. She was too terribly tired as a rule to have any feeling. The only times she used energy to talk to them was when she had to reprove them for some dangerous misdeed. That was all wrong. It seemed wicked; but how could she help it? With the work draining the very life out of her, strong as she was.

John came in heavily, and they ate in silence except for the children's chatter. John hardly looked up from his plate. He gulped down great drafts of the warmed-over coffee and then pushed his chair back hurriedly.

"I'm goin' to try to finish the harrowin' in the south field," he said.

"I'm at the tomatoes," Jennie answered. "I've got them 'most all picked and ready for takin'."

That was all. Work was again upon them.

It was two o'clock by the sun, and Jennie had loaded the last heavy basket of tomatoes on the milk wagon in which she must drive to town, when she heard shrill voices sounding along the path. The children were flying in excitement toward her.

"Mum! Mum! Mum!" they called as they came panting up to her with big, surprised eyes.

"Mum, there's a lady up there. At the kitchen door. All dressed up. A pretty lady. She wants to see you."

Jennie gazed down at them disbelievingly. A lady, a pretty lady at her kitchen door? All dressed up! What that could mean! Was it possible someone had at last braved the stony land to buy fruit? Maybe bushels of it!

"Did she come in a car?" Jennie asked quickly.

"No, she just walked in. She's awful pretty. She smiled at us."

Jennie's hopes dropped. Of course. She might have known. Some agent likely, selling books. She followed the children wearily back along the path and in at the rear door of the kitchen. Across from it another door opened into the side yard. Here stood the stranger.

The two women looked at each other across the kitchen, across the table with the remains of two meals upon it, the strewn chairs, the littered stove—across the whole scene of unlovely disorder.

They looked at each other in startled surprise, as inhabitants of Earth and Mars might look if they were suddenly brought face-to-face.

Jennie saw a woman in a gray tweed coat that seemed to be part of her straight, slim body. A small gray hat with a rose quill was drawn low over the brownish hair. Her blue eyes were clear and smiling. She was beautiful! And yet she was not young. She was in her forties, surely. But an aura of eager youth clung to her, a clean and exquisite freshness.

The stranger in her turn looked across at a young woman, haggard and weary. Her yellowish hair hung in straggling wisps. Her eyes looked hard and hunted. Her cheeks were thin and sallow. Her calico dress was shapeless and begrimed from her work.

So they looked at each other for one long, appraising second. Then the woman in gray smiled.

"How do you do?" she began. "We ran our car into the shade of your lane to have our lunch and rest for a while. And I walked on up to buy a few apples, if you have them."

Jennie stood staring at the stranger. There was an unconscious hostility in her eyes. This was one of the women from the highway. One of those envied ones who passed twinkling through the summer sunshine from pleasure to pleasure while Jennie slaved on.

But the pretty lady's smile was disarming. Jennie started toward a chair and pulled off the old coat and apron that lay on it.

"Won't you sit down?" she said politely. "I'll go and get the apples. I'll have to pick them off the tree. Would you prefer rambos?"

"I don't know what they are, but they sound delicious. You must choose them for me. But mayn't I come with you? I should love to help pick them."

Jennie considered. She felt baffled by the friendliness of the other woman's face and utterly unable to meet it. But she did not know how to refuse.

"Why, I s'pose so. If you can get through the dirt."

She led the way over the back porch with its crowded baskets and pails and coal buckets, along the unkempt path toward the orchard. She had never been so acutely conscious of the disorder about her. Now a hot shame brought a lump to her throat. In her preoccupied haste before, she had actually not noticed that tub of clothes she had put to soak a week ago and forgotten. And the overturned milk cans and the rubbish heap! She saw it all now swiftly through the other woman's eyes. And then that new perspective was checked by a bitter defiance. Why should she care how things looked to this woman? She would be gone, speeding down the highway in a few minutes as though she had never been there.

She reached the orchard and began to drag a long ladder from the fence to the rambo tree.

The other woman cried out in distress. "Oh, but you can't do that! You mustn't. It's too heavy for you, or even for both of us. Please just let me pick a few from the ground."

Jennie looked in amazement at the stranger's concern. It was so long since she had seen anything like it.

"Heavy?" she repeated. "This ladder? I wish I didn't ever lift anything heavier than this. After hoistin' bushel baskets of tomatoes onto a wagon, this feels light to me."

The stranger caught her arm. "But—but do you think it's right? Why, that's a man's work."

Jennie's eyes blazed. Something furious and long-pent broke out from within her. *"Right!* Who are you to be askin' me whether I'm right or not? What would have become of us if I didn't do a man's work? It takes us both, slaving away, an' then we get nowhere. A person like you don't know what work is! You don't know—"

Jennie's voice was the high shrill of hysteria; but the stranger's low tones somehow broke through. "Listen," she said soothingly. "Please listen to me. I'm sorry I annoyed you by saying that, but now, since we are talking, why can't we sit down here and rest a minute? It's so cool and lovely here under the trees, and if you were to tell me all about it—because I'm only a stranger—perhaps it would help. It does sometimes, you know. A little rest would—"

"*Rest!* Me sit down to rest, an' the wagon loaded to go to town? It'll hurry me now to get back before dark."

And then something strange happened. The other woman put her cool, soft hand on Jennie's grimy arm. There was a compelling tenderness in her eyes. "Just take the time you would have spent picking the apples. I would so much rather. And perhaps somehow I could help you. I wish I could. Won't you tell me why you have to work so hard?"

Jennie sank down on the smooth green grass. Her hunted, unwilling eyes had yielded to some power in the clear, serene eyes of the stranger. A sort of exhaustion came over her. A trembling reaction from the straining effort of weeks.

"There ain't much to tell," she said half sullenly, "only that we ain't gettin' ahead. We're clean discouraged, both of us. Henry Davis is talking about foreclosin' on us if we don't pay some principle. The time of the mortgage is out this year, an' mebbe he won't renew it. He's got plenty himself, but them's the hardest kind." She paused; then her eyes flared. "An' it ain't that I haven't done my part. Look at me. I'm barely thirty, an' I might be fifty. I'm so weather-beaten. That's the way I've worked!"

"And you think that has helped your husband?"

"Helped him?" Jennie's voice was sharp. "Why shouldn't it help him?"

The stranger was looking away through the green stretches of orchard. She laced her slim hands together about her knees. She spoke slowly. "Men are such queer things, husbands especially. Sometimes we blunder when we are trying hardest to serve them. For instance, they want us to be economical, and yet they want us in pretty clothes. They need our work, and yet they want us to keep our youth and our beauty. And sometimes they don't know themselves which they really want most. So we have to choose. That's what makes it so hard."

She paused. Jennie was watching her with dull curiosity as though she were speaking a foreign tongue. Then the stranger went on:

"I had to choose once, long ago; just after we were married, my husband decided to have his own business, so he started a very tiny one. He couldn't afford a helper, and he wanted me to stay in the office while he did the outside selling. And I refused, even though it hurt him. Oh, it was hard! But I knew how it would be if I did as he wished. We would both have come back each night, tired out, to a dark, cheerless house and a picked-up dinner. And a year of that might have taken something away from us—something precious. I couldn't risk it, so I refused and stuck to it.

"And then how I worked in my house—a flat it was then. I had so little outside of our wedding gifts; but at least I could make it a clean, shining, happy place. I tried to give our little dinners the grace of a feast. And as the months went on, I knew I had done right. My husband would come home dead-tired and discouraged, ready to give up the whole thing. But after he had eaten and sat down in our bright little living room, and I had read to him or told him all the funny things I could invent about my day, I could see him change. By bedtime he had his courage back, and by morning he was at last ready to go out and fight again. And at last he won, and he won his success alone, as a man loves to do."

Still Jennie did not speak. She only regarded her guest with a half-resentful understanding.

The woman in gray looked off again between the trees. Her voice was very sweet. A humorous little smile played about her lips.

"There was a queen once," she went on, "who reigned in troublous days. And every time the country was on the brink of war and the people ready to fly into a panic, she would put on her showiest dress and take her court with her and go hunting. And when the people would see her riding by, apparently so gay and happy, they were sure all was well with the Government. So she tided over many a danger. And I've tried to be like her.

"Whenever a big crisis comes in my husband's business—and we've had several—or when he's discouraged, I put on my prettiest dress and get the best dinner I know how or give a party! And somehow it seems to work. That's the woman's part, you know. To play the queen—"

A faint *honk-honk* came from the lane. The stranger started to her feet. "That's my husband. I must go. Please don't bother about the apples. I'll just take these from under the tree. We only wanted two or three, really. And give these to the children." She slipped two coins into Jennie's hand.

Jennie had risen, too, and was trying from a confusion of startled thoughts to select one for speech. Instead she only answered the other woman's bright good-bye with a stammering repetition and a broken apology about the apples.

She watched the stranger's erect, lithe figure hurrying away across the path that led directly to the lane. Then she turned her back to the house, wondering dazedly if she had only dreamed that the other woman had been there. But no, there were emotions rising hotly within her that were new. They had had no place an hour before. They had arisen at the words of the stranger and at the sight of her smooth, soft hair, the fresh color in her cheeks, the happy shine of her eyes.

A great wave of longing swept over Jennie, a desire that was lost in choking despair. It was as though she had heard a strain of music for which she had waited all her life and then felt it swept away into silence before she had grasped its beauty. For a few brief minutes she, Jennie Musgrave, had sat beside one of the women of the highway and caught a breath of her life—that life which forever twinkled past in bright procession, like the happenings of a fairy tale. Then she was gone, and Jennie was left as she had been, bound to the soil like one of the rocks of the field.

The bitterness that stormed her heart now was different from the old dull disheartenment. For it was coupled with new knowledge. The words of the stranger seemed more vivid to her than when she had sat listening in the orchard. But they came back to her with the pain of agony.

"All very well for her to talk so smooth to me about man's work and woman's work! An' what she did for her husband's big success. Easy enough for her to sit talking about *queens!* What would she do if she was here on this farm like me? What would a woman like her do?"

Jennie had reached the kitchen door and stood there looking at the hopeless melee about her. Her words sounded strange and hollow in the silence of the house. "Easy for her!" she burst out. "She never had the work pilin' up over her like I have. She never felt it at her throat like a wolf, the same as John an' me does. Talk

about choosin'! I haven't got no choice. I just got to keep
goin'—just keep goin', like I always have—"

She stopped suddenly. There in the middle of the kitchen floor,
where the other woman had passed over, lay a tiny square of white.
Jennie crossed to it quickly and picked it up. A faint, delicious fragrance like the dream of a flower came from it. Jennie inhaled it
eagerly. It was not like any odor she had ever known. It made her
think of sweet, strange things. Things she had never thought about
before. Of gardens in the early summer dusk, of wide fair rooms
with the moonlight shining in them, of pretty women in beautiful
dresses dancing and men admiring them. It made her somehow
think with vague wistfulness of all that.

She looked carefully at the tiny square. The handkerchief was
of fine, fairylike smoothness. In the corner a dainty blue butterfly
spread his wings. Jennie drew in another long breath. The fragrance filled her senses again. Her first greedy draft had not
exhausted it. It would stay for a while, at least.

She laid the bit of white down cautiously on the edge of the
table and went to the sink, where she washed her hands carefully.
Then she returned and picked up the handkerchief again with
something like reverence. She sat down, still holding it, staring at
it. This bit of linen was to her an articulated voice. She understood its language. It spoke to her of white, freshly washed clothes
blowing in the sunshine, of an iron moving smoothly, leisurely,
to the accompaniment of a song over snowy folds; it spoke to her
of quiet, orderly rooms and ticking clocks and a mending basket
under the evening lamp; it spoke to her of all the peaceful routine
of a well-managed household, the kind she had once dreamed of
having.

But more than this, the exquisite daintiness of it, the sweet,
alluring perfume spoke to her of something else which her heart

understood, even though her speech could have found no words for it. She could feel gropingly the delicacy, the grace, the beauty that made up the other woman's life in all its relations.

She, Jennie, had none of that. Everything about their lives, hers and John's, was coarsened, soiled somehow by the dragging, endless labor of the days. Suppose . . . suppose . . .

Jennie leaned forward, her arms stretched tautly before her upon her knees, her hands clasped tightly over the fragrant bit of white. Suppose she were to try doing as the stranger had said. Suppose she spent her time on the house and let the outside work go. What then? What would John say? Would they be much farther behind than they were now? *Could* they be? And suppose, by some strange chance, the other woman had been right! That a man could be helped more by the doing of these other things she had neglected?

She sat very still, distressed, uncertain. Out in the barnyard waited the wagon of tomatoes, overripe now for market. No, she could do nothing today, at least, but go on as usual.

Then her hands opened a little; the perfume within them came up to her, bringing again that thrill of sweet, indescribable things.

She started up, half-terrified at her own resolve. "I'm goin' to try it now. Mebbe I'm crazy, but I'm goin' to do it anyhow!"

It was a long time since Jennie had performed such a meticulous toilet. It was years since she had brushed her hair. A hasty combing had been its best treatment. She put on her one clean dress, the dark voile reserved for trips to town. She even changed from her shapeless, heavy shoes to her best ones. Then, as she looked at herself in the dusty mirror, she saw that she was changed. Something, at least, of the hard haggardness was gone from her face, and her hair framed it with smooth softness. Tomorrow she would wash it. It used to be almost yellow.

She went to the kitchen. With something of the burning zeal of a fanatic, she attacked the confusion before her. By half past four the room was clean: the floor swept, the stove shining, dishes and pans washed and put in their places. From the tumbled depths of a drawer Jennie had extracted a white tablecloth that had been bought in the early days, for company only. With a spirit of daring recklessness she spread it on the table. She polished the chimney of the big oil lamp and then set the fixture, clean and shining, in the center of the white cloth.

Now the supper! And she must hurry. She planned to have it at six o'clock and ring the big bell for John fifteen minutes before, as she used to just after they were married.

She decided upon fried ham and browned potatoes and applesauce with hot biscuits. John used to love hot biscuits. She hadn't made them for so long, but her fingers fell into their old deftness. Why, cooking was just play if you had time to do it right! Then she thought of the tomatoes and gave a little shudder. She thought of the long hours of backbreaking work she had put into them and called herself a little fool to have been swayed by the words of a stranger and the scent of a handkerchief, to neglect her rightful work and bring more loss upon John and herself. But she went on, making the biscuits, turning the ham, setting the table.

It was half past five; the first pan of flaky brown mounds had been withdrawn from the oven, the children's faces and hands had been washed and their excited questions satisfied, when the sound of a car came from the bend. Jennie knew that car. It belonged to Henry Davis. He could be coming for only one thing.

The blow they had dreaded, fending off by blind disbelief in the ultimate disaster, was about to fall. Henry was coming to tell them he was going to foreclose. It would almost kill John. This was his father's old farm. John had taken it over, mortgage and all, so hopefully, so sure he could succeed where his father had failed. If he had to leave now there would be a double disgrace to bear. And where could they go? Farms weren't so plentiful.

Henry had driven up to the side gate. He fumbled with some papers in his inner pocket as he started up the walk. A wild terror filled Jennie's heart. She wanted desperately to avoid meeting Henry Davis's keen, hard face, to flee somewhere, anywhere, before she heard the words that doomed them.

Then as she stood shaken, wondering how she could live through what the next hours would bring, she saw in a flash the beautiful stranger as she had sat in the orchard, looking off between the trees and smiling to herself. "There was once a queen. . . ."

Jennie heard the words again distinctly just as Henry Davis's steps sounded sharply nearer on the walk outside. There was only a confused picture of a queen wearing the stranger's lovely, highbred face, riding gaily to the hunt through forests and towns while her kingdom was tottering. Riding gallantly on, in spite of her fears.

Jennie's heart was pounding and her hands were suddenly cold. But something unreal and yet irresistible was sweeping her with it. "There was once a queen. . . ."

She opened the screen door before Henry Davis had time to knock. She extended her hand cordially. She was smiling. "Well, how d' you do, Mr. Davis. Come right in. I'm real glad to see you. Been quite a while since you was over."

Henry looked surprised and very much embarrassed. "Why, no, now, I won't go in. I just stopped to see John on a little matter of business. I'll just—"

"You'll just come right in. John will be in from milkin' in a few minutes an' you can talk while you eat, both of you. I've supper just ready. Now step right in, Mr. Davis!"

As Jennie moved aside, a warm, fragrant breath of fried ham and biscuits seemed to waft itself to Henry Davis's nostrils. There was a visible softening of his features. "Why, no, I didn't reckon on anything like this. I 'lowed I'd just speak to John and then be gettin' on."

"They'll see you at home when you get there," Jennie put in quickly. "You never tasted my hot biscuits with butter an' quince honey, or you wouldn't take so much coachin'!"

Henry Davis came in and sat in the big, clean, warm kitchen. His eyes took in every detail of the orderly room: the clean cloth, the shining lamp, the neat sink, the glowing stove. Jennie saw him relax comfortably in his chair. Then above the aromas of the food about her, she detected the strange sweetness of the bit of white linen she had tucked away in the bosom of her dress. It rose to her as a haunting sense of her power as a woman.

She smiled at Henry Davis. Smiled as she would never have thought of doing a day ago. Then she would have spoken to him with a drawn face full of subservient fear. Now, though the fear clutched her heart, her lips smiled sweetly, moved by that unreality that seemed to possess her. "There was once a queen. . . ."

"An' how are things goin' with you, Mr. Davis?" she asked with a blithe upward reflection.

Henry Davis was very human. He had never noticed before that Jennie's hair was so thick and pretty and that she had such pleasant ways. Neither had he dreamed that she was such a good cook as the sight and smell of the supper things would indicate. He was very comfortable there in the big sweet-smelling kitchen.

He smiled back. It was an interesting experiment on Henry's part, for his smiles were rare. "Oh, so-so. How are they with you?"

Jennie had been taught to speak the truth; but at this moment there dawned in her mind a vague understanding that the high loyalties of life are, after all, relative and not absolute.

She smiled again as she skillfully flipped a great slice of golden brown ham over in the frying pan. "Why, just fine, Mr. Davis. We're gettin' on just fine, John an' me. It's been hard sleddin', but I sort of think the worst is over. I think we're goin' to come out way ahead now. We'll just be 'round to pay off that mortgage so fast, come another year, that you'll be surprised!"

It was said. Jennie marvelled that the words had not choked her, had not somehow smitten her dead as she spoke them. But their effect on Henry Davis was amazingly good.

"That so?" he asked in surprise. "Well now, that's fine. I always wanted to see John make a success of the old place, but somehow—well, you know it didn't look as if—that is, there's been some talk around that maybe John wasn't just gettin' along any too—you know. A man has to sort of watch his investments. . . . Well, now, I'm glad things are pickin' up a little."

Jennie felt as though a tight hand at her throat had relaxed. She spoke brightly of the fall weather and the crops as she finished setting the dishes on the table and rang the big bell for John. There was delicate work yet to be done when he came in.

Little Jim had to be sent to hasten him before he finally appeared. He was a big man, John Musgrave, big and slow moving and serious. He had known nothing all his life but hard physical toil. He had pitted his great body against all the adverse forces of nature. There was a time when he had felt that strength such as his was all any man needed to bring him fortune. Now he was not so sure. The brightness of that faith was dimmed by experience.

John came to the kitchen door with his eyebrows drawn. Little Jim had told him that Henry Davis was there. He came into the room as an accused man faces the jury of his peers, faces the men who, though of the same flesh and blood as he, are yet somehow curiously in a position to save or to destroy him.

John came in, and then he stopped, staring blankly at the scene before him. At Jennie moving about the bright table, chatting happily with Henry Davis! At Henry himself, his sharp features softened by an air of great satisfaction. At the sixth plate on the white cloth. *Henry staying for supper!*

But the silent deeps of John's nature served him well. He made no comment. Merely shook hands with Henry Davis and then washed his face at the sink.

Jennie arranged the savory dishes, and they sat down to supper.

It was an entirely new experience to John to sit at the head of his own table and serve a generously heaped plate to Henry Davis. It sent through him a sharp thrill of sufficiency, of equality. He realized that before he had been cringing in his very soul at the sight of this man.

Henry consumed eight biscuits richly covered with quince honey, along with the heavier part of his dinner. Jennie counted them. She recalled hearing that the Davises did not set a very bountiful table; it was common talk that Mrs. Davis was even more "miserly" than her husband. But, however that was, Henry now seemed to grow more and more genial and expansive as he ate. So did John. By the time the pie was set before them, they were laughing over a joke Henry had heard at Grange meeting.

Jennie was bright, watchful, careful. If the talk lagged, she made a quick remark. She moved softly between table and stove, refilling the dishes. She saw to it that a hot biscuit was at Henry Davis's elbow just when he was ready for it. All the while there was rising within her a strong zest for life that she would have deemed impossible only that morning. This meal, at least, was a perfect success, and achievements of any sort whatever had been few.

Henry Davis left soon after supper. He brought the conversation around awkwardly to his errand as they rose from the table. Jennie was ready.

"I told him, John, that the worst was over now, an' we're gettin' on fine!" She laughed. "I told him we'd be swampin' him pretty soon with our payments. Ain't that right, John?"

John's mind was not analytical. At that moment he was comfortable. He had been host at a delicious supper with his ancient adversary, whose sharp face was marvelously softened. Jennie's eyes were shining with a new and amazing confidence. It was a natural moment for unreasoning optimism.

"Why, that's right, Mr. Davis. I believe we can start clearin' this off now pretty soon. If you could just see your way clear to renew the note mebbe. . . ."

It was done. The papers were back in Davis's pocket. They had bid him a cordial good-bye from the door.

"Next time you come, I'll have biscuits for you, Mr. Davis," Jennie had called daringly after him.

"Now don't you forget that, Mrs. Musgrave! They certainly ain't hard to eat."

He was gone. Jennie cleared off the table and set the shining lamp in the center of the oilcloth covering. She began to wash the dishes. John was fumbling through the papers on a hanging shelf. He finally sat down with an old tablet and pencil. He spoke meditatively. "I believe I'll do a little figurin' since I've got time tonight. It just struck me that mebbe if I used my head a little more I'd get on faster."

"Well now, you might," said Jennie. It would not be John's way to comment just yet on their sudden deliverance. She polished two big rambo apples and placed them on a saucer beside him.

He looked pleased. "Now, that's what I like." He grinned. Then making a clumsy clutch at her arm, he added, "Say, you look sort of pretty tonight."

Jennie made a brisk coquettish business of freeing herself.

"Go along with you!" she returned, smiling, and started in again upon the dishes. But a hot wave of color had swept up in her sallow cheeks.

John had looked more grateful over her setting those two apples beside him now than he had the day last fall when she lifted all the potatoes herself! Men were strange, as the woman in gray had said. Maybe even John had been needing something else more than he needed the hard, backbreaking work she had been doing.

She tidied up the kitchen and put the children to bed. It seemed strange to be through now, ready to sit down. All summer they had worked outdoors till bedtime. Last night she had been slaving over apple butter until she stopped, exhausted, and John had been working in the barn with a lantern. Tonight seemed so peaceful, so quiet. John still sat at the table, figuring while he munched his apples. His brows were not drawn now. There was a new, purposeful light upon his face.

Jennie walked to the doorway and stood looking off through the darkness and through the break in the trees at the end of the lane. Bright golden lights kept glittering across it, breaking dimly through the woods, flashing out strongly for a moment, then disappearing behind the hill. Those were the lights of the happy cars that never stopped in their swift search for far and magic places. Those were the lights of the highway which she had hated.

But she did not hate it now. For today it had come to her at last and left with her some of its mysterious pleasure.

Jennie wished, as she stood there, that she could somehow tell the beautiful stranger in the gray coat that her words had been true, that she, Jennie, insofar as she was able, was to be like her and fulfill her woman's part.

For while she was not figuring as John was doing, yet her mind had been planning, sketching in details, strengthening itself against the chains of old habits, resolving on new ones; seeing with sudden clearness where they had blundered, where they had made mistakes that farsighted, orderly management could have avoided. But how could John have sat down to figure in comfort before, in the kind of kitchen she had been keeping?

Jennie bit her lip. Even if some of the tomatoes spoiled, if *all* of them spoiled, there would be a snowy washing on her line tomorrow; there would be ironing the next day in the clean kitchen. She could sing as she worked. She used to when she was a girl. Even if the apples rotted on the trees, there were certain things she knew now that she must do, regardless of what John might say. It would pay better in the end, for she had read the real needs of his soul from his eyes that evening. Yes, wives had to choose for their husbands sometimes.

A thin haunting breath of sweetness rose from the bosom of her dress where the scrap of white linen lay. Jennie smiled into the dark. And tomorrow she would take time to wash her hair. It used to be almost yellow . . . and she wished she could see the stranger once more, just long enough to tell her she understood. . . .

As a matter of fact, at that very moment, many miles along the sleek highway, a woman in a gray coat, with a soft gray hat and a rose quill, leaned suddenly close to her husband as he shot the high-powered car through the night. Suddenly he glanced down at her and slackened the speed.

"Tired?" he asked. "You haven't spoken for miles. Shall we stop at this next town?"

The woman shook her head. "I'm all right, and I love to drive at night. It's only—you know—that poor woman at the farm. I can't get over her wretched face and house and everything. It—it was *hopeless!*"

The man smiled down at her tenderly. "Well, I'm sorry, too, if it was all as bad as your description; but you mustn't worry. Good gracious, darling, you're not weeping over it, I hope!"

"No, truly, just a few little tears. I know it's silly, but I did so want to help her, and I know now that what I said must have sounded perfectly insane. She wouldn't know what I was talking about. She just looked up with that blank, tired face. And it all seemed so impossible. No, I'm not going to cry. Of course I'm not . . . but . . . lend me your handkerchief, will you, dear? I've lost mine somehow!"

Agnes Sligh Turnbull
(1888–1958)

Agnes Sligh Turnbull, author of best-sellers *The Crown of Glory, The Bishop's Mantle,* and *The Golden Journey,* wrote of a world where values were crucial. Critics might accuse her of lacking realism, but she always maintained that her books and stories mirrored the gentler world she grew up in—a world she felt had much to teach us in our frantic-paced society. The fact that she is still read half a century later is proof that she may have been closer to the mark than were some of her cynical critics.

STEPMOTHER

Mabel Bryden

$\mathcal{D}$avy hated his new stepmother; she was always trying to look prettier than his mother had. And Beauty, her snow white cat, was just like her.

Now, there was an idea. He'd fix Beauty!

*T*he old flour sack that hung over Davy Enstrom's shoulder humped and sagged as the cat in it tried frantically to escape. The sun beat hot on his back, and he could feel the heat of the bricks in the alley through the soles of his shoes. He lowered the bag to the pavement and paused to rest a moment. He was a rather stocky boy of twelve, a little short for his age, with unusually large brown eyes and a shock of dark red hair. His face was flushed with the heat and his exertion. His destination was about seven blocks farther up the alley, a vacant lot near a new building, where he had noticed a puddle of water the day before. It was now two o'clock in the afternoon, and the hot sun would have left nothing but a glistening black circle of mud about two yards across.

The alley was quiet, and the small residential side streets he had to cross were almost deserted. The roof of a garage near him exuded the pungent odor of fresh tar. The alley sloped gently, and from where he stood he could look back on his home. It was a low, rambling bungalow of brown shingles, partly covered with vines. His mother, who had died three years ago, had designed it, and every detail of its arrangement reflected the quiet, faultless taste of the retiring and unassuming little woman who had been its first mistress.

A muffled, angry whine came from the bag at Davy's feet. At the sound his expression became a blend of bitterness and satisfaction, for his mission was revenge. The cat was Beauty, his stepmother's pet Angora. He hated Beauty because she belonged to his stepmother. And he hated his stepmother.

Davy swung the bag over his shoulder again and plodded on resolutely. As he walked, his thoughts took up the familiar review of a long-smoldering resentment.

He would not hate his stepmother so much, he reflected bitterly, if she would stop trying to be so pretty. If his *own* mother had fixed herself up, she would have been just as pretty. All the ladies who had come to the house when she was there had said that it was lovely and that she had "taste." But she had never worn dainty dresses like his stepmother, and she had never waved her hair. His stepmother wore such pretty clothes! He remembered the first night he had seen her. It had been one evening last September at the end of a summer vacation. When school had closed in the spring, he had gone to spend the summer on his grandmother's farm, and shortly after he left, his father had married Lila, whom he had met on a business trip to another state.

On Davy's return, his father had met him at the train. She had remained at home to get the dinner. When they were only a block from home, his father had talked to him very seriously about her.

"I'm sure you won't hold any grudge against her just because she's your stepmother," he had said, "and your own mother would not want you to grow up without a woman's care. Lila is very anxious to win your love. I think it would be nice if you called her 'Mother'—you always called your real mother 'Mama,' so it's not the same, you know. And remember, Son, this is just as hard for her as it is for you. You'll help all you can, won't you?"

Davy had nodded dumbly and followed his father up the walk and into the house.

The long living room was a lovely sight. The waxed floor softly reflected the brass andirons before the fireplace and the flickering light of a small fire. A big brass bowl of goldenrod stood on the low bookcase. At the far end of the room the walnut gateleg table was set for three. Davy noticed that it was daintily set with his mother's doilies and fine glassware.

As he glanced swiftly around the room, his eye caught only two changes: His mother's picture had been removed (he found it later in his bedroom), and curled up in a comfortable chair before the fire was the largest white Angora cat he had ever seen. She must belong to his stepmother. Oh, what *would* his stepmother be like, and what would she think of him? He was so frightened that his knees knocked together, and after that first swift survey of the room, he could not look up. He heard the refrigerator door slam.

"Lila," his father called, "here we are. We're home!"

Quick steps and a slender figure entered the room.

"Davy," his father said, "this is your new mother."

There was a delicate scent of powder, a soft brush of silk, and a light kiss. "Hello, Sonny," she said. Her voice sounded strange, and he wondered if she, too, were frightened.

They sat down to dinner, and Daddy told him about his friends and all he had heard about the new schoolteachers. Davy kept his eyes on his plate. He knew his face was red and that he was handling the silver awkwardly. Finally his father asked about the farm, and Davy contributed his most important news.

"Ol' Blackie has three black puppies, Dad. Uncle Bert's sold 'em all, but if there had been four he was going to give me one."

His father spoke to the woman across the table. "Davy's just crazy about all kinds of pets, Lila."

"How lovely! I was afraid maybe he wouldn't like Beauty. Here, kitty," she called.

The cat stretched luxuriously, opened her topaz eyes, licked her paw with a tiny pink tongue, and curled down again in the depths of the big chair.

"I love Beauty," she went on; "she's the first pretty thing I ever owned."

Davy hardly heard her last words. For the first time he fought down his embarrassment long enough to look at his stepmother. For a full two minutes he stared at her, taking in every tiny detail of her appearance. She looked back at him steadily. She did not blush, nor smile, nor speak—just looked back at him—but when he silently dropped his eyes to his plate again, his heart was already warm with resentment. And this was the woman his father wanted him to call "Mother." This woman who was deliberately trying to be prettier than *his* mother.

Without a word, he resumed his dinner. His daddy seemed to know that something was wrong. He had begun to tell about the fat man in the parade band that he had seen on his last trip. Daddy hummed a line of music and tapped his fork against the glass. He waved his napkin to show how the parade was stopped. There were a lot of little boys about Davy's age there, and Daddy had wished Davy was with him.

At this point Lila carried out their dinner plates and brought in the dessert. It was chocolate ice cream. When she set his down, her hand brushed him and he noticed that it was icy cold. From carrying the ice cream, he thought. But when she spoke, her voice sounded almost as if she were trying to keep from shivering, and he knew, without looking up, that her eyes were searching his face.

"I hear you're very fond of chocolate ice cream, Davy. Isn't that right, Daddy?"

So she was calling his father "Daddy." And he was supposed to call her "Mother." Miserably he ate his chocolate ice cream, unmindful of its flavor, conscious only of something cold that he held in his mouth until it trickled down into his stomach. He was glad when the meal was over. With an effort he raised his eyes. He could not look at his stepmother again. Looking directly at his father, he mumbled something about seeing 'th' fellas' again and started out of the room. As he passed the chair, Beauty yawned lazily. She was the prettiest cat he had ever seen. *Her cat* was pretty, too! He hated them both.

Three hours later, when his father entered Davy's bedroom to tuck him in for the night, she came with him. She wore a pale yellow robe with a soft feathery collar and big soft cuffs. She tucked the blanket around him and leaned over to kiss him.

"Good night," he said in a hard little voice. "Good night, Mrs. Enstrom!"

"Davy!" His father was really angry.

His stepmother laughed nervously. "Don't scold, Ben. This is hard for him, you know, and he's little. And I don't care at all— honestly I don't."

She laughed again to prove it and snapped out the light in Davy's room. Her husband followed her out silently. Left alone in the dark, Davy sobbed heartbrokenly into the pillow.

"Mama . . . Mama . . . I *never* will think she's prettier than you, Mama . . . no matter how hard she tries."

The winter had dragged on, a series of hidden struggles and heartaches, hidden because of the love both he and his stepmother bore his big, jolly daddy. And she had been nice to him. Sometimes Davy felt that he couldn't bear to have her be nice to him any longer. Every morning she gave him a frosty glass of orange juice; when his father was gone on his frequent trips, she cooked only Davy's favorite dishes; she gave a birthday party for him and invited without question all the boys he wanted, said nothing about their noise, and gave everybody a second large dish of ice cream. She invited them all back again, and now she had the reputation in his gang of being "an awful nice lady." She had taken his side against his father in an argument over a new suit, but he didn't want the suit after she favored it and veered abruptly to his father's choice. She had cried a little over that when his father went to look at shoes. And she stroked his hair lightly when she passed his chair—that is, at first she had, but he tossed his head impatiently, and she stopped.

She still called him "Sonny" most of the time, especially when Daddy was there, but Davy always spoke directly to her and said only "you," and to his father, "her." Not since the first night he met her had he called her "Mrs. Enstrom," but not once in all the months that followed had he called her "Mother."

Becoming once more aware of his surroundings, Davy saw that he had almost reached his destination. Only a few feet away from him was a dilapidated old coal shed, built on the extreme rear of the vacant lot. Through a door that sagged open on the alley he entered. The old shed was small and empty save for one or two old boxes. One of these he dragged out of the corner and turned upside down.

With a sigh of relief he lowered the bag to the floor and, sitting down on the old box, reached in his pocket for twine and scissors. He cut the twine into two pieces about two feet long and made a sliding noose at the end of each piece. Then he carefully opened the bag and pulled Beauty out, holding her firmly by the neck. He swung her clear of the ground, and as she hung limp, he slipped one noose over her forepaws and the other over her hind paws, drawing the twine down tightly. She growled and spit at him angrily and lashed the ground with her tail. She was so strong that she was very difficult to hold, but Davy went about his task with grim determination. He cut all the long hair off the plumy tail and sheared a broad band up the middle of her back. Then he sheared the left forepaw and the right hind paw and all her head and face except the throat, which gave her the effect of a long white goatee. Beauty had not only lost all claim to her name; she had become a laughingstock.

The shearing over, he lifted the heavy cat carefully and stepped out of the shed. About ten yards in front of him was the mud puddle, which, as he had anticipated, the hot sun had reduced to a glistening black batter. Scattered over the vacant lot were several planks from the building next door. Picking up one about four feet long, he walked to the edge of the puddle. Here he laid the plank on the ground, and loosing the nooses on the cat's feet so that she could easily work herself free, he tossed her into the center of the puddle. The soft mud splashed only up to her head, but Davy, snatching up the plank, used it like a paddle to shower her with more. She stood motionless for an instant, then, jerking her feet free, she darted across the vacant lot and headed toward home.

He stood watching her till she was out of sight then, pitching the plank into the puddle, muttered, "Some time before you'll be pretty now," and started on a run for the ballpark.

It was after six when Davy reached home that evening, and his stepmother was waiting dinner for him. His father was on one of his frequent trips out of town. As he stepped inside the door, he looked quickly around for Beauty and to his surprise saw her curled up in her favorite chair. She had been scrubbed to her usual snowy whiteness. He wanted to shout "Scat!" to see her run across the room, but he knew that he must feign ignorance. He quickly washed his hands and face and brushed the shock of red hair.

"Wasn't it almost too hot for ball today, Sonny?" his stepmother asked a few minutes later as they sat down to dinner.

"A fellow forgets all about the heat when he's playin' ball."

He noticed that she wore a cool green crepe dress. She had changed since lunch. She had worn a white one then. Always changing her dresses. She looked tired. Possibly it had been a lot of work washing all that mud off Beauty. He didn't care. He wondered if she suspected him and decided that she would not. He wanted to talk about Beauty, or rather he wanted his stepmother to talk about her. Dinner was dragging on in silence. Suddenly she did.

"Davy," she said, "who would want to hurt Beauty?"

"Wh-What?" he stammered, startled by the directness of her remark. Maybe she had seen him going up the alley.

"Beauty came up to the back door about three this afternoon entirely covered with mud. And when I washed her, I found that she had been partly sheared. Whoever sheared her must have done it with the idea of making her look ridiculous. I can't understand it."

Davy's heart thumped suffocatingly. Where was the pleasure he anticipated finding in this revenge? Certainly he was not experiencing it now; instead he felt guilty and miserable. Lila was evidently expecting him to speak, but he could find no words.

In a moment she continued: "I suppose to a great many people the affection I feel for Beauty is rather hard to understand. No one could understand it without knowing about my childhood, too, and I've never said much about that because it wasn't very happy. I never had any of the pretty things most little girls have. My parents both died when I was quite small, and Aunt Lucinda took me to live with her. She was a very good woman, but she believed that all pretty things were vain and wicked. So I had to wear dull, ugly clothes when the other children had bright dresses and hair ribbons. I was almost grown up when my Aunt Agnes came to pay us a visit and brought Beauty to me as a present, a little fluffy white kitten. No one can realize how delighted I was. And then when Aunt Agnes left, she took me to live with her and bought me pretty things like the other girls wore. But Beauty was really the first pretty thing I ever had."

Davy could not speak. His heart felt like a lump of lead, and he could hardly swallow. His stepmother went on hesitatingly.

"My Aunt Lucinda had thought that pretty things were wicked, but my Aunt Agnes taught me just the opposite. She said that the body was the temple of the soul, and that we owed it to our soul and to God to keep that temple as beautiful as possible. She taught me that it was our duty to others, too, and I have tried to remember that always, especially since I married your father. He has never told me anything about your mother except that she was a lovely woman, and I know she must have been from the atmosphere of this home. And ever since I came here I've tried very hard to live up to her example. Sometimes when I've felt tired or ill, it's been rather hard to do, but I've always felt I would be shirking my duty and disappointing you and Daddy if I didn't look as nice as I could."

She smiled across the table at him. Davy slumped suddenly in his chair and slid off onto the floor. Hidden from her sight by the edge of the table, he leaned his head against the chair and burst into tears. She *wasn't* trying to be prettier than his mama. She was trying to be pretty because it was her duty to him and Daddy. She had said Mama was lovely and an example. And she loved Beauty because—

He felt an arm go around him. She pulled his head over against her shoulder. "There, there, don't cry," she soothed. "I'm so sorry I mentioned your mother. I didn't know it would make you feel so bad."

She patted him softly on the back and kissed him. She *kissed* him! After what he had done! Now he'd *have* to tell her.

"It was me that threw Beauty in the mud," he confessed brokenly. "An' I sheared her that way, too."

His stepmother sat very still for a minute, then kissed him again. "Why?" she asked quietly.

She hadn't slapped him—she had even kissed him again. He would have to tell her why.

"Because she was pretty—and you're pretty, and I thought you were trying to be prettier than my mama."

His voice broke again, and he sobbed wildly. Would she hate him now? Would she perhaps tell his father? Why had he been so quick to misjudge her? Then he felt her arms tighten around him sympathetically. His sobs quieted down.

Presently she spoke in a voice that strove to be casual. "It's been so hot lately that I've often thought Beauty should be completely sheared. Maybe you'd like to get it done before Daddy gets home and surprise him. . . . And now let's finish dinner. I bought chocolate ice cream for dessert."

Davy hugged her convulsively. "You're an awful good sport—Mother."

MOTHER'S VICARIOUS GRADUATION

Josephine Cunnington Edwards

ew things in life bring us more anguish than long-cherished dreams that prove impossible to achieve. As a child on the prairie, Jennie had longed for the day when she could go away to college and study music; but somehow, when that time came, the money just wasn't there.

She married, and the work was brutal and constant. On one never-to-be-forgotten day, she cleaned her hands . . . and, trembling with anticipation, sat down at her organ to play—but was heartbroken to discover that her parboiled fingers could no longer perform!

But some dreams just take longer to come true.

She sat there so quietly that few noted her presence. Her hair was smoothed back, and her hands were folded on her black-taffeta lap.

Her hands.

One noticed them.

Knobby and gnarled, the fingernails trimmed close, they were to a casual observer just the work-worn hands of an ordinary farm woman. Yet they were different. Somehow under the rough armor there was a delicate and fairy loveliness, weak and impotent as if it had long lain in chains.

Class-night exercises were in full swing. Whenever someone went to the piano or drew the bow across the strings or gave a beautiful reading, her fists clenched and her knuckles went white. A strange look of frustration came into her eyes. A look of frustration mingled with triumph.

Just then a girl graduate, capped and gowned, rose and went to the piano. Her fingers were wings, touching the keys with the airy grace of butterflies. Music like waterfalls, like choirs of birds and angels, melted and flowed as smoothly as water. One caught one's breath at the sweetness coaxed out of the ivory keys by the flying white fingers. Then the young musician rose, smiled, and bowed amid a thunder of applause. One noticed *her* hands, too, poised beautifully now upon their return from a flight after loveliness. Like carved ivory they were.

Then one looked at the *other* hands. Their roughened knuckles were white.

Who is that woman?

"She? Oh, she is the mother of the girl who just played the piano solo."

The road that went by the house was typically 1885. There were ruts and chuckholes and an occasional declivity that had been washed out by the heavy rains. Jennie did not find any fault with it because it was as good as the other roads thereabouts. Of course, she could remember better roads back in Ohio, but the railroad land had been cheap, and Father said that folks could get rich if they went out there and proved up. So they went—three wagonloads.

In the first wagon was the furniture, and through the flapping back curtains, Jennie could see mother's bureau, the feather beds, the cupboard, the old organ, and the chest of drawers lurching perilously about.

At last they arrived at their destination. They bought a piece of land on a broad prairie about eighteen miles from the thriving little town of Junction City. The land was flat and uninteresting, but Father said that the soil was very fertile.

The nearest neighbors came and helped to "raise" the house. It was made of logs and was two stories high—a sitting room and a big kitchen downstairs, and two big bedrooms upstairs. Mother set up a loom out in the shed, and Jennie helped to stretch the homemade carpet over the new parlor floor.

They set the organ in one corner. There were little shelves on each side of its front, which were fenced in by tiny knobs. On one of these Jennie proudly set a vase of everlasting flowers, and on the other the big china parlor lamp with the roses painted on it. A stand with a red-chenille cover bordered by dangling little wool balls sat in the exact geometric center of the room. Then there was the patent rocker covered with Brussels rugging, and two other rockers on the backs of which were stiffly starched cro-cheted tidies. A tufted sofa was placed grandly against one wall, and stiff Nottingham lace curtains were hung at the windows. Mother and Jennie surveyed the room proudly. Then Jennie went to the organ and, pumping vigorously, achieved "Money Mus,"

"Old Dan Tucker," and "Turkey in the Straw" in a very ecstasy of delight at having a home again.

Jennie did not fully realize all that the move involved for her. Ever since she was a little child she had planned on getting a good education and on entering a profession. As she grew older, it became almost an obsession. She would try it out on paper sometimes, just for fun. Jennie Eaton, Ph.D. Jennie Eaton, M.D. Jennie Eaton, M.A. Now they were far removed from any educational opportunities. What might have been achieved with a little effort in the small Ohio college town of her birth was an impossibility out there on the prairie. Jennie was soon to see it, sick at heart.

The new farm was laid out and fenced in. Father worked early and late, his shining plowshares cutting deep into the sod and turning it over. Jennie helped him many a hot summer day, following after him and dropping four grains of corn in each hole, often saying childishly as she did so:

"One for the mole,
One for the crow,
One to rot,
One to grow."

One day she saw a big snake coiled up in the furrow ahead of her. He was holding up his little rattle and was warning her vigorously, his malignant eyes sullen and angry. She screamed and ran, and Father killed it with a rail from the fence.

When Jennie saw that her dream of an education could never be realized, her hungry little soul turned eagerly to the fine things that *were* within her grasp. She always cleaned up carefully in the evening and went in to her organ. She was tireless in her practicing. One, two, three, four; one, two, three, four; one, two, three, rest. She took no note of the passage of time. Tirelessly she worked at a piece of music until she mastered it. It was a compensation to herself for her precious dreams. If she could not be a great teacher, or a doctor, she could make the little organ talk to her of streams, of waterfalls, and of a heaven where one's hopes were never baffled and where one could go on and on and on in the entrancing path of learning. It was to her little organ that she cried out her disappointment, often making up little wailing melodies of her own and finding a sweet comfort therein.

Father never failed to get new music for her every time they sent an order to the mail-order house. Then Jennie would be in a fever of excitement until the things came. She watched the road when Father went into Junction City for them, fairly on edge with impatience.

"Open it quick, Father," she would cry, hopping first on one foot and then on the other.

"Yes, do open it. She's got a new coat and shoes and skirt there. And that pretty length of dress goods—"

Jennie would stop and look at her mother uncomprehendingly.

"No, Mother, not that. My music book!"

Father and Mother would laugh and laugh over this episode and would tell it again and again.

"More interested in a music book than in new clothes," they would chuckle, and the neighbors all joined in the laughter.

Jennie played for programs at school, for church, for funerals, and for weddings. Everywhere she was in demand in that tiny new community where the streets were two wagon tracks with sod in the middle, and the trees were just buggy whips.

It wasn't until after she was married that a good music teacher came to town. But by then she didn't have time to practice. There was the endless chain of duties that compose the life of a farm woman, particularly one who has none of the new laborsaving devices. There were butter and bread and soap to make, meals to prepare, and heavy, coarse work garments to wash and iron and mend. The strong water had stiffened and coarsened her supple fingers. She yearned toward her organ so terribly sometimes that it actually pained her. One day, yielding to a sudden impulse, she took her hands out of the scrub water, wiped them dry, and went in and tried to play. But her poor fingers were so parboiled, and she was in such a fret lest her bread burn or lest she should wake the baby, that she finally closed the precious instrument with a sigh, lowered the parlor shades, and went back to her work.

Then she folded up the dear old daydreams and put them away in lavender. She yearned over them sometimes with a sad, sweet pain, as if it were really some loved one who had died and whom she was sorely missing. Her husband was a silent man, good-natured and kindly. He did not dream of the depths of her frustration. He was too unimaginative.

Hazel, the little girl, was her delight now. She loved to dress her in pink gingham, brush her shining curls, and send her out to play.

When Hazel was nine, Jennie let her begin music. The little girl amazed her teacher, her parents, and the whole town. Even the local paper published an account of her first recital and called her a "musical prodigy." Her tiny fingers seemed to have been created to make music.

Mother was bursting with pride, and big, silent Daddy was so "puffed up" that he drove clear to Junction City in his big farm wagon and brought back a fine mahogany piano. You could hardly pry Hazel away from it. She practiced every spare moment she had.

Watching her, Jennie felt the old desire to "be something," to "do something," steal over her with overwhelming force. Then she would look at her roughened hands with the broken nails. Futility! But she brightened as she thought, *I shall do it—through Hazel.* And she began to play a little game with herself. Every little victory that Hazel had was hers.

They sold three cows to start Hazel in college. Then they worked like slaves to keep her there. Her letters home, full of little allusions to a life that Jennie had so longed for, filled her heart again with that pain of a terrible defeat. But she played her little vicarious game again.

When she went to Hazel's graduation, she felt that her heart would bubble over with joy. *She* was going to graduate! She sat through the exercises inconspicuously and quietly, with her hands folded on her black-taffeta lap.

But her hands.

One noticed them. They grew white at the knuckles and clenched into fists whenever anyone touched the piano.

After the exercises, while she was going out of the chapel with the crowd, a hand was laid on her arm.

"If it isn't Jennie Graham! How did you come to be here? I haven't seen you since you were married!"

And Jennie looked into the face of a girlhood chum.

She laughed tremblingly.

"Hello, Ellen. I just graduated from the music cour—" Here Jennie stopped in confusion for a minute, but, hastily correcting herself, continued, "My daughter, Hazel, is graduating. See? That is she." And the proud little woman indicated her daughter.

"Not that one who made the piano fairly talk?" marveled the friend.

"Yes," answered Jennie proudly. "Yes, we—I mean she did. She certainly did!"

Josephine Cunnington Edwards
(b. 1904)

During the first half of the 1900s, Josephine Cunnington Edwards was one of America's most prolific writers of inspirational literature. She was also a teacher, a missionary to Africa, a traveling lecturer, and a Hollywood scriptwriter.

I CHOOSE YOU

Author Unknown

Jenny, a child nobody wanted, could not accept the fact that at last someone—two someones—really wanted her.

And Carol, who yearned to be a mother, was hiding something in her own past that not even her husband knew.

If three people were to become a family, one of them— perhaps two—would have to become vulnerable and make the first move.

*W*hen Carol awoke, it was after nine o'clock and the spring sunlight was streaming in at the bedroom window. She did not think of the little girl at all. As usual, her first glance was at Alan's rumpled bed. She smiled, remembering that Alan was at the hospital this morning operating.

She had kissed him when she got back from her concert at two o'clock this morning, and he had kissed her back, without opening his eyes. Suddenly, she remembered what he had said to her before he'd dropped off to sleep again: "Hey, darling, tomorrow we will be parents."

She sat up suddenly, frowning as she remembered: This was the morning Alan was bringing home the little girl. She dressed and went downstairs. From the hall, Carol could hear Sadie in the kitchen, trying to make humorous chatter with the child. The swinging door of the kitchen was open, and Carol stopped in the doorway. The little girl sat on a tall stool, watching Sadie prepare Carol's breakfast. She had not touched the glass of milk on the table in front of her, or even the cookies that had been baked so lovingly yesterday, hearts and gingerbread men and long-eared rabbits.

Sadie was cutting thin slices from a cinnamon loaf. "Why don't you eat a cookie?" she said. "Cook spent all day baking yesterday because today is her day off and she wanted you to have some on your first day. Try one of those lemon hearts, honey. They're terrific."

"No, thanks," Jenny said flatly. "I ate a big breakfast before he came for me."

Carol winced at the cold "he" for Alan, who wanted so much to be called "Dad."

Alan had found Jenny at the orphanage two weeks after he had assumed a volunteer job. He had come home elated. "Carol, I like this kid so much," he had said. "She is shy, frightened, but she has real character. She is the most alone kid I have ever seen. But she walked straight into my heart. And, darling," Alan paused, laughing, and rumpled Carol's hair, "Miss Jenny Doyle has red hair, too."

"How old is she?" Carol had asked, her throat dry. It had been completely fantastic and heartbreaking when she had discovered finally that she could never have a child. And it still hurt to hear Alan speak of a child and smile about one.

"She is eight," he had said. "Freckled, skinny, and translucent. But it is all strictly armor, poor kid. She has been there in the home since she was two. Time enough to grow a real suit of armor, eh?" He had touched Carol's cheek softly. "Will you go there and see her?"

"Of course," she had said, and smiled at him.

Sadie had gone with her. Sadie had taken to the child at first glance. "Now there is a child who would just as soon punch the world in the nose as I would," she had said.

Carol, gazing at the child who stood alone among the other children in the big room, had been deeply touched by Jenny. Instantly she had been afraid of her. It was like looking into the cold and hungry eyes of a child she had sworn to forget.

Sadie and Carol had almost reached home when Sadie's rough affectionate voice broke the silence. "Baby, why didn't you ever tell Alan you came from an orphan asylum?"

"I could not bear to. I still don't want to." She remembered how she had told Alan that he had proposed to a girl with no family, no past, no nothing. He had smiled and answered, "That makes life simple. You can marry me and share my past."

Now, standing in the kitchen doorway, it was the memory of Alan's smile that helped her to walk into the kitchen and say very gaily, "Good morning, Jenny. Welcome to your home." She saw the girl start and glance up quickly. She lowered her eyes again without speaking. She seemed very pale and almost hostile in her faded pink dress and heavy shoes. Carol looked at her helplessly.

"Did you have fun with Dad this morning?" she said.

"Sure," Jenny said, her voice so flat that Sadie said hurriedly, "Al sure looked happy when he dropped her off. 'Take good care of my daughter,' he said, 'till her mother wakes up.'" Jenny still said nothing.

Sadie cleared her throat. "Won't it be swell to get a lot of new clothes, honey?" she said.

"Yes, ma'am."

"And tonight—did Dad tell you what is happening?"

Jenny nodded indifferently. "We are going to eat out. At the place where you sing."

"The Peacock," Sadie said. "It's a supper club. Did you know your mom is a real famous singer? Known all over the country: New York, Miami, and the West Coast. . . ."

"Oh, Sadie, hush up," Carol said, laughing.

Jenny was staring at her so intently that Carol smiled encouragingly. "Dad thought it would be fun for you to hear me sing tonight. Besides, it's sort of a homecoming party, dear. Your grandmother, us, Sadie—your family. Sadie will be glad to help you get ready, too."

"Sure I will," Sadie said eagerly.

Jenny did not respond. Deliberately, Carol finished her coffee, and then she said, "Jenny, dear, I have to practice my new song before we shop. Would you like to go outdoors with Sadie?"

"Sure," Jenny said and jumped down off the stool.

"Come on, honey," Sadie said, and took Jenny's hand.

For a few minutes, Carol watched them through the window

and saw the tense, awkward little girl walk stiffly past the beds of daffodils and narcissuses, her hair flaming in the sunlight.

If I can only meet her halfway, Carol thought. *If only she does not shut Alan out, too.* Her husband was only thirty-two and had already made a name for himself as a fine surgeon. Alan had inherited money, had been born into one of Chicago's oldest families. Now he was possessor of all the things he wanted except a child, the gift he wanted most.

Before she began working on her song, she called her mother-in-law, Mrs. MacDonald. Carol loved her, for she had welcomed her so sweetly into the family at the time of her marriage to Alan. She was going with Carol to get Jenny her first clothes.

When Mrs. MacDonald had hung up, Carol went to the piano and ran quickly through her new song. Before she had met Alan, singing had been her whole reason for existing in the world. Now there was no longer the frantic need to be recognized by a worldful of people, to be applauded and photographed wherever she went. Now it became merely something she enjoyed doing and doing well.

They had been married three years. Dr. Alan MacDonald had walked into the Bronze Room with a party one night and had come back every evening after that during her six-week engagement there. He had followed her to Detroit, to Cleveland, and to New York courting her, and she had fallen in love with him. Singing her song now, Carol knew with sudden clarity why she had been so frightened of taking this little starving waif into her home. It was because she did not know how to take her into her heart.

The shopping trip was a dismal failure. As Carol and Mrs. MacDonald picked out dresses, shoes, and underclothes, Jenny watched indifferently, as if all the clothes were for someone she did not know.

At first Carol was excited. When they had assembled a complete outfit for Jenny, she said eagerly, "Come on, dear, let's get all dressed up now."

She helped the girl into a forest green linen dress, new socks and shoes; she adjusted the matching hair ribbon. "Lovely," Mrs. MacDonald said happily, and Carol waited for Jenny to look at herself in the long mirror, waited for her guarded eyes to brighten with the sight of the pretty new clothes.

But Jenny barely glanced at herself. As she turned toward the saleswoman who was holding her old clothes, she said, "I'll carry them. May I have a bag, please?"

"Oh, we will have them sent," Carol said. "We are going to carry all the new clothes so we can have them at home right away."

"No, I want my old stuff," Jenny said harshly. "I'll carry it."

With startling abruptness, as she looked at the child's set expressions. Carol remembered herself in the Orphan's Home, sneering inwardly at the cheap, ill-fitting dresses passed out twice a year from the big charity crates that had been sent in. *Jenny resents us,* she thought grimly. *She thinks this is charity, too, and she doesn't want it.* Carol felt the raw hurt that remembering her childhood always brought. She had managed for years to keep from thinking of it, and was this red-haired waif going to force her back?

At home she and Sadie carried all the boxes up to the newly furnished bedroom. Jenny followed, clutching her bag of old clothes.

Carol was able to leave the child calmly, but as soon as she closed the door, the tears came, and she went quickly to her room. Sadie was there to help her get ready to go to the club.

"Hey, baby," she said, "Jenny doesn't mean to be such a cold potato. She's a good kid, if you ask me."

"She hates being here," Carol said. "I know she doesn't like me. Poor Alan. Sadie, it is not going to work out." She sat on the edge of the bed and wiped her eyes with the back of her hand.

"Sure, it'll work out," Sadie said. "You have just got to give her time. Remember what a tough little customer you were once, that day you walked in for your first job."

"Was I this tough, Sadie?" she asked.

"Sure, you were, you thought. It was a wonderful job of acting, like Jenny is doing now." Sadie laughed and handed her a handkerchief. "You were lots older than this kid, and not so skinny, but there's a real resemblance."

They smiled at each other, remembering. Carol had been sixteen, but looked nineteen; a tall, slim girl with stunning red hair and creamy skin. It had taken her years of planning to perfect her runaway escape from the Detroit orphan home. She had been sent there at five with only a misty memory, like a dream, of a beautiful mother who had disappeared.

She had hitched rides to Chicago and had studied the newspapers to find the name of the best supper club in the city. Then, with almost insolent calmness, she had applied for a job as a waitress—and she had been lucky. Not only had she gotten the job, but one of the waitresses had been a teacher and a big sister to her almost from the start. Her name was Sadie White, and she was the first real friend Carol had ever had. She was homely and good-natured and one of the best waitresses in town.

Sadie had offered her the first unquestioning love Carol had ever known, and she had snatched at it greedily. It was Sadie who had recognized the sweet haunting quality in her voice and had urged and threatened until Carol finally asked the manager for a tryout. Sadie had bought the evening dress Carol wore the night she opened. At seventeen, Carol had been the hit at the Emerald Room.

"It took you almost two years," Sadie reminded her now, "even to tell *me* about that orphan asylum, and me your best friend. And, baby, you were lots older than this kid. What do you want from her the first day—the works?"

Carol went quickly down the hall and knocked on Jenny's door. After a moment, the girl called hesitantly, "Who's there?"

"It's Mother," Carol said, and opened the door and stepped in. Jenny had changed back to her old clothes. Carol was over-whelmed by her feelings of tenderness and pity, but she managed to be casual.

"Hi, dear," she said. "Shall we get your clothes unpacked?" Chattering gaily, she unpacked the boxes, hanging up the dresses, putting the underclothes away. Jenny did not offer to help. When she had finished, Carol turned to look at her.

"Say," she said, "have you ever baked a cake?"

Jenny blinked. "No, ma'am," she said, surprised and a little wary.

Carol's smile did not waver. "Neither have I," she said, "and the kitchen is ours today. Wouldn't it be fun?"

She held out her hand, and after an instant, Jenny got to her feet. As they went downstairs together, Carol felt giddy with this first small triumph.

"Let's try Dad's favorite cake," she said, "chocolate. The worst that can happen is that we may have to eat it before he sees it."

Jenny giggled faintly.

In the kitchen, Carol doubled one of the cook's huge aprons and tied it around the child's thin body with a flourish.

In a moment, the table was littered with ingredients. Carol

lifted Jenny onto a kitchen stool and gave her a mixing spoon. She began reading directions aloud and cracking eggs and sifting flour into a large bowl.

"Shall we bake it two layers or three?" she asked.

"Three," said Jenny as she stirred, "like a birthday cake."

Her face was flushed, and for the first time, her eyes showed excitement. She peered into the bowl, up at Carol, and then back at the batter she was mixing. Enveloped in the white apron, she suddenly looked pert and adorable.

"What dress are you wearing this evening?" Carol asked after a moment.

Jenny stopped stirring. Finally she said in a low voice, "I don't know."

"The organdy?" Carol said. "It's awfully pretty."

There was another pause, and Jenny said cautiously, "The silk one's fancier. Is . . . is that a fancy place where you sing at?"

"Sort of," Carol said. "By the way, Sadie wants to help you dress. I won't be here, you know."

"Oh," Jenny said. "You have to go early?"

"Yes, dear, but Sadie will be here."

"Will he be going, too?" Jenny said.

"Dad? Of course. He is escorting you and Grandma."

She poured the batter into the cake pans and put them into the oven.

"Now, let's lick the bowl," Carol said. She ran a finger around the rim and licked it thoughtfully. After a second, Jenny did the same.

"Hey, it's good," Carol said, and laughed.

And in a moment, Jenny began to laugh, too. "We won't have to eat it before he comes," she said.

They both had chocolate smeared around their mouths and

on their aprons. There was a dark blob of batter on Jenny's forehead, and Carol bent to wipe it off.

The little girl stared up at her, her eyes so wondrous that Carol paused a moment with her hand on Jenny's hair. Then quickly, she kissed her cheek. "When are you going to call me Mother?" she said softly.

Jenny seemed to wince. "I don't know," she said, and slid off the stool and ran out of the kitchen.

Carol and Sadie came home from the Club at about midnight, and Sadie was helping her out of her dress. As usual, they spoke in whispers.

"Alan has an operation at eight, and that is the reason I wanted them to leave early," she said to Sadie.

"The kid looked like she wanted to stay," said Sadie, chuckling. But Carol felt lonely, though usually an evening's performance exhilarated her. She had sung at their table, which Alan always enjoyed. But she had really sung to Jenny, seeing in the child's eyes a dream of beauty and color she had dreamed of so much in her childhood. Looking into the child's hungry eyes, she had thought, *How can I feed such sad eyes? Dear God, tell me how.*

She finished undressing, and instead of going to her bedroom, she went out into the hall and started to Jenny's room. The door was a bit ajar. She pushed it open and, seeing the tiny light on the dresser, she walked on tiptoe to the bed and bent over it.

Jenny sat up with a jerk. "I didn't talk when you came in because you might have been scared," she whispered. "Because you thought I was sleeping."

Carol sat on the edge of the bed. "Couldn't you fall asleep?" she asked.

"I didn't want to," Jenny said. "Too much to think about. Boy, you looked beautiful—like a princess, honest. It wasn't hardly for real. I mean, you know how it is when you think maybe you are dreaming?"

"Yes, I know," said Carol.

"And I just never had to wake up," Jenny said gleefully. "When we came home, he told me stories for a while. Oh, and all of us had cookies and milk, and I took a bath."

"Grandma, Daddy, and you?"

"Yeah. And she helped me wash my back. And he tucked me in, and then I could lie here and think about everything that happened as many times as I wanted to."

Jenny clutched her knees and rocked happily until Carol said, "Time to go to sleep now, dear. It is awfully late."

"Okay," said Jenny, and promptly lay down again. "I will shut my eyes right after you go."

Carol stood up. She wanted to kiss Jenny good-night, but she did not dare. Instead she said shyly, "Did you say your prayers?"

Jenny's smile disappeared. "No."

"Oh, don't you say your prayers?"

Jenny looked at her thoughtfully. "Well, I always used to pretend," she said. "When Mrs. Wheeler came in every night, she always said, 'Time for prayers, girls; sit up and clasp your hands.' So thirty of us sat up and let'er rip."

Staring up at Carol, she said defiantly, "I used to just move my lips. Some of the kids did *buzz buzz* or *bang bang,* and in a minute it was over and we could lie down again, and the lights went out. Mrs. Wheeler did not listen anyway, she was always too busy checking on stuff."

Almost before she knew it, Carol said, "Want us to say our prayers together on our knees? That is the way I used to want to when I was little."

Jenny was out of bed immediately.

"Dear God," said Carol hesitantly, "thank you for this happy day. Bless our family. Now we are a real family."

Somehow she managed to steady her voice, and with a new feeling of peace, she went on, "Oh, God, we thank you so much for our daughter. We thank you that out of the whole wide world of children we were permitted to choose her to be our child. We thank you for our happiness. Amen."

When Carol opened her eyes, Jenny was staring at her almost incredulously. "You wanted to choose me?" she said. "You said it in your prayer, and that is like crossing your heart."

"Yes, cross my heart, and cross Daddy's heart," Carol said.

"Oh, you picked me . . . me. . . ." Jenny flung her arms around Carol and kissed her face over and over. For several minutes she clung and pressed her face against Carol's.

Then Carol said, "I am going to tuck you in for good, my darling. But you are so wide awake, how will you sleep?"

"I won't," said Jenny joyously. "Tell me a bedtime story. Tell me about when you were little."

"I was very much like you," Carol said so quietly that Jenny suddenly lay very still. And then Carol told her about the place called an orphan asylum and how the little girl named Carol Scott had been able to bear everything but the special days.

Special days came the first Sunday of every month. All the children lined up on that day, scrubbed and combed and dressed in the best of their charity clothes, and waited for the people to come and pick. The men and women would come then and walk slowly among the boys and girls, staring at each one. They walked like an endless procession of judges. Every once in a while a couple would stop and point to some child and say, "I choose you." But never, never, did anyone say to *her* the magic words, "I choose you."

As she finished her story of the special days, reliving the fear and the hatred she had felt, Carol was aware that Alan was standing in the doorway of Jenny's bedroom. She knew he had heard. She had never told him about Carol, the orphan.

Jenny was holding her hand tightly, and Carol smiled at Alan and told the rest of her story to both of them. How the little girl had grown up and run away to work, and how she had made friends with Sadie and discovered inside herself the gift for singing that made the world want her.

Finally, she stopped talking. She had wanted to go on to tell how love had come at last to the girl, love and happiness, and even a daughter. But she could not go on.

"Please don't cry, Mother," Jenny said. She was sitting up and patting Carol's hand.

Then Alan came quickly across the room. He knelt in front of his wife and turned her face toward his.

"No, don't cry," he said gravely. "Jenny and I, we both choose you."

WHITE LILACS

Leota Hulse Black

*I*t was Mother's Day . . . and the church was grand.
Light streamed through the stained-glass windows, turning
them to flame. The organ thundered into Handel. And
rarely beautiful roses and carnations perfumed the air.

Only one object was out of place: a little old lady
(seated in a pew towards the front) wearing a faded gray
dress and a shabby hat; one wrinkled hand holding a
listening trumpet to her ear—and the other clutching a
huge bunch of white lilacs.

An officious usher icily steered her to a remote pew at the back, refusing to listen to her importunings.

And then . . . the young minister began to speak.

*I*t was Mother's Day. The chimes played softly as the little old lady crept slowly up the steps and entered the cool dimness of the church. The fashionably dressed worshipers that thronged the vestibule glanced curiously at the tiny figure in the faded gray dress and shabby hat. One wrinkled hand held to her ear an old-fashioned trumpet; the other, a huge bunch of white lilacs. Darting timid glances here and there, she passed through a doorway and moved slowly up the aisle. Near the front of the church she paused uncertainly, then slipped into a pew. An usher appeared, his bulk blocking the aisle.

"I'm sorry, ma'am, but you can't sit there—that is a rented pew. There are good seats in the back of the church."

"Eh?"

"I said there are good seats in the back—you'll have to move back."

"Oh, I'm sorry—I ain't used to such a stylish church. I thought it was all right to set in any seat in the Lord's house. I wisht they was a seat nearder the front—my hearin' is so poor, an' I do want to hear the sermon. You see, my—"

"I'm sorry, lady, but you'll *have* to move back!"

He led the way to a pew far back in the church and piloted her into a niche behind a pillar. The little old lady laid a detaining hand on his arm, "Mister—I wonder if you'd mind puttin' these lilacs up where the preacher kin see 'em? You see, it's Mother's Day, and I thought he'd like to be smelling white lilacs while he's apreachin'. They been picked quite a spell but I kep' 'em nice and fresh with this wet rag, and they'll look right purty up there amongst the roses an' carnations."

The usher made a gesture of annoyance.

"We can't do that—our florist has arranged the flowers and your bouquet would spoil the—er—symmetry."

The little old lady nodded disappointedly.

"I—I didn't quite git what you meant, but I wouldn't want to be aspoilin' anything."

She slipped to her knees behind the pillar for a moment. Then the organ, pealing forth the throbbing notes of Handel's "Largo" brought her to her feet. Drawing a sobbing breath, she whispered, "My—it's—BEAUTIFUL—it's like Heaven—and this is where Johnny is keepin' my promise to the Lord."

The choir in white vestments poured into the loft. There was an expectant hush—then the door by the chancel opened softly, and a tall man in clerical robes appeared. As he mounted the platform, his footsteps kept time with the beating of the little old lady's heart. The minister glanced over the congregation with a smile like new sunshine. Though it was not for the little old lady, it swept into her heart so utterly that she placed a withered hand over the spot. Pride welled up in her so that she could hardly breathe. Then suddenly the church was filled with the strains of the opening hymn. She clutched the arm of a beautifully gowned woman who sat by her side.

"My, ain't it just BEAUTIFUL? Heaven can't be no sweeter with the light pourin' through that stained-glass window of Mary kneelin' at the cross—and the choir singin' like angels—an'—an' Johnny with the light from that yellow pane a-shinin' on his head! It makes him look like the picters of Christ with the halo around Him—"

The woman glanced with annoyance at the little figure, then

whispered to her escort: "Some demented creature that has wandered in. The ushers should be more careful!"

The hymn ended; the congregation bowed in prayer, rose again—the minister came forward. Smilingly he read the words of his text.

"'And He stretched forth His Hand unto His disciples and said, Behold my Mother and my brethren.'"

The little old lady chuckled happily as she whispered to herself, "Law, if Johnny had of knowed I was to be here he couldn't have picked a more fittin' text. Wouldn't he be su'prised if he knew I *was* among the brethren."

Beautiful phrases were falling from the minister's lips, the story of that mother who had followed the Man of Sorrows to the cross.

The little old lady peered around the pillar but was able to catch only scattered fragments. Then the weariness of seventy-two years coupled with two days of travel proved too much for the tired body and she nodded sleepily. Was she sleeping or was it a vision that passed through her subconsciousness in swift panorama? She was back on the old farm, young and happy. Three little curly heads clustered around her as she snipped the blossoms from the white lilac bush at the corner of the house. Then the dreadful scourge of diphtheria—and she folded the hands of Jimmy and Mary in the last sleep. Only Johnny, the baby, was left, and she was kneeling by the bed where he lay choking and raving in delirium. In agony she cried out, "Oh, God, spare me this *one!* Don't take my baby, and I'll give him to Thee. I'll give my whole life to preparin' him to do Thy work. I promise, Lord, if you'll only spare him to me."

And Johnny had been spared. Then followed years of hardship and poverty. Just she and Johnny to till the soil and eke out an existence on the old place. But she never forgot for one moment *the promise.* Every penny that could be spared must be saved for Johnny's education. The days and weeks behind the plow, the nights when the weary old back bent over the washboard, had always the same objective: that a few more pennies might be earned for Johnny's education.

The ear-trumpet slipped to her lap, again she nodded, and now they were sitting on the old porch in the twilight. Johnny was speaking.

"Ma, don't the lilacs smell nice? They—they seem kinda human—they make me want to do something to try to help people to be good—an'—an'—*pure*—like the white lilacs."

"Yes, Johnny, Ma understands. You see, you're promised to the Lord, to do His work. It jest don't seem like it's gonna be possible to give you the education you'll be needin' to git you fer His service—but if you do your part—He'll do His."

"But, Ma, do I need such a good education? Lots of men in the ministry don't have. I'm not wantin' to be a burden to you. Mebbe I could serve a country church."

"Why, Johnny, *the idea!* Folks in the country have the same kind of souls that city people have. No matter where you labor, you got to have the right preparation. You're goin' into the highest callin' known to man, and yer gonna be prepared! There's nothin' cheap about the Lord's work an' yer not goin' into it in ignorance! I'll manage somehow!"

Again the scene changes, and she sees herself, more bent, more frail, seated under the white lilacs. The gate opens, and Johnny, suitcase in hand, enters. With a sigh of discouragement, he slumps down by his mother.

"Well, Ma, I'm home to stay."

"Why, Johnny, what's wrong?"

"Everything. Ma, you can't make good in college unless you have money—and a pull! They don't want paupers like me there. They laugh at me—at my clothes. I tell you, Ma, I can't stand it!"

"Why, Johnny! I'm ashamed of you! Wantin' to throw in the sponge because someone laughed at you! If that's all the grit you got you're not the kind of timber that's needed in the ministry! You'll be facin' plenty of scoffin' an' discouragements, an' if you ain't got the will to overcome 'em it's better to find it out now than to fail later. Hand me your suitcase, Johnny, I'll unpack it. . . . Look, Johnny, the white lilacs are bloomin'! They're beckonin' to you, like people."

"Ma, I'm sorry. I didn't look at it right—I'll go back—and *I'll stick!* I can catch a ride back to school with the same fellow I came down with. Good-bye, Ma. I'll make good!"

And true to his word, he had made good. The little old lady nodded on, then sat up with a start. Where was she? She adjusted the ear-trumpet and peeped around the pillar. Why—why—what was Johnny saying? "Mother—toiling night and day—mortgaging the old farm—the fulfillment of a promise—Mother's Day—the old farmhouse—*white lilacs*—I want to see the lilacs—Mother—homesick—"

She leaned farther around the pillar that she might see his face.

"Why—why—he's cryin'! There's tears runnin' down his cheeks! He's nothin' but a boy, and he's *cryin'*—"

The little old lady hadn't heard it all, but she had heard enough to know that her Johnny was homesick and needed her. She squeezed past the pillar and stepped into the aisle. She advanced toward the platform, holding white lilacs at arm's length and calling tremulously: "Johnny, darlin', don't cry! I'm comin' with some white lilacs—from the old place! I wanted to su'prise you—"

But "Johnny darlin'," after one incredulous gasp, was halfway down the aisle, where he gathered the little old lady in his arms and carried her to the platform. The faded hat was sadly askew, and the wet rag from the lilacs streamed limply toward the floor. A ripple of surprise flowed and darted over the audience—and mellow light from the window fell slantwise across their faces; that window where another Mother knelt at the foot of a cross.

The usher who had seated the little old lady stepped in from the vestibule and saw the lovely tableau.

"Who—who *is she?*" he inquired of a fellow usher.

The other, with a constriction mounting in his throat, answered . . . *"The minister's mother."*

NOVEMBER WINDS

Joseph Leininger Wheeler

Money. Media and sports superstars are paid millions—so are many corporate CEOs. Then there are teachers. What in the world would cause someone to go into the teaching profession? What would cause someone to stay with it? What would cause someone to give up everything else because of it?

A woman, no longer young, stood leaning against the windowpane—seeing, yet not seeing, the bleak November world outside: the overcast sky; the icy wind whipping the Severn River to a blue gray froth; the trees standing almost naked, their shredded garments fluttering restlessly at their feet.

In the fireplace was a warm crackling fire—but it brought no warmth to the silent woman. To the right and left of the fireplace were row after row of inviting books, well-worn by loving hands down through the years—but they brought no comfort today. Above the fireplace was a seascape depicting an indigo blue morning on the Amalfi Coast—but its beauty brought no response either.

It was only September in the woman's life, but it might as well have been November, judging by her mood, by the winter in her eyes.

After a time, she turned from the window and sought out her favorite chair by the fireplace, sinking down into its softness with a sigh.

Not even the leap into her lap of Alfred, Lord Tennyson (disrespectfully shortened to Tenny), nor the postleap purr, softened the hard cast of her face.

Her thoughts winged their way backward into time, as they did more and more often these days, it seemed. Out of the blur of the rewind came a scene she had not revisited for a long time. She was a child again, and eight lighted candles were on her cake. "Make a wish!" commanded Daddy, so she hesitated a moment before blowing them out. *Oh, Lord . . . do let me be a teacher someday!* was her heartfelt prayer. How long she had wanted to be a teacher, she never knew—but she *did* remember that one candlelit moment, frozen in time.

Today, for some unexplainable reason, she wanted to follow
that little pigtailed girl down through the years. Her favorite
childhood game had been School, with herself playing the role of
Teacher. When her friends balked at being her students—which
they did all too often—she drafted her dolls and pet animals. *They*
behaved—which was certainly a lot more than she could say for
her friends!

Tenny cold-nosed her into awareness of his need for her, so
she came out of her reverie long enough to scratch his head,
neck, and back—then she sank back into the past again.

She was sixteen, waiting in the wings for her turn to go onstage.
Then her name was announced and perfunctory applause could
be heard, welcoming her and her contribution to the amateur
hour. Somehow she found her way to the lip of the stage and felt
sure everyone out there could hear the pounding of her runaway
heart. Where was Dad? Where was Mom? She licked her dry lips
. . . and the applause ceased.

She froze. For the life of her, she couldn't remember the
words! The words that she knew backward and forward; sideways
too, for that matter . . . The silence in the high school auditorium
grew deafening, broken only by a nervous cough and someone
clearing her throat. That *had* to be Mom (she'd recognize her
unique rasp anywhere!).

The prompter, positioned just inches away on the other side
of the curtain, hissed the words.

Oh, yes! The door to her memory opened again, and the rest
of the words obediently came when she was ready for them.
Within minutes she had hit her stride, forgetting her audience in

her total identification with John Alden and the lovely Pilgrim maiden, Priscilla. So much so that when she came to those coy words, "Why don't you speak for *yourself,* John?" . . . a storm of applause swept the auditorium—applause that only grew louder rather than diminished.

She never did finish it, feeling that the rest of Longfellow's long poem was anticlimactic anyhow. The judges obviously agreed; otherwise they would never have awarded her the Grand Prize.

A coolness at her feet reminded her that the fire was almost out.

Sorry, Tenny! she apologized as she emptied her lap of his warm and comfy presence; then she stepped out into the cold wind sweeping down the river and brought in another armload of split oak.

The fire restoked and Tenny sulking somewhere because of his abrupt eviction, it was harder this time to find her place in her "Book of Years."

She was twenty, and the moon etched a path of silver across Dream Lake. At her side, with his arm around her, was Bob. She knew it was coming before he spoke the words—*had* known it was coming for weeks now. Yearned for it. Dreaded it. Even in her dreams, she knew no peace, no acceptance. Only confusion, apprehension, frustration, and turmoil.

Just last night, knowing this moment was nearing, she had watched her mother and father with the eyes of awareness, studying intently this relationship she had always taken for granted. She had mused, *By what divine miracle could the love Dad has for Mom and the love she has for him fuse into me? . . . And, it is a love that has but grown stronger with the passing years . . . They have lived for the Lord, for each other, for me . . . Do I have that kind of love for Bob? Would I want a life that is framed by all the things that he is? . . . Am I a "whither thou goest" woman like Mom is? . . . Do I want children? Bob certainly does! He would be devastated were he never to have any of his own.*

And I know full well that if I let Bob get away, I'll never even consider looking for another to replace him. No, it is either Bob . . . or I'll never get married at all. Never have children of my own . . . Lonely. I'd get lonely. Awfully lonely!

That had been the night before, and she had cried herself to sleep, unable to bring the matter to resolution. But now the moment had come. He pulled her closer to him and, after what seemed forever, had gazed into her luminous eyes with such intensity of desire and longing that she felt all resistance ebbing away. And when his lips claimed hers, all pretense at rationality ceased.

Finally, breathing raggedly, he broke away and smiled that slightly crooked smile she had adored since the day he had moved next door when he was twelve and she was nine. He took his hand from her shoulder and reached into his pocket for something she *knew* would be a little square box, and within that box would be a thin piece of metal that would symbolize lasting promises. Promises that would grow into marriage and family and endure as long as their lives should last. Unthinkable for her to approach marriage in any other way than for life. No, it must be either *all*—or it would have to be *nothing!*

When he opened the box and handed her his heart on a moonlit platter, she was almost torn in two by the tug-of-war between her heart and mind. So she had temporized: "Give me some more time, Bob . . . I'm . . . I'm just not ready yet to make such a decision."

"Not ready?" He was disbelieving. How could she, his soul mate, not be ready for a question they had talked about ever since they had been children? . . . But grudgingly, he had accepted it, with the hopefulness of youth assuming that there could be but one answer.

There was—but it was not the answer he had expected. She *just couldn't do it.* . . . It was the hardest thing she had ever done; it was the hardest thing she would ever do. In the end, she had been honest both with herself and with him; there would now be no husband, no children of her own, in life. Teaching—that would be her all in all. Hers would be a ship that sailed alone.

The wind-driven rain began to slash at her windows, the sky to darken. Involuntarily she shivered—but it was not just because of the storm outside. It was because only now was she beginning to realize how high a price she had had to pay.

Teaching had indeed become her life—her *whole* life. There had not been room for anything else. Not even research or administration, which were, to so many of her colleagues, more important than "mere" teaching: far more significant than teaching in the race for honor, prestige, money, and tenure. She was just one of those simpletons who were dumb enough to believe that the highest calling in education was—to teach.

And now she realized how foolish she had been. *For what?* Who among all those students she had given her very lifeblood to . . . cared two figs? They probably laughed at her behind her back.

Oh, they were nice enough to her face, said all kinds of complimentary things to her on all the appropriate occasions. But who could possibly be sincere where grades were concerned? Every last one of them had an ulterior motive behind all those honeyed words. Unconsciously her lips contorted into a cynical smirk.

How quickly had passed the years! Ten years, twenty years, and now thirty years . . . Ahead, in not too many more years, loomed that unfathomable thing akin to death, nursing homes, and Alzheimer's—*retirement!* What then? She would have given up all the things that men and women yearn for—love, marriage, children, grandchildren, companionship—just so she could dedicate *all* her energies to this strange thing called "teaching."

And now—ahead—were only the lonely years. And she, like Esau, had sold her familial birthright for a mess of pottage!

And she wept.

What in the world! Silently they filed past her one after another. *How had they opened the sliding door so quietly?* They kept coming, familiar faces all. And among them were two colleagues, each giving her, in passing, a conspiratorial wink. The long snaky line of students (past and present) did not end until her house was full. Those at the end lugged in food. Enough for an army.

How they revelled in her initial blank look; nothing registered at first—it was almost as if it were but an extension of her dreaming. Then came, in waves, recognition of who they were, followed by puzzlement as to why.

Perversely they left her dangling there with that look of utter bewilderment on her face, relishing the opportunity to reverse roles on her for once.

As often as these students had been in her home before, they knew it inside and out. In a matter of moments, they had commandeered her kitchen, and hilarity reigned supreme. In the long living room, each had found a chair, a sofa, an unspoken-for stretch of carpet and begun to talk to whomever was in range. It was bedlam with everyone talking at once.

The blessing represented the first clue as to why they had come:

"Dear Lord, we ask You to bless this food and we who are about to partake of it. But, more importantly, we ask a special blessing on our dear Prof. May we have her with us for at least thirty *more* years.

"In His name, Amen."

So *that* was it! Now that she knew, she could begin to relax and enjoy the impromptu party. But not *completely* relax, for there were mysterious subcommittees meeting here and there and objects surreptitiously passed around. Through it all, she smilingly played the game and pretended to be oblivious to all the sideshows.

Finally, the food and drink devoured, the clutter picked up, and the remains boxed, there was no longer any excuse for keeping her in suspense.

As if by magic, suddenly everyone found a seat—and all conversation ceased. She, seated on the floor, found herself surrounded.

Miriam, now a corporate executive, stood up. *Might have known she'd be in charge,* she thought to herself. *At the College, she ran everything—from Loaves and Fishes to Teach a Kid to the yearbook to the Student Association . . . But I'd better quit this woolgathering and find out what all this is about!*

Miriam smiled at her before she spoke; then, good adminis-

trator that she was, her eyes panned the room to see if everything and everyone were ready. Only then did she open her
mouth.

"We are here on this cold winter evening" (it was sleeting
outside now) "for a special purpose—a *very* special purpose:
to celebrate thirty years of teaching on our campus by our own
dear Prof."

Miriam paused until the applause and cheers died down and
then proceeded: "We have some tangible things, gifts, for you at
the end . . . but we felt you would appreciate even more some
intangible things. Each of us in this room has a story to tell, a
memory. We'd rather share them with you now rather than . . ."
And here she paused, choosing her words carefully, "rather than
when you get old."

Irrepressible Steve burst out, "Old! She'll *never* get old!" And
everyone laughed, lightening the serious mood.

"So," Miriam continued, "who'd like to be first? . . . Oh,
Lauri?"

"Yeah, I'll start," said Lauri, who as a collegiate leader was
used to starting things. "I'll never forget my first day on campus.
I didn't know a soul . . . and I was *so* homesick. I was standing
forlornly in the basement of Wilkinson Hall, trying to hold back
the tears, and I heard a gentle voice just behind me, saying, 'Hi!
Can *I* help?' I looked up, wiped my eyes with my handkerchief,
and mumbled something inane—I was dreadfully embarrassed to
be caught sniffling."

"Oh, come now, you cry just watching commercials!" teased
Janelle.

"Yeah, guess I do at that." Lauri smiled. "But, anyhow, she
seemed so interested in me, and her eyes were so friendly . . . and
. . . kind—suddenly I wasn't so lonely anymore. She took me

down to her office, had me sit down, and soon had me telling my life story!"

"She must know a lot of 'em!" quipped Sal.

Ignoring him, Lauri concluded, "Anyhow, thanks to her interest in me, I decided to stay and make a go of it. And that chance meeting was no fluke; she's been there for me ever since."

Next to get the nod was Ed. "What I remember most about Prof are her homilies."

"Hear! Hear!" came from half a dozen throats.

"Somehow, whenever she spoke to us, she'd weave us in by name. None of us were safe from her wicked homilies," he chuckled. "Prof has a steel-trap mind—*nothing* escapes it! But it isn't just the name thing that I remember . . . She always has something special to say—something deeply moving or devastatingly witty! And her voice is so low, there is always dead silence when she speaks—no one wants to miss a word!"

Seeing that Ed was done, Randy broke in. "I'd just like to add something to what Ed said. What I appreciate most about her homilies is the time she spends preparing to speak. *Every word* is always well chosen—and I know from experience that it takes a lot of time and work to speak like that!"

"And," added Starla, "let's not forget how hard it is to ever forget what she says! Her homilies are always about things we're concerned about—at least, that *I* am concerned about," she qualified.

"I remember a time," interjected Jeannie, "when you-know-who was giving me such a bad time. . . ."

"One guess!" quipped Lauri. Everyone knew who Jeannie's nemesis was.

Blushing, Jeannie continued. "Well, it looked like the end for me! It was my word against his, and obviously, his counted a lot more than mine did. A *lot* more! Anyway, as a last resort, I walked over to Prof's office, almost unbelievably, finding her alone.

(Laughter)

"Prof quickly got to the root of the problem, and as she did, I could sense her rising anger. . . ."

"Yeah, when someone picks on one of her lambs, that someone better watch out!" interposed Dorothy.

"Anyhow," Jeannie continued, not missing a beat, "when I left her office, it was with a tremendous sense of relief. I was no longer alone—I now had an advocate. She called in reinforcements—the English Department took a united stand on my behalf . . . and, well," she sputtered, "I'm still here."

In the silence that followed, Danny stepped in: "You'll have to go a lot farther than just those of us gathered in this room . . . before you'll find someone Prof *hasn't* been an advocate to! I know *I* certainly wouldn't still be here if it hadn't been for her!"

Softly, Charity then spoke up. "I don't know most of you, as I graduated about ten years ago, but Prof has *always* been our advocate. I remember with shame one time when I did a dumb thing—no, it was far worse than dumb! Anyway, I had been called before the Discipline Committee . . . and I knew it was curtains for me. In only hours I'd be gone . . . And my folks! How could I possibly face my folks? Anyway, even though it was late at night, I called Prof up at home and told her what had happened—not really expecting help . . . but just letting her know—because she had been from the first the one faculty member who really *believed* in me!"

"You were in good company," broke in Ryan. And heads nodded all around the room.

Charity continued, "Well, I'm sure you guys know what followed. In minutes, she had driven to her office and met me there. We had a long talk . . . and did she ever talk turkey to me! She took me to the woodshed—" and here her voice broke— "but then she hugged me, told me she believed in me, that she loved me . . . and then she asked in her quiet voice, 'Is it all right if we bring the matter before the Lord, Charity?' I could only nod because I was crying by then. Well, she prayed for me . . . and then I prayed, too, between sobs; I prayed that the Lord would help me not be such a fool again." She paused, finding it hard to go on.

Recovering, Charity concluded, "I don't need to tell you what came next. . . . She went to bat for me—went with me to the Discipline Committee. Got 'em to settle for probation instead of expulsion. Had I been expelled, I hate to think what would have become of me!"

There followed a long silence. No one, it seemed, wanted to follow that impassioned testimonial.

Steve, bless him, changed the mood! "What I'd like to know," he mused, "is where she finds her cards!"

(Laughter—tension-releasing laughter)

Steve continued, "She must either own a card shop . . . or *live* in one. At just the right time, she manages to find just the right card—a card made for the occasion, for whatever I was going through! Some are funny, some are inspirational, 'encouragy'. . . ."

(Smiles—Steve was known for his Steve-isms.)

"And some are thanking me, praising me—and some are 'Go directly to jail. Do not pass Go; do not collect $200.'"

(It was some time before order was restored.)

It was then that Claire blurted out, "You know what impressed me most about Prof? Whenever she was talking to any of us, no one else—not even the President of the College—took precedence over us! She'd never even answer the phone during the discussion. And on the other side of the door would be a big sign IN CON-FERENCE—and *nobody* dared knock when that sign was on her door!"

(Sounds of agreement everywhere)

In the silence that followed, Danny spoke up. "Nobody has yet mentioned her classes. She is a hard teacher, but she is fair, tries to never show partiality, to give everyone an equal chance to speak, to participate. And what she says is always interesting, always provocative, always well worth hearing . . . I come away from her class feeling I am the better, the wiser, for having been there."

"And the kinder," added Kim. "She is the kindest person I have ever known!"

Kim continued, "And I also appreciate the fact that she *always* prays before class starts. Even though this is a Christian College, it always amazes me how few teachers open their classes with prayer."

"I want to get back to her fairness," announced Joan. "In all the years I have known Prof, I have never known her, in a case where it was her word against a student's—or her memory against a student's memory—not to give the student the benefit of the doubt! . . . I imagine she has been taken in, from time to time, because of it, but it always meant a lot to me to know that here was one teacher who believed in me, *trusted* me."

"As an alumnus—of a number of years," injected Brad, "what has impressed me most is that her friendships are not limited to the years we are in her class . . . but are for *life!* No matter where I go, no matter what I do, I always know she is still there for me. Even now," and he smiled reminiscently, "she's always pulling me out of ditches. . . . And I've dumped enough recommendation forms on her to have sunk a battleship!

(Laughter)

"Whenever I come home to my dear ol' alma mater, her office is the first place I head for! And it's like homecoming week every time I knock on her door. And I take one look at her library—the only one I know more monstrous than mine!—and I take heart. There *are* crazier people in the world than me."

"Yeah, but she parts with 'em, too," volunteered Camille. "I can nearly always manage to deliver a good enough sob story—well, I *am* nearly always broke, after all!—to get her to loosen up with one of the books I have been coveting."

"How does she ever find time to do all that she does . . . and still show up at so many of our functions?" asked Lauri rhetorically. "Chapels, assemblies, vespers, athletic events . . . convocations, special programs, honor society investitures, weddings, she's *there!* Oftentimes one of the only faculty who *are.* Where *does* she find the time?"

"And she'll always find time to go the second and third mile," added Jeannie, "to follow up a written recommendation with a personal phone call to the person doing the hiring, telling that person that we can do all but walk on water!"

"She did that for me, too," agreed Wendy, "and it got me my job. And a good one it is! But what has impressed me most about Prof is the close personal walk she has with the Lord, how she brings Him into everything she does and says. Had it not been for her, I would not be a Christian today. She is my mentor, my mother, my sister, my guiding light . . . I just hope I can become someone she'll be proud of and minister to the Lord's sheep as she has . . . and . . . uh . . . ." and her voice broke.

Again there was a long silence.

Finally, Claire cleared her throat and summed it all up: "I just wanted to say how much I personally appreciate Prof's life of service, the blessing she has been, is, and hopefully *will be—for many, many years to come!*"

(Thunderous applause)

Well, it was *over!* The tributes added by her two colleagues—and her own tearful response. And then the kisses, the hugs, the smiles, the tears.

Oh, yes, and the gifts. The wonderful gifts! Especially the ones they had written in or on themselves. But none of them could begin to match—what was it Miriam called them?—those "intangible" gifts. Those wonderful words—surreptitiously recorded for her by Wendy—that, that . . .

She noticed that the storm had intensified. *Be funny if it would snow this early,* she mused. *Oh, the fire has gone out*—and she had not even noticed!

Sinking back down into her favorite chair, almost immediately she felt a familiar furry caress on her legs! "Oh, Tenny! You funny thing—now that the company's gone, you come back to me." And she lifted him to her lap, where he began to purr seraphically, kneading his claws into her in ecstasy.

After he had been reassured of her love for him, her thoughts went back to the last couple of hours. What had happened? What was the meaning of it all?

In memory, she replayed each testimonial. *What dear students, what dear friends!*

As she continued to scratch Tenny's head, she wondered if that was it—the secret of life:

> *Just to have served*
> *Just to have cared*
> *Just to have believed*
> *Just to have trusted*
> *Just to have encouraged*
> *Just to have nurtured*
> *Just to have loved*

Awakening some time later to the twelfth gong of her grandfather clock, she rubbed her eyes (November eyes no longer—but June) and murmured, "For shame, Tenny, I'm getting as lazy as you!" But the smile on her face as she said it radiated joy and acceptance of her life: *Lord, if I had it to do over again, I would not have it any other way.*

Then she stood up on legs that wobbled, carried Alfred, Lord Tennyson to the sliding door, and flicked on the floodlight.

"Look, Tenny—it's *snowing!*"

*If these stories for moms touched your heart, you will
enjoy Joe Wheeler's other collections of timeless stories:*

HEART TO HEART STORIES OF LOVE

From the tale of an army lieutenant's test of
faithfulness to the story of an old Victorian
rocking chair with a secret, this collection is sure
to touch your soul as you enjoy the stories time
and again. Representing several different eras
and cultures and depicting love at various stages
of life, this collection of stories is all about the
different ways that love can be shown.
0-8423-1833-X (Hardcover available July 2000)

HEART TO HEART STORIES OF FRIENDSHIP

A touching collection of timeless tales that will
uplift your soul. For anyone who has ever
experienced or longed for the true joy of
friendship, these engaging stories are sure to inspire
laughter, tears, and tender remembrances. Share
them with a friend or loved one.
0-8423-0586-6 (Available now)

HEART TO HEART STORIES FOR DADS

This collection of classic tales is sure to tug at
your heart and take up permanent residence in
your memories. These stories about fathers,
beloved teachers, mentors, pastors, and other
father figures are suitable for reading aloud to
the family or for enjoying alone for a cozy
evening's entertainment.
0-8423-3634-6 (Available now)

CHRISTMAS IN MY HEART
Volume VIII

These stories will turn hearts to what Christmas—
and life itself—is all about. Powerful and
inspirational, each story is beautifully illustrated
with classic engravings and woodcuts, making the
collection a wonderful gift for family members
and friends. Reading these stories will quickly
become a part of any family's Christmas tradition.
0-8423-3645-1 (Available now)